RIVER FORGED

DOUGLAS P. SMITH

KINGFISHER PRESS LLC

River Forged by Douglas P. Smith

Prequel to the Fisher of Time series

Published by Kingfisher Press LLC

Fairview, North Carolina, United States of America

Visit the author's website at www.douglaspaulsmith.com

Cover by MiblArt

Print ISBN: 978-1-7373680-4-5

A previous version of this story was published as *Resilient* in 2021. This new book is a substantial rewrite with new content.

Dedicated to all those that think anything is possible.

Chapter One

I moved behind him and snapped his neck with a satisfying crunch. His body crumpled in front of me, and I didn't bother to break his fall. Not that he would feel it.

I looked down at the body and thought about options. What were my risks in leaving evidence and getting caught? My balaclava was down over my face so that should negate any visual evidence. I did not see any camera domes nearby, anyway, which made sense since this piece of garbage I had just offed had chosen this location to dump a body.

That left DNA evidence. No one had my DNA on file anywhere in the world, but that was no reason to get sloppy. Either I made the body disappear, or I placed it where innumerable other strands of DNA would cover the corpse. Amsterdam had a population of a million residents and seventeen million visitors, so a lot of DNA found its way into the canals and rivers. The canal it was. A brisk swim down an Amsterdam canal after midnight, with a dead body, was not how I had envisioned my evening unfolding. Certainly not how most international business investors got their exercise. But sometimes you had to improvise.

I pulled his body over to the canal and dropped it, then myself, into the water. As I grabbed the body, I caught a whiff of an odd odor, like a bad cologne. Then I set off swimming to a place I knew I could stash him while decomposition should erase any evidence. I also thought about some of the drug crimes conducted in other places and how they dismembered the competition. It made sense to copy some of their work. Good insurance just in case someone discovered the body. It had paid off for me over the centuries to be careful with this type of task.

I swam us to a concrete ledge under some thick bushes where the canal opened up to the larger water of the Ijssel River. I stood on the water's edge while I pulled the body up on the ledge. Out came my favorite razor-edged knife, and I severed his hands and head. My knife stayed sharp because I knew how to use it. You had to slice through the soft tissue and work the blade carefully through the joints. Hitting cartilage was OK, but one false slice to the bone dulled the blade. I was from a time when a dull blade could get you killed, so I learned to prevent that mistake.

I put the severed parts into his jacket and then zipped it shut and tied the arms together to keep the package all tidy. That would enable me to swim easier. The rest of the body I tucked under the ledge and wedged it in among the loose large rocks and rusty rebar. He wasn't going anywhere soon, at least not this part of him. I worked a chunk of concrete free from the rubble that had a piece of rebar embedded. I bent the rebar over to make a loop, then tied the jacket arms to the loop.

I then swam further down the canal into the river with my grisly and heavy bag of goodies, although it was slowing my progress. When I felt like I was in deep water, I dropped the package. Sleeping with the fishes, like Luca Brasi from the famous mobster movie. The good part of the plan was that the parts would not bloat and float up in the near-freezing water. The bad part was that decomposition was very slow in cold water. But I calculated the chances of a dredge pulling it up were beyond slim. The typical dredges used to clear the canals of drowned bicycles and trash would not operate this far out into the river.

With my unplanned chores finished, I turned around and swam up the canal several hundred meters. I noticed a trail of phosphorescent light in the water in my wake. That was strange, but I did not think it was important to my task. I climbed out of the canal in a dark area, so even if there were cameras, they would not get a good view of me. It was a few blocks from where I had killed him and did not want to get any closer. I started the long, cold, damp walk home. It was not my first time for that, and I wondered how many times I had been in freezing cold canals or rivers. I stopped thinking when I realized it was often, and most of those times also involved a body. I did not do this kind of thing much anymore, but tonight I had acted in a rage. Should have stayed in control, I told myself. But this guy had deserved everything that had happened to him tonight. He crossed the line, enraging me, and now I was mad at myself for my reaction. The swim and now the weather were cooling me off rather quickly.

The night was one of those March monstrosities, with wind blowing in from the North Sea, whipping the intermittently falling mist into my face. It felt like snow was coming. As I walked across the ancient cobblestones and pavers, I looked around at the house facades along the streets. Amsterdam was always beautiful, even on an ugly night. The heavy glossed paints, dark but colorful, decorated each door and window trim, and each house was a different color. Huge dark windows, like dead eyes, faced the street. It was a town worth loving, but tonight it seemed less inviting than usual. Ice formed on my clothes, and I wiped it off as I walked and fumed about my evening.

Once home, I changed clothes and sat on the comfortable leather sofa. Out came my favorite cashmere wool throw. I wasn't cold, but the idea of being cold bothered me, and I had good reasons for that. I watched the snowfall through the window. The canals didn't ice over most winters anymore, so the night portrayed them as black, endless roads. The snowflakes were disappearing into infinity. Altogether a typical late winter evening in the Netherlands.

The name seemed odd; for most of my existence, I had referred to this part of the country as Holland.

Amsterdam had a lot of positives, but much of winter was soul-crushingly bleak after the holidays, especially as March crept along without a break for nicer weather. And I had just spent the evening backstroking down a freezing canal; the winter seemed more immediate. The swim tonight would have killed most humans from hypothermia, but it was just annoying to me.

I thought back over the evening and tried to think if I had made any mistakes, for the tenth time. I felt I was in the clear, unless something had slipped by my attention prior to my attack. That thought took me to the events that preceded this evening.

The small-scale but murderous little drug lord had come to my attention a few weeks ago. Police reports had linked him to the body of a kid, barely a teenager, a junkie, found dead in a local canal. I decided the dealer was worthy of more scrutiny, since it was my home turf. I followed and documented his typical day of dealing and distribution. Anonymously, I forwarded two weeks' worth of observational evidence to the police. That gave them probable cause to make an arrest. It also kept me from having to kill again.

They took no action, which was odd for the Amsterdam police. Although often mistaken for amateurs because of their good nature, they were always quick and thorough when dealing with certain illegal drugs. Especially if the activity involved a murder, since capital crime was rare here. You had a much better chance of dying in a bicycle accident or hot-air balloon crash than being murdered in the Netherlands.

Then a second body was found two nights ago. Another kid, aged fifteen, dumped in an industrial area near Sloterdijk. She had been a carrier, or mule, for my surveillance target. I needed to up my game and follow this creep more closely if he was killing teenagers. He must have someone at the police protecting him or was a confidential informant since he was still free and in business.

Tonight was his unlucky night, as I had been hunting. I was walking up a dark street beside a canal where I knew he conducted business and hung out with customers. I saw him a block away, with my enhanced night sight, and he was putting something in the trunk of his BMW. Damned if it was not another dead kid. Something in my brain snapped. That is when I pulled down the balaclava over my face and dashed up behind him. My speed was inhuman, so he never saw or heard me approach. A fleeting thought crossed my mind whether what I was about to do was right. That thought did not last long enough to save him. Despite what most people thought, and religions taught, I felt society was a better place with certain people removed.

I left his car there with the trunk open and the body revealed. It was my way of making a point to the police; they should be able to follow this lead. It perturbed me they had not acted and arrested the dealer before now, forcing me into action. They would find the body in the car rather than fishing it out of the canal. But they would not find the perpetrator.

I needed to let go of the evening's event and try to relax. I would have had a nice brandy, but I'd grown tired of alcohol over the years. There were only a few liqueurs left that had any appeal, mainly because of associations of previous good times. I had an occasional cider, served cloudy, but usually in warmer weather. Another vice grown old over the years and only continued for tradition's sake. But I now sipped an ice-cold Baileys, while thinking about body part disposal. It seemed more difficult these days than it had been in ages past.

I got up later and slipped into bed under beams that were four hundred years old. They seemed young for a house, somehow. I needed little sleep, so again it was more for tradition than need. Tonight, I could not sleep, so I experienced that wonderful state of tiredness where an endless loop of random thoughts chased around inside my brain.

I wanted to go outside and see the stars, but one of the few things I did not like about the Netherlands was the lack of a truly dark night sky. The snow clouds wouldn't even allow any attempt on this evening. That led me to thoughts about my home in Asheville, where I could more easily see Orion and the Milky Way. My memory blinked back to a past life in America, to a story of how the black path of the Milky Way trapped evil souls for eternity. Maybe the little drug lord was up there right now, or did Europeans even go to Native American hell?

All this nonsense spinning through my head tonight could be useful fodder for a dissertation, but I really didn't need another PhD, despite the attraction of the subject. I also was running out of universities that I liked and where I could spend a few years in residence. Leiden, University College Cork, Padua, Edinburgh, and several others had all been a worthy investment of time. Great, now my brain was off on an academic tangent.

But I would like to go back again, if something new came along worth starting a fresh study. Dark matter sounded interesting, and I was waiting for some department to get around to studying the corollary of dark time before embarking on another six years in a program. Because I had lots of dark time to spend in spades. I would have already published something theoretical about the subject, but I had to be very careful. It would be risky for me to gain notoriety as some sort of authority or pioneer. I needed to leave the minimum footprint necessary to continue as a successful predator, continuing my un-fettered existence. And I knew the real reason I was thinking about another program; another cycle of deep melancholia was struggling to sneak in the edges of my consciousness. An age-old foe that I had fought for longer than most countries had existed.

I felt the oppressive weight of time. Perhaps I should find some new pursuit or go hunting to allay the deadening press of the years. Hunting no longer had the appeal it once had, but it needed to be done. I desperately wanted some nicer weather and sunlight to lighten my mood. I was not sure of my future course, but I needed a positive change of some sort.

I got out of bed. There would be no sleep for me tonight. My mind was still spinning so I might as well be productive. I made a coffee and turned on the computer to begin the search for trends and patterns of criminal activity. They were always there, hiding in plain sight. It just took a lot of experience to notice them; in my case, centuries of experience.

By morning, I had a short list of new possibilities for investigation. Hopefully, one or more of them would lead to a hunt. I needed the distraction from the incredibly boring job of investing money and reliving hundreds of years of memories that only depressed me.

Over the next few weeks, as the North Sea calmed and the storms rolling across the lowlands relented, I found several interesting leads. But I still needed time to piece together some disparate reports coming in from Utrecht. Finally, the weather gods smiled on Amsterdam and long, warm days full of sun made the winter seem a surreal dream as May approached. The month of May was hard to beat in the Netherlands and was liberally sprinkled with holidays. Even on regular days, the workday usually stopped after lunch so colleagues could walk out to grab a Heineken, cappuccino or Aperol spritz and sit in the sun. Interesting how such industrious people could take so much time off for enjoyment yet be so productive. It put the British and American job environments to shame. The Dutch had adapted well to their environment, basking in the sun almost as if they were turtles enjoying the cloudless days and sunlit warmth. They were happy turtles with happy and well-adjusted turtlettes in tow. They definitely knew something that everyone else should learn or relearn.

I thought about throwing the kayak in the canal but decided a bike ride would be better. I took the train to Woerden and walked to my other residence in the Kazerne, the town's former barracks. Something about a 1700s brick building constructed with massive beams was comforting for me. I changed into bicycling attire and started north to the familiar river. It was now a glorified big ditch with beautiful houses, although it was once a wide and marshy river full of wildlife. I wasn't sure which was better, but I enjoyed both for different reasons. At the river I turned right for Harmelen, then south to Montfoort, across to Oudewater. Then back up to the river west of Woerden to complete the circuit and home. I had to pace myself, even though I wanted to open up. However, even in the Netherlands with many near-Olympic sprinters, it wasn't normal to see a rider pushing ninety kilometers per hour on the flats. Besides, with all the other riders out, it could be dangerous for them if we collided. I'd had a few near misses in the past, especially from the younger kids joyriding with a cigarette in one hand and a cell phone in the other. Neither of those hands were on the handlebars.

I finished my ride and took a shower, found a book in my stash of floor-to-ceiling bookcases, and settled in a comfy old leather chair. Skipping dinner was easy enough, as I could go three days without eating. Although if I was spending a lot of energy, I would need somewhere around twelve to fifteen thousand calories on day four to catch up. I cooked when I wanted, ate when I wanted, but skipped several meals a week.

Such was my life; centuries of existence distilled down to a daily grind of cooking, bike riding, hunting humans, making money, and fighting depression. Most people's daily grind lasted fifty years, whereas mine, so far, was thirty-five times that. Too much more of this and I worried that I might have to explore the limits of my immortality.

Chapter Two

My life revolved around a house in Amsterdam, an apartment in Woerden, and a house in Asheville. I had family in America that I must keep secret, and rarely saw anyway. Other than that, I had a very few close friends. My hobbies, interests and talents were traveling, cooking, and collecting academic degrees to research my biological peculiarities. I wasn't sure what order I preferred, but all had their highlights. But underlying them all in various ways was a widespread boredom of life, sometimes masquerading as depression. Too much time spent alive had its drawbacks.

The territory I claimed as mine, as a predator, was the northern half of the Netherlands. The home in Amsterdam I considered my lair, and I always had at least one backup, which for a long time had been in Woerden. That allowed a lot of freedom of movement while I could still stay anywhere in my range comfortably. Each place had a special "mud room" with a stainless-steel table, plumbing for spraying down and a floor drain, and a few sharp instruments. I had each place equipped with an oversized freezer and refrigerator. Lots of cleaning supplies to eradicate all blood and even a lot of the DNA that might be loose in the area. Each freezer also had at least half a side of excellent beef to explain any interest the authorities might have had in the mudroom. Home butchery was uncommon, but still practiced in Europe. I did not even eat much beef anymore, but my friends and neighbors still appreciated the few cookouts I held or the meals I delivered to them.

I had not used the mud rooms the past few years. They were only in the rare cases after the War when a body had to disappear with no trace, and I had no time for other measures. But I had little stomach for that anymore. In my mind, I had already shut them down. I planned to add a sauna and expand the laundry rooms in those spaces.

But now it was time to hunt. The set of disturbing stories I had been following the past few weeks of researching sent me back to Amsterdam, where I had more secure equipment to conduct research. I wasn't much of a computer person, but I was a predator, which is the same thing as being aggressively paranoid, so I took precautions. My computer equipment and networks were as secure and anonymous as money and threats could make them. And though the Dutch weren't known for such, they had made incredible advances in the computer area. They consistently embarrassed the Russians and surprised the Americans, yet they were good enough to survive both. So, I felt confident my efforts on the networks would be safe enough. Besides, I had a guy that I called Monk. He was the best computer geek I had ever found, and he kept me covered.

Since the person of interest was showing up mostly in Utrecht, I could physically operate from either Amsterdam or Woerden to start the hunt. I stayed in Amsterdam just to keep a lower profile, since the population was much greater, and it was easier to blend in and move around in the big city. It was possibly easier to be seen by the authorities, or their cameras, on trips back and forth to Woerden. With the weather warming, I would head to Woerden later in the week to relax after my hunt.

My target I called Wormtongue, based on the slimy Tolkien character. He was something unusual. Typically, I found a vicious criminal fairly easily after they committed some heinous act, got away with it and then tried it again.

But this guy was different. He seemed to be around a lot of petty criminals, everything from drugs, guns, minor assaults, and credit card theft. But then those minor crooks inexplicably escalated their actions to major crimes. Utrecht was not a place normally known for crime. Alarmingly, serious things had happened there in the near past. A Middle Easterner known for having minor problems had suddenly decided rape and gun violence was his forte and then he started shooting at random strangers. Others like him began kidnapping women, forcing them into the sex trade, then offing them with drug overdoses for sport. Gun battles over drugs showed up in the same neighborhood. Some of these guys even knew each other, and the crimes were so stupid and obvious that the police could catch them within a few days. Because of that, I didn't need to involve myself and hunt. Soon I realized one person linked up with everyone involved in each of the crimes, yet he had never committed a known crime. It seemed everyone he came into contact with became a mindless beast within weeks.

My lead on Wormtongue was from reports that most of the recent rash of trouble came from taxi drivers known to frequent a certain area of town. I'd kill some time and money and ride the taxis for a day to random parts of town, walk back and try another. Somebody might talk. Plus, I could call Ahmed. He was a regular driver I'd used often and gotten to know. Ahmed could give me some general information, but I was going to steer clear of anything specific and keep him out of the entire mess. He and his family in Vleuten needed nothing at all to boomerang on them.

I went to the Utrecht train station, then down the steps to hail a taxi. The first one was older, but not very talkative. Small talk went nowhere, so I figured asking him about an unusual character he might have picked up or knew from the neighborhood wasn't a good idea. The next ride was a younger driver with an interest in using his English. We talked quite a lot, but he seemed to know nothing about any odd happenings in his area. Turned out he was from the other side of Utrecht near Houten, so he wouldn't know much unless through other drivers. Four more rides later, I was tiring of getting nowhere. Although I was enriching the community, in the interest of efficiency, I made the call.

Ahmed answered, and we exchanged pleasantries. Then I asked him my questions, and he went silent. That was odd. He was clearly thinking, and I suddenly wasn't sure this was a good idea. However, spending a few hours in taxis had not worked either.

"There could be a young person that flows with trouble. One such as he could be found in or around a market shop on the Vleutenseweg near the station."

"Thanks, I know of that place. I appreciate you letting me know about this, while I also want you to know that you've told me nothing, my friend. Go with God."

He seemed relieved and replied, "Inshallah."

I had a special regard for what all faiths taught, at least in their truest forms. In each fundamental text, of all beliefs, were clues about things other than men. So, I had studied most all the early religious texts and found general truths in all of them beyond just the supernatural aspects. For a brief time, in the deep past when I had been on Crusade, I had been in an excellent position to learn about and grow to respect the Muslim faith. That kind of thing happens when your enemy becomes your great friend.

I walked down the sidewalk just before midnight that evening. The station crowds had all thinned out by then, as it was a Thursday. I'd spent the later afternoon walking the old streets in Utrecht. And having a bite and a cider at Pickles restaurant. But now it was time for work. I had my trade tools under my lightweight long jacket.

I noticed someone that seemed to slough off my look. He felt completely off somehow, just like a black plastic bag floating low in the water that I had once come across in a canal while kayaking. The closer I drew to the bag, the weirder the feeling got, like I was both attracted to see what it was, but also repulsed by the horror that it might be. When I drifted over to the bag, I realized my feeling was accurate. It was a dead, bloated puppy inside the bag, swirling slowly and heavily in the current.

I now had that feeling again and knew Wormtongue was standing and smoking outside the shop. He was by himself and although the shop was open, I didn't see anyone up front or at the counter. This would be over quick, and I grabbed my favorite antler-handled knife blade. But a car door opened just a few feet away from my target. Out stepped a younger white guy, clean-cut and well-built with blonde hair. Couldn't have stood out more inappropriately than a drunk former boyfriend of the bride at a wedding. Wormtongue instantly tensed up and hurried around the corner of the shop into shadows. The blonde guy followed quickly. Well, hell, there went my easy opportunity. I followed, as I figured something interesting was about to happen. Whoa, that was some bad cologne wafting from the alley. Reminiscent of a burned, sickly sweet spice sprinkled over a slightly dead animal. Seemed familiar from somewhere, but I did not have time to think about it.

When I arrived in the shadowy side alley, Wormtongue was already rounding on his follower, quickly moving toward and under his guard, to place a chokehold and sweep the legs. Definitely moving like a trained martial artist. The other guy pulled countermoves incredibly fast and almost escaped, so he was good, too. My turn, so I sprinted forward and hit Wormtongue with three shots to the face, my fist moving incredibly fast into the lower, middle, and upper face. Anybody else would have been down with a broken jaw and cheekbone. Wormtongue grunted and bench-pressed the blonde guy right into me, then sprinted down the alley with supernatural speed. I could have caught him, but blondie was unconscious after the quick but brutal stranglehold. I grabbed him and laid him prone, elevated the head, and cleared the air pipe. Just then he wheezed and started coughing so hard he blew chunks. One thing I am is fast, so I stepped back and remained chunkless while rolling him over to his stomach. After a minute, he rolled back over and sat up. He was already clear-eyed, so he must have practice doing this, or at least had experience getting his ass kicked regularly. He was looking at me like a cop watches a drug deal as I squatted nearby.

I started off in English. "Good evening. You must be the guy that goes around to all the bad spots in town to get his ass kicked," I said. See, I could be civil. Now he was really looking like a mean cop. As his breathing slowed, he pulled out a silver baton and eased himself up the wall his back was against.

"Now don't make me take that away and turn it into a suppository for you as a reminder to be kind to strangers," I said. Now the charm was flowing.

Suddenly his eyes widened, and he collapsed the baton and put it back in his pocket. "I thank you, sir, for your assistance. My premature attempt to apprehend what I mistook for a man nearly ended me. I am pleased to meet you."

What the hell? This night had gone even more sideways than I expected. And who talked like that these days? "You seem to have me at some disadvantage, since I don't think I know you."

"Yes, please excuse my familiarity. I am Brother James, and I don't know you, but I know about you. Thank you again for saving me from that creature. Rarely do we survive a mistake as the one I made tonight."

"OK, now that we are talking, I believe the conversation needs a bit more background. Apparently, I am lagging behind in this story. Next block down is a coffee shop that is still open, and I bet you'd like to clean up before climbing back into that nice car."

"You are correct. I should cleanse myself. Then I would share a beverage with you during a brief conversation, but then must report in regarding my failure."

Again, who talks like that? He must not be from around here, but I was about to find out. His English was good, but an occasional odd word told me he wasn't native to it. Of course, the very name Brother James signified he was from the Church or an affiliate group, and those guys could be recruited from anywhere in the world. He certainly gave off a religious vibe. We ambled down a hundred yards and both ended up with hot tea. With no small talk, he began.

"I am afraid that I cannot tell you very much. I probably should not be conversing with you, but I am out of sorts, yet very grateful. The Church, in our training specific to Netherlands operations, informed us you were in this area. Briefings usually include people, places, and things that we may encounter in the field. We weren't told exactly who or what you are, just a brief background and a photograph, and told that you are here and not a threat to us. If contact ensued, we were to take no action against you. In fact, most of us admire your practice of wreaking vengeance on the worst criminals, getting rid of those we would like to see adjudicated but don't terminate ourselves."

The revelation stunned me. I had been careful to an extent but not overly so, as I expected little scrutiny from the average person or from law enforcement. The Church had quite extensive networks and resources at a certain level but didn't realize I was on their radar. I'd definitely need to do things differently and up my game. I wasn't too concerned about them specifically, but I knew they did trade information with specific governments. Not good from my perspective. I had actively stayed away from their perceived areas of influence, such as universities affiliated with the Church, and had never gone to Rome, even though I really wanted access to their archives. But my interest in the archives just took a hit since Brother James admitted they didn't know what I was. The question of my origin was my primary interest in those records.

"Well then," I answered, "I'm glad I get a pass from the big guy for now. So, what do you guess I am?"

"I do not know. From our education of entities, creatures, and paranormals, I am not sure where you would fit. From what we have been told, and this is the only potentially confidential thing that I will say tonight, is that you are the only individual in your category. There are many other categories beyond humans, including things that go from bad to evil to unspeakable. Those lower categories are the ones due to receive justice, and usually on sight when we find them."

"What about the guy tonight? Where does he fit? Obviously, he was not human."

"We have been tracking a most problematic jinn here in the city. They assigned me to pick up his latest human disciple, or convert, before he harmed anyone. I misidentified the jinn for the human, a mistake I will not make again. Most jinns are in a neutral category, but this one is dangerous based on crimes we have associated him with."

I thought about Brother James' earlier words. Hmm, I thought, I'm the sole owner of my category. I was glad they didn't know everything.

"What do you think you are?" Brother James asked. "I am only curious, and you do not have to respond."

"I'm just a guy that has been around a while and that doesn't mind exterminating those that require it. Since my ethics mostly predate the Church, I'm not doing it for your side."

He seemed stunned, and I realized I'd made a mistake. "Maybe you have been mis-categorized. If you speak the truth, normally only the evilest entities realize that long of a lifespan."

I realized they had been tracking me for a lot less time than I thought. Probably more like since the 1600s, perhaps even later. I'd have to ask when conditions were better. "I speak the truth, but the length of my life is not what it seems," I answered. "Actually, I wasn't awake for a lot of that time, as I've spent some of those centuries comatose."

He seemed perplexed, but let it drop. I'm sure somebody at the Vatican would soon get an update.

"If you are not my enemy, then I thank you for your help this night. The Church also thanks you. At least for now. But there may be questions in years to come."

"I wish you well tonight and in the future. I will continue hunting for this one unless your people are taking over, as I've always desisted the chase when law enforcement intervened. For any further questions, it seems your people know where to find me."

"Of course. Regarding this creature, I must report to my superiors. But I believe we will pursue this jinn. Perhaps you can discontinue the hunt for forty-eight hours. It is possible we will apprehend him alive for questioning before administering termination."

"Sure, that works for me," I said. "I assume you or someone will let me know by next week either way?"

"Yes, a message should arrive soon. Goodnight and good luck to you."

"Good luck to you as well." I had a strong feeling my life was now much more complicated. I had secrets to keep and was well aware the Church must have thousands of their own secrets, and I wasn't confident that we could keep out of each other's way.

The evening was quiet as I strolled back to the train station. But I felt my life was likely to soon get complicated. I stepped on the Intercity to Amsterdam and slouched in my seat. I had multiple contingency plans for various threats, but with the reach of the Church, especially in Europe, I would need to be calm and let things play out a bit.

CHAPTER THREE

The man sitting on the bench with me, enjoying the sun, was older but fit. I thought he had strong features and tall, gray and solid was his look. Because his coloring was just slightly off, I was not sure he was native Dutch. We were both much too serious for two guys on a bench fronting the canal in Woerden's Westdam Park, watching the kids invade the warm canal water with glee. That he had tracked me here spoke volumes about his network.

"Hello, I'm Michael. I'm with the Church Benevolence Association." I chuckled at his affiliation but had no further response. His English was just slightly accented, but not with the normal Dutch inflections. So probably not a Dutch native. "Regarding the matter last week in Utrecht, your help to our brother and your willingness to allow us to proceed in our own way is much appreciated."

I'd never heard the head of what was likely a group of assassins speak so well about what I assumed was a termination. "Always happy to help the CBA. I assume the jinn is no longer an issue. I had never met one before, but he seemed like a tough customer. But I guess you guys have the experience and manpower to have finished the problem."

"A curious case. We have excellent people and centuries of experience with these matters, yet the jinn escaped us."

"Ah, so the hunt is on. Can I get another shot at him or are you guys still calling dibs?"

He paused for a few seconds and considered a reply. "While I say he escaped us, what I really mean is that he seems to have escaped this world. He disappeared from in front of us, and there is no trace of him anywhere. So, I think we are both relieved of this pursuit for now."

"OK, I know almost nothing about them, but don't jinn normally do that?"

"No, not in this case. They took all the precautions to keep him from escaping in all the ways that jinn travel. This one simply disappeared despite all the safeguards."

I had no response to that. I had extremely limited experience with almost all supernatural beings, but I figured this Michael guy knew plenty. And if he was confused, then something was odd. And not something he would probably tell me about, anyway.

"It is not normal procedure for me to meet and discuss our operations with you, but I think we can both agree this is not a normal situation. As a thanks for last week specifically, and for other past matters, I thought we could have a conversation about some items of mutual interest. Or answer questions that you may have. Of course, there are many specific topics that are off limits, but I will be happy to chat in general about most things."

That sounded like a circular word twist worthy of a politician. But I needed to play along. "I have a question based on something your man said. It seems your organization has observed me for some time. How and when did I come to your attention?"

"Originally, a parish priest reported a man that did not age as others in the village. Over the years, the man disappeared, and the priest died, but another priest reported the same occurrence in another village, and his description of the man was quite similar to the previous priest. And then again. Our clerics are slow but steadfast, and eventually a pattern became clear to those in Rome. Agents began reviewing deeds, inheritances, accounts—all the usual earthly bureaucratic documents that dog us unto death. Patterns emerged and this man, you, kept coming back in other places and, in later, sequential times. Our office was then alerted, and we have kept up passive observation, since those such as you have shown the potential to do great harm."

I automatically tensed up as I felt a threat was emerging. He immediately noticed my reaction.

"Wait. During our intense investigations, a pattern emerged that was exactly opposite to our expectations. Our measures include tallies of all crimes against humans and property in the areas you inhabited, and we expected the typical increase in rapes, murders, disappearances and thievery. Even animal disappearances, treason, and buggery were included in that analysis."

I smiled at that, which I hoped unnerved him a little. Harmless fun at a priest's expense.

"In each case where we located you, over two hundred years, the only potential crime that increased were disappearances. All other criminal activity markedly decreased. The disappearances were one of two groups—known criminals and the very wealthy. And those missing wealthy turned out to have a rather dark histories in retrospect. During those periods, police arrests and convictions significantly increased, as it seems evidence of those guilty of crimes was supplied to the authorities."

Crap. He had me dead to rights. For an ancient, and very slow organization, it seemed they were also very thorough. "Yes, I help the police when possible. Otherwise, those disappearances would have escalated considerably. And potentially put me in jeopardy if noticed, plus weighing slightly heavier on my conscience."

It was his turn to smile. We assassins get along really well in the daylight. "We also appreciate your efforts during the War. We conservatively estimate you saved a few thousand souls, just that we know of, in 1944 and 1945. Which explained why German officers in Holland had both the highest suicide and accidental death rate of all occupied countries," he continued.

Yeah, some of those endings I dealt out were quite memorable. But I didn't think this was the time to reminisce.

"I appreciate the history lesson and some insight into your organization's techniques," I said. "But what I'm missing here is why you are telling me all this. I doubt that your group, whatever it is within the Church, normally chats with those under surveillance like me."

"You are quite right. This is a gesture of goodwill. Nor is any repayment necessary. I would ask that when or if you are comfortable doing so, you would provide a general idea of your history. As the sole member of a Church category, you have aroused some interest further south. But we also respect your right to privacy. There will be no coercion. And no repercussions as we feel confident in Rome that you are not a threat to our flock of humanity, and in your own way, might be a shepherd. Although a rather stringent one." He smiled after he said that.

Damn, the old guy had just called me a killer shepherd. Something was off here, but I wasn't sure what it was. I needed to stall and decide how to react to what I felt was an offer or a threat. Maybe it was both?

"You've given me a lot to think about. I suppose after all this it would be in poor taste to wander over there and eat one of those kids?"

"Not advisable. Likely one of my snipers would take you down before you were within three steps of the nearest child."

Yep, he could play the game, too, and he might not even be bluffing. No poker on Saturday night with this guy.

"Nice talk. I'm heading for a long walk. And no snacks."

I left him sitting on the bench with that peppy riposte as we mutually waved adios. He seemed content sitting there. Like a boa constrictor deciding whether to trouble itself with strangling some random rodent.

I walked to the other side of the canal and stood in the sun and tried to think. Michael had done his homework. That he knew about my general whereabouts for a couple of centuries, plus the details of the World War II exploits, made me think his sources were remarkable, considering all the information and data that he had compiled predated computers. The conversation with Michael had stirred up my old brain. I started walking in the sun to let my thoughts rise from the memory fog of so many centuries.

My memory was good, it was just the quantity of memories that crowded my brain. Sometimes I wondered how many were accurate, or whether local drift was occurring in my recollections. Whether memory or written history, everything depends on the observer and changes over time and with attitude. I thought back again to the night when I became something not human.

My best guess was that something had attacked me. Possibly it was a creature that was much later called a vampire. Which might make me a vampire, or possibly a hybrid, because of what happened afterward. Immediately falling into an icy river and fighting a massive fish in the mud all those centuries ago could have altered a proto-vampire virus. Or I might be something with no relation to a vampire. I just was not sure. Whatever it was that happened, I was now nearly immortal.

Ironically, the events leading to my current condition might, at a stretch, even be scientifically feasible. Regardless, I knew my condition was not something to advertise. Especially not when such a dangerous man had just been sitting in my quiet park. I contemplated giving my story, or at least the short version, to Michael. I wondered if that was his actual name. But my story sounded preposterous even to me.

I kept walking a long time, to the far park on the northeast side of town. Circling back toward my apartment, I stopped at the market and picked up some fresh tomatoes, cheese, and basil. I'd throw in some avocado and make my version of Caprese salad. My only simple decision of the day.

For years, all I had to do was to live a dull life, catch a few criminals, manage my investments, and never get too involved with friends and family. I found that a long life didn't guarantee a good life. But now it seemed I would have to adapt again. Moving money and creating new identities would be necessary to hide from the Church. I sat in my kitchen and began some meandering plans and some long-range contingencies. I decided that caution was the better option and I should keep my details to myself for now. But I needed a story in case this developed into something more, and if I complied with Michael's request to provide more of my background. What should I divulge versus keep secret? I decided I could provide a brief history, plus a description of my physical enhancements. I would not now, or possibly ever, reveal my history in America or my family there.

The Church's involvement in my life would likely lead to complications, one of which could be termination if they deemed me a threat. I had seen the Church in action at times, and even longer periods of inaction. I didn't always agree with what they did, yet I had to give them credit for holding things together across bleak and dangerous times over hundreds of years. Like any mega-corporation, they had their good guys and bad guys, and even definitions of those seemed to change over time, as societies changed. Very early in my life I had made a conscious decision to stay out of religious or political activities. The exception was crime; I considered crime just a lower form of politics.

I spent a sleepless evening in my Woerden apartment. I looked over my wall of books, then opened up my safe room and looked at the weapons I had collected over the years, all of them personal favorites and well used.

The only ones not present were a couple of priceless items well hidden in a combination double safe in the foundation of my Asheville house. Nothing was relaxing me, however, so on went the coffee again. I settled into my favorite chair and began mulling over my life so far.

I could not explain the original attack that opened my neck up, but that did not stop me from searching for answers to questions about what I was. Something had occurred that was not completely explained by current science. Mostly, I kept looking for those answers to prove to myself that I was not a vampire. I had spent on doctoral degree on the science behind European folklore and supernatural beings, another on fish proteins, a third on the microbiology of mud from a certain river in Holland, and another on human virology. And a recent dissertation on a new topic that seemed promising.

I also did a degree in archaeology at Leiden. It was just a lark at first to see how much they had dug up, literally, in the Roman period in old Holland. There was a definite lack of documentation and significant loss of content that had happened over the centuries. I never saw a reference to myself; my passing was of no consequence. Individuals missing from the Legions were common enough and could look bad for the patron, so easier to just show loss to disease or accident.

All the effort was to search for an explanation of my condition, yet there was no answer. The only thing I hadn't tried so far was DNA analysis. I thought it best not to have my genome sequence information floating around cyberspace in case anyone like the Church or any governments were looking at interesting anomalies. That hadn't kept me out of the Church's sights as much as I had thought, however.

I lived a quiet life like a regular person. Living a prudent life also helped me maximize my ambush predator skills instead of running around like Rambo and getting shot and noticed. I had seen mobs in action before during public executions. Being drawn and quartered was a real thing that used to happen, and the forerunner of the reality television show. Nothing entertains the masses like blood, screams, and entrails in the public square.

I did appreciate my physical enhancements. Several times stronger and faster than other humans, proportional hand-eye coordination, and extremely quick healing. Excellent night vision, enhanced hearing, and other sensory improvements, including a sixth sense of where people were in my vicinity. All good stuff for a predator.

Overall, I had lots more time and resources to travel, study, and kill when necessary compared to ordinary humans. When you finally accept that you might have a few centuries to live, rather than a part of one, new opportunities arise along with a plethora of problems. Which meant life, just longer. And other things, like remorse, build up only to get pushed down. It's bad enough to do that for a decade, but I'd had centuries to repress significant events and emotions.

By the time I mulled over all those thoughts, it was late at night. I spent time planning financial arrangements to make my investments more liquid, in case I needed to leave the country quickly. That thinking applied to documents and other assets. Successful predators needed escape plans.

CHAPTER FOUR

I was walking in Utrecht as it was another brilliant day in May, and everyone was out enjoying the weather. On days like this, I would ride the train in, stroll through the town, then walk the paths through the parks and villages back toward Woerden. When these especially nice and mild sunny days came around, at least when the wind died down, I would sometimes walk all the way home. That time was always my solace and time to think. But right now, I was walking through the Dom, the massive tower in Utrecht. The scaffolding was gone, but probably due back in another fifty or a hundred years.

As I stepped beyond the tower, I heard, "Good day. Might I walk with you a moment, and perhaps buy you lunch or an apéritif?" Michael had found me again. It was a pretty good and quiet sneak up for a large old man.

"Michael!" I said with a big grin. "Fancy meeting you here." I figured I might as well try to tease him a bit and see if that implacable look would slip. It did not. He had that boa constrictor look on his face again. "I'd love a walk and a bite."

"The offer still stands if you can behave yourself." He didn't seem bothered at all, despite his words.

"OK. Let's wander down to Pickles and grab something. Hopefully, we can sit outside."

We turned left and walked past shops and a couple of galleries. People were definitely out and enjoying the sun. May in a Netherlands city was made for people watching. I would bet someone was watching me right now, probably through a rifle scope.

At Pickles, we got a table outside on the margin of the crowd. The sun had slid over enough that the alley was no longer fully lit. I had an Aperol to start while Michael ordered a cappuccino. I guess he didn't drink on the job.

When the server returned, I ordered the turkey burger and coleslaw. Michael surprised me by getting a burger and frites with mayonnaise.

He caught me looking at him after his order. "I try to eat unhealthy food once a month lest I forget to commit other sins during the month."

"Fries, mayo and beef fat will fit that bill."

"How are you doing since our last visit?"

"I'm doing well. I am enjoying this weather like every other soul in the country, but I must confess that I was getting a bit bored. Might have to go on the Camino again, the long version this time, or a hike and bike in Ireland. I could fly to the Faroes since I've never been but had planned that for a special occasion." I paused while the server came back with a tea for me and another cappuccino for Michael. "And how are you doing?" I asked.

"Staying busy as it seems we always are, with new situations arising and old situations resurfacing." Our food arrived, and we dug in for a few moments. "I believe I can relieve you of your boredom issue."

Oh hell, this could get sideways in a hurry. But it intrigued me enough to stay quiet and let him continue.

"Is this a job offer, or do you have a sister that needs a blind date?" I could never resist the urge to throw a curve at the unflappable Michael.

"My sisters are happy and not looking for companionship. As for a job, I would like to discuss potential opportunities, even though you don't fit the applicant profile we typically use for hiring."

"Why do you think you can trust me?"

"A couple hundred years' worth of passive background checks for one. And that ring you are wearing for a second reason."

"This ring?" That seemed unlikely. It was significant only to me, made by a silversmith I used to know, and had absolutely no intrinsic value I could think of.

"Yes. That silver band vouches for your character."

"You might have to explain a little more about that. As far as I know from the movies, it just means I'm not a werewolf."

"Exactly. Not a werewolf or several other things we worry about. That you can wear silver and not even be aware of it means a great deal in some quarters. And that we are having this conversation in the sunlight." There went my naive feelings of safety on those long overnight walks in the fall or in the mountains after a snowfall. Maybe some of those predators and monsters in the movies were real and larger than me. This guy would know. "But before we delve into any specifics, I would like to walk over to a quieter and safer location," he said.

Each of us paid our own bill after we finished our meal, as we went Dutch, of course, and then walked back to the main canal and southwest past another canal into a residential area. We came to an ancient blue door in a brick wall and he punched in a code on a very expensive stainless keypad. I followed him into a courtyard that you can sometimes glimpse in these old cities when someone passes through a door. They had paved this courtyard with ancient bricks, and it contained a massive old sycamore in one corner, and a fountain closer to the middle of the space. Several containers overflowed with flowers and the bees and butterflies were working overtime on the blooms. It looked, smelled, and sounded wonderful. And, of course, there was a nice bench in a strategic location giving a view of everything.

"Nice digs."

"It fits nicely within our profession to have safe houses scattered in a city. Luckily, the brethren take pride in the upkeep of these spaces. No reason not to have a beautiful safe house rather than just a plain space."

I thought it was true but didn't mention that these kinds of spaces were easier to keep if you had access to free labor.

As we sat, Michael continued the conversation from lunch. "There are beings and things that most are either not aware of, or through conscious choice, wish not to know about. In your case, you may not have encountered many of these beings, but given your longevity, it was probably either by luck or because of the reclusive nature of most of these creatures. By reclusive, I mean that they likely sensed your nature as an apex predator and shied away before you noticed them."

"I suppose that is strangely encouraging, but what is the opportunity?"

"First, I would like to ask you a few basic questions to establish if this is even a good fit."

I nodded acceptance.

"In your encounter with Brother James and the other individual two weeks ago, did you sense anything unusual at all about the creature?"

"Yes. When I got closer, he seemed less distinct than a human, like his skin was oily or inky and moving around unnaturally. He was also giving off a very off-putting vibe, similar to what I've experienced with subsonic sounds. And a smell, perhaps burned cardamom, or when cilantro blooms just before turning into coriander. Last, when I popped his face a few times, I should have broken his facial bones, but he seemed barely hurt."

"Hmm. What you saw and felt was a reaction to his nature. It takes years for us to develop that skill except for the few adepts that naturally possess that talent. What you encountered was a jinn and human hybrid, a scion."

I nodded agreement.

"You don't seem surprised at that information."

"A very long time ago, my best friend taught me some things about the jinn."

Michael looked intrigued but did not ask for anything further. When I added nothing else, he continued with his questions.

"Have you ever been in a location or situation where you developed a quick and short headache, your vision went white, and you smelled something like burning plastic?" Michael asked.

"Yes, I was taking an extended hike in the Lake District. I was on the ridge just above a town called Wythburn and passed a small group of people on the trail. They were overdressed for the occasion. At least the women were. I remember the headache, white vison with aching eyes, and that odd smell."

"The Lake District," he repeated back to me. He pulled out a leather binder from his pocket with a small notebook full of writing on one side and a mini tablet on the other side. "Was that sometime between 1969 and 1984?"

"1972."

"Very good. A strong coven of witches lived there, and they produce exactly those symptoms to adepts. They might have even been the group you passed." He continued with his questions. "What about a time or place where you developed a bitter taste in your mouth, your teeth hurt, and possibly saw something moving somewhat indirectly, almost as if it was in the corner of your eye?"

This one I would have to be a little more careful about. "Yes. Driving and visiting areas out west of Asheville, I've encountered that. In some of the mountain 'hollers', the term they use there to describe the narrow valleys."

"Shapeshifters inhabited those places," Michael said. "They look human but have supernatural abilities, including changing into animal forms. The other possibility is you encountered the Native American shamans there that hunt the shapeshifters, as they have a similar type of energy that mimics the shapeshifters."

I certainly had a lot more additional information, but wisely kept quiet.

"Just two more questions to conclude this. Ever experience a smell, like something dead and fermented, strong enough to stagger you, plus your ears were ringing?"

"Not exactly. Unless you are referring to one of those anchovy-paste plants like the one I passed by in the Philippines. So, what delightful creature could that have been?"

"It is not important. Most of us do not encounter that one but thought I would ask, anyway. My last question is whether you have had any other unusual experiences, similar to what we have discussed. Or any powerful unexplained feeling along those parameters?"

"Moffett, Oklahoma, 1996. Sunlight felt oddly dimmed although the fog was coming in from the river, a quick onset of anxiety, and a strange sweet smell like fresh dirt and plants, but noxious somehow."

"We don't do all that much in Oklahoma, so probably not one of ours. I'll look it up, anyway."

Out came the binder again, and he typed into the tablet what I assumed was the town's name. He looked shocked a second later. "Oh my, I had no idea."

I gave him a minute. "What we got cooking over in Oklahoma?"

He still didn't respond for a moment. "There is something unknown but most unsavory in that location. I would caution you to not travel there again anytime in the next century. We have quarantined our people from that area."

"Well Michael, you certainly have my attention and no more trips to Moffett. Whatever is there, it's bad. I really wasn't ever planning on traveling back there, anyway. I drove through there after hearing about all the strange deaths and disappearances that had taken place over the past one hundred and fifty years."

"Wise choice," was his response.

We both took a silent moment to watch the insects assaulting the flowers, while a pair of grackles set up a noise contest in the sycamore. The tree did not seem to care.

"Now that I firmly believe you are an adept, besides your other desirable traits, I would like to discuss an opportunity that could benefit both of us," Michael said.

"Sure," I replied. This was going to be interesting.

"Based on what we know of your past and present, plus now knowing you are an adept at picking up certain signals from those we are interested in, we can offer a contractual relationship. The Church is very large but ancient, meaning that it has compromised management systems. It is slow to respond to threats and inefficient in handling unusual situations. My particular branch is partially immune to that, but the tradeoff is that we are also understaffed and annually fight other departments for resources and budgets."

"Sounds like every other major corporation I've ever dealt with," I said.

"Exactly," he continued. "With the additional burden of nearly two thousand years of additional inertia, we need a faster response time than we currently have. We would not bind you to us in any way other than by a simple contract, cancelable by either party without penalty."

"And what do you see as the purpose of this proposition?" I asked.

"Investigate abnormal happenings and, if appropriate, apprehend the entity responsible. And, I stress, you must do this discreetly, and without collateral damage to the general population. We fully believe you are capable of those terms, otherwise we would not be discussing this."

"Do you have any examples of what you may consider me for in the near future?" I asked. "Just in case I need to prepare."

"Nothing imminent," he said. "But for an example, there has been trouble in northern Mexico, mostly involving the drug cartels. We believe a small group of very disagreeable shapeshifters are being used as enforcers. They may need to be removed."

I sat quietly and considered the options. I had been thinking about this for a few days, as it had seemed a likely play for Michael to make. Not only would it help them out of some jams, but they would also get to keep me close for observation. And termination if things went sideways. A win-win for the big guy.

From my side, the work sounded interesting. I needed the activity to stave off boredom and depression. But I needed to tread carefully. The devil was going to be in the details.

"I have a few conditions first," I said.

"I would think so," Michael replied.

"First, I have the right to refuse any job for any reason."

He nodded affirmatively. I assumed that was a yes and continued.

"Second, each job comprises two parts. If I accept, I will do the investigation. You will compensate me for that, regardless. Then I will decide on whether to proceed on the takedown portion separately. I can refuse to capture or kill the bogeyman. That, of course, would negate the second part of the payment."

He speculated about that for a moment. "I think we can accept that," he said. "If your investigation is fruitful, that puts us in a much better position for planning a capture or termination if you decide not to proceed."

"Third, compensation can be in gold, silver, or barter."

He paused and considered that. "Bullion or coins are not an issue at all for us. I am intrigued by what you think we can offer in trade for your services."

"I need documents and information. Keeping my documents current, such as my passport, has become expensive and time-consuming. Plus, I have liability through increased exposure to the criminal enterprises that I employ to forge the documents. I need passports and other forms of identification that are clean and, where possible, legal. Other than periodic name changes to protect my longevity, I would prefer everything be legal to prevent unwanted scrutiny." Although the Church's help would give them the opportunity to keep a closer watch on my movements. I thought it was a safe bet Michael would agree.

"We can do that. With treaties and agreements, we work closely with many governments. I assume you would need documentation for both the Netherlands and the United States?" he asked.

"Yes," I responded. "Plus, another set from somewhere else, possibly Portugal or Malta, or a similar country of your choosing. I like to keep my options open in case of emergency travel."

"Done," he said. "Now, what type of information are you seeking?"

"I am not sure," I answered honestly. "I don't yet know enough to even start with inquiries. I am requesting a librarian to begin my research."

He grinned. "Librarians, we have in droves. However, I suspect you are considering something special?" he asked.

"Yes, somebody versed in the occult and supernatural," I said. "What you are asking me to do will probably be more successful the better prepared I am, plus I would like to do further research in other arcane areas."

"I have precisely the person in mind. They already work with us, so that will expedite your requests. I understand you wish to do your own research, but we will provide training to get you up to speed."

"Thanks, I appreciate that, as I have some things I want to look into myself. A lot of material I have searched for is either nonexistent or incomplete, and if any organization in the world has such records, I think it is yours."

"Done," he said. "With the usual caveat that we seal some records, both for your protection and ours. If you get into some of that material, we will have to negotiate release to minimize threats."

"I agree," I said. "Since I don't know yet where I will go with this, I will respect your boundaries, and reserve arguments over specifics for a later time."

"Good, I think we have a basis for an agreement," he said.

I nodded, and we sat for a few minutes. The grackles had finally moved on to annoy another courtyard.

"There are many details to be determined in the next few weeks, so I will assign one of my people to start that process and arrange a place to conduct the first training on Church logistics and methods. Soon, we should be able to prepare materials and give you some background training for assignments. For your information request, that can be accomplished faster. Any day after tomorrow I can introduce you to the librarian," Michael said.

"Sounds good, and I look forward to what I am sure will be an interesting life in the upcoming months," I said.

"Oh, I can assure you of that," he said. "The site is not too far from Woerden as it's near the village of Meije by the river. A pleasant place still far enough out in farm country that the activity and noises sometimes occurring are not as alarming as they would be in the city."

"Sure, what day and time?" My mind was still in the past, even as I was trying to take part in the conversation.

"Tuesday at ten am. I will forward the address to your new email account we will have set up by then." He handed me a card with an email address, username and password printed on it.

"You seem pretty sure of yourself talking me into this job, as you already had the card printed."

"I had two cards ready, this one and a red one. If I had handed you the red one, then my colleague would have shot you through the forehead."

I just glared at him, as I was not sure if he was joking, and he knew it. "You're kidding, right?"

"Perhaps." He was wearing another half-smile.

Once again, I was not sure, but I categorized it as a joke. I just had nothing witty or profound to come back with to prod him. My response was weak. "I owe you one."

I stood and walked to the door, pressed the green button to unlock it, and stepped onto the street. It turned out to be a long and thoughtful walk home. Lucky for me, the days were already long this far north, even in Ma

Chapter Five

I drove through Meije, which was a village so small as to not really exist except as a name on a map. Mostly farmland, with some beautiful older homes placed right on the meandering river. The river was much diminished from centuries past. But it wasn't too hard to find from a distance. Just head toward the massive white tower that dominated the landscape. From a distance, it looked like a medieval marvel, but it was only a fairly modern water tower. A white spire erupting from the green heart of the Netherlands.

I found the address and came to a drive with a gate. I touched the pad, and it automatically opened. The cameras mounted on either side announced my presence. The drive was between two dense hedgerows and ended at a large circular turnabout in front of the cottage.

The "cottage" was actually a vast house with extensive grounds and one border on the river. This part of the river was marshy enough in most places that the house was set back from it nearly two hundred meters. There was a grassy berm from the house out to the river ending in a dock big enough for several boats. Large garden spaces surrounded the house, and massive green fields were past that on all sides but the river. Separating the garden grounds from the fields was a short but thick hedgerow. In the far distance, trees and tall hedgerows marked the property boundaries. There were no other houses on this portion of the road or river. The entire layout, including the driveway in, was perfectly situated to act as a passive ambush zone. I catch on to those things quickly. If the estate was as guarded with sensors and technology as I suspected, then nothing could get in without detection.

The front part of the house, the original building, was Dutch style with stone and brick walls and a thatched roof. They had added a large section to the rear, perpendicular to the old house, so the entire structure was T-shaped. The new section was brick with a metal roof. In one corner of the T was a large brick paver courtyard, while on the opposite side was a formal garden with grass paths.

I parked and walked to the heavy door, which opened just as I approached. "Welcome," Michael said. We shook hands.

"Nice cottage. And very well placed, I think."

"It serves our purposes well. Come in and I'll show you around."

Inside, the builders had utilized the common post and beam style. Massive ancient timbers and beams were exposed from the plaster of the walls and ceiling. The structure allowed lots of unobstructed wall space, most of which was filled with windows. The Dutch liked to maximize the sun since it wasn't around often. Furniture was leather or upholstered in the older tradition rather than the modern Nordic style. A variety of wooden chairs surrounded a very large plank table. I could glimpse what looked to be walls full of books toward the back. I quickly glanced at the collection and made an approving sound, then turned to Michael.

"You can see the rest of the house in the back, and the outer grounds later. Let's step over to the library to wait for your requested guest. Our librarian is being temporarily assigned to the Netherlands, so you should have sufficient access over the next few weeks. Longer, if needed. You can work out how much time the two of you need during the weekdays when you are not otherwise engaged in additional training exercises, which should begin in two weeks. Ah, good timing. Let me introduce you."

A woman walked into the room from a door to the back wing. She was petite but well-muscled with blonde hair and marbled blue eyes, wearing a navy pantsuit and carrying a leather case. She looked like an athletic university professor.

"Joanna, I'd like you to meet your new assignment," Michael said. I noticed, as assuredly did she, that he did not disclose my name.

She looked coolly at me. "Pleasure to meet you." Her accent was very much North England.

"Good to meet you. I am grateful for your help."

She said nothing. She was all business, or not happy to be here, or both.

"I will leave you two now in order for you to acquaint yourselves. Joanna will be here during the week, but you two can arrange the days and times to your liking," Michael said, and then he left the room.

I looked her over discreetly and thought about how much she represented northern England, with its waves of Roman, Saxon, and Norman inhabitants. But I did not think she would appreciate me describing her as a history lesson. She was also quite attractive, but again, best not to mention. At least she didn't have glasses, or the attractive librarian cliché would have been laughable.

I went over to the sideboard table set up with a kettle, teapot, two tea canisters, condiments, and a large flask of water.

"Would you like some tea?" I asked.

"Yes, thanks." Nothing else, so I was not winning any points yet.

"Great. There is English Breakfast or Earl Grey. I prefer a fruity tea like the Harney and Sons Paris or the Osterlandsk Mermaid. It goes with my bubbly personality."

She just looked at me. My humor was not working either.

I realized I should treat my librarian, the person who controlled the flow of the world's largest library, more professionally. I was sure she was in no mood to joust with me and my poor attempts at small talk and humor after getting pulled off her regular job.

"I'm sorry. My age has rendered me impertinent. I will be happy to place the leaves as soon as you decide which you prefer. I see there is also sugar and cream. Let me know your preference and I'll make you the perfect cuppa."

"The Breakfast is fine, with one sugar. And you don't look old enough to be so grumpy."

I started laughing while she looked perplexed. "Someday we will discuss that further."

When the kettle water reached boiling, I poured the water into the teapot with a generous helping of leaves in the screen filter. I grabbed two cups, added a sugar cube, and after a minute, I poured each cup half full of boiling water. And then filled each after another minute passed. It was an old trick I knew to get the tea to release the oils and flavors in a delicate balance, since the leaves released different flavors at different times and temperatures. I put two small spoons in each and walked over to the table and handed a cup to Joanna. We both sat at a regular size table by the window overlooking the garden.

"I sense you are not thrilled about being here. I'm not offended but I am curious why. The arrangement may not be optimal for you, but perhaps I could amend the days or hours to better suit you."

She would not make eye contact, so my guess was right. "You are correct that I would rather not be here. I have both family obligations back home and some research that I would prefer to continue. An assignment here is interfering with both."

"I appreciate the honesty and will try to accommodate your schedule where possible. Do you want to proceed with any introductions, or should we begin?"

"I prefer some introductions, as Michael has not told me anything other than to be here, and to keep an open mind," she said.

"Fair enough," I said. "Please, go first."

"I am Dr. Joanna York, as you likely know already. I went to university in Manchester and spent some time at Cambridge in the graduate program. My field of research is in arcane and occult myths and stories, predominately those of northern Europe. I followed some leads to the Vatican, and during my second trip there, Michael introduced himself and offered me a position. With the offer, I could continue living in England but have access to their records and resources for my studies. I have been doing this for over nine years. Now I find myself here today with no adequate explanation."

"Nice to meet you. I normally go by Senecus. What is your specific topic or project?"

"Origin and development of the myths surrounding ancient transformations of humans, particularly the werewolf myth and how it relates to vampire legends. Most previous work states that the werewolf myth preceded and eventually evolved into the vampire stories across Europe. But I have some evidence from early oral traditions that the opposite may be true, or both myths possibly co-evolved from a common source."

"Very interesting, and now I understand why Michael chose you."

"Well, I do not. Ordering me here to teach one of his students about a premature hypothesis of human transformation seems ridiculous. And pardon my directness, but aren't you too old to be a student, or are you late to working on your doctorate?"

"I am not exactly a student in the traditional sense. When we get back around to that age topic, then perhaps your assignment will make more sense."

She looked confused. "If you are not a student, then what are you here for?"

"I'm doing some freelance work for Michael. Actually, I am troubleshooting some of those transformations found in your research. And in return, Michael is lending me access to you for more information that I'll need to carry out that task. I also plan to do some research on a side project. Last, I may have some old but unrevealed knowledge to transfer back to you."

"Troubleshooting those transformative humans. That is nonsense. Those are just myths. And how do you think you could even find one if they existed?"

"I'm not sure yet. However, the Church seems to think this is a worthy cause and that I can help."

She sat there looking at me like I was an idiot. I realized I once again was taking the wrong approach. "Once again, I must apologize. I am being vague, as I know little about my assignments yet. My position here is to learn from you, and to prepare myself for the occasional project with Michael to find and fix some of his problems. I'm not one of your transformationalists, or whatever the proper term is, but I have other attributes to assist me in pursuing them. You will discover more about all these topics as we work together. Beyond that, I can't answer many questions as I am new to this organization. In fact, this is my first day."

She looked more comfortable, but I could tell her dislike of me was not dissipating. It was also a bad sign that I was talking more than her. I typically was the least talkative person in the room. Time for a slight change in direction.

"You look like a runner. Care to go for a quick run this afternoon?" I asked to change the subject.

She looked doubtful.

"It would just be around the grounds, all within camera view," I said to reassure her.

"That would be acceptable," she said.

"Now, before lunch, I basically need to know everything you have discovered from your studies, from graduate school until the present." I quickly jumped in as I noticed the incredulous look on her face. "Just a summary. Whatever you can fit into an hour. More like a thesis synopsis."

She looked a lot less angry. "Absolutely." She pulled out of her leather case what looked like a thesis publication and opened it. "To begin with..." The rest of the hour went quickly and was quite interesting. Her summary was better than anything I had come across in many years of research on the subject.

Lunch was a typical Dutch board of bread, spreads, cheeses, cold cuts, and fruit. They laid it out on the plank table in the large room of the main house. I made myself a sandwich and got several types of fruit. Then I made more tea. Joanna had gotten a yogurt and some fruit, then had gone through the door to the back of the house, so I walked out a side door into the garden. I sat and ate and thought about how to show Joanna what she needed to know about me without antagonizing her. A half-hour later, she came back in and had changed into an athletic outfit with leggings and a shirt, plus running shoes.

"Do you need to change?" She was looking at my jeans and leather shoes.

"No, I'm good. I didn't bring a change today, but I'll be fine." I actually hated running just to run, but I hoped jogging together would get her to feel more comfortable around me.

She turned around and walked out the front door, and I followed.

"Take off from here, down the drive to the gate, then around the perimeter? There is a lane just inside the outer hedgerows."

"Sure."

We took off at a decent pace. It was a pleasant enough day, now slightly ruined by having to jog around in it. We looped around the perimeter twice, then back to the cottage to get in thirty minutes of running. She was barely breathing hard, and I wasn't at all. So, our lack of talking was not from being taxed by the run. She went inside and then through to the back of the library to the other section of the house. I sat at the table and mentally placed bets on how long I would need to make Joanna like me. Two weeks to a month was the safe bet.

Joanna came back to the library, or study as I was now thinking about it, an hour later. She had taken the time to change and probably check messages. I behaved myself the rest of the day, and we had a cordial afternoon while she introduced her extensive work on one of my favorite topics. She seemed surprised that I knew a fair amount about some subjects we discussed. I decided not to tell her that one of my PhDs was on a similar topic.

The next two days were similar in tone. I got two short walks with Michael to discuss general topics. He was interested in both my investigative and martial skills. He needed to line up some of his people for training sessions. We discussed a little more about my personal life. I believe it was as much to give Joanna a break as it was to share information.

Joanna, meanwhile, continued telling me about her observations and analysis, and I continued asking endless questions about the who, when, how, and why of her results. I thought all the interruptions would perturb her, but she seemed glad that someone was taking an interest in her work. And it was indeed a work. I had found nothing close to the amount of relevant information and neat summarization in any of my previous quests among a dozen different libraries. I attributed that both to her intellectual acumen and the access she must have had to arcane sources. It impressed me to the point of distraction. Her physical presence was also distracting in another context. I began thinking that in the future we should spend a little less time together or get out of these confines. My best move was to just get past any feelings of attraction and move into the friend stage as quickly as possible. I had the powerful impression that she had no interest in me at all, so I should follow her direction.

Between tea breaks and lunches, we had enough small talk where I learned she still lived in northern England, near her family. The youngest of five, she had two brothers and two sisters, her mum, and a small army of nieces and nephews. Running was a passion, as was her work. I stayed in my lane, tried to limit my sarcasm, and as long as we kept to safe small talk and work topics, it went smoothly. A pleasant and productive way to spend a few days. I offered to drive her around or lend her a bike for a joint ride off the grounds, but she declined. So far, she was all work and no play. Which, of course, was the safe play for both of us. But I was concerned our stilted professionalism might stifle the discussion.

By Friday she was getting stir crazy, or just tired of the routine. I was asking about the werewolf vampire myths again, and whether any of them had taken place while submerged in water.

"I really don't see where this is going. I have just about exhausted all the research, and you keep asking questions about aspects of transformation that are not addressed anywhere in any material that I am aware of."

"I know. I'm just looking for something that probably does not exist. Your work is about the last hope I have of finding it, other than the library in Rome. But since you have gone through their material, I now doubt I will ever find my answers."

"Your answers? What exactly are you trying to find? Is this for a particular entity you need to track for the Church? If you tell me explicitly, I may remember something or dig something up on my next trip to Rome."

"I know my questions are wearing thin. My search in this case is of a more personal nature. I think I just need to accept that the unknown will remain so."

"We have only known each other for a few days, but I think you need to tell me specifically what you need so I can help you find it."

"I am not quite ready to do that yet. But you are right, you need to know more about me to make this venture more likely to succeed. Let us take a run now while I explain."

She looked skeptical but left to go change. We met back at the front door a few minutes later.

"OK, try to keep up." Nothing like snark to win the friendship of a librarian.

She glanced at me like I was something she might have stepped in at the dog park. We jogged off across the front grounds and into the driveway proper. I left her there as I sped up, touched the gate at the end of the driveway, then met her as she was only halfway down the drive. I wasn't breathing hard. "You still have a way to go. Should I wait here for you?"

She just stopped and stared at me. "Nobody is that fast. What the bloody hell are you playing at?"

"Well, I am just being myself, finally," I said. "Plus, making a point that there are things that aren't easily explained but do really exist. In some ways, I am one of those anomalies."

"Yet you are working with Michael," she stated with an interested look on her face. "Does that make you one of..."

"Oh, hell no," I said quickly, worried that she was about to ask me if I was some kind of angel. She looked startled, so I needed to explain myself.

"Many years ago, something changed me. I'm not exactly with the Church. We both chase after bad things, so we are on the same general side, but not exactly the same team, except when I'm on contract with them. I'm trying not to impersonate an angel or warrior priest or whatever. There's probably a steep fine if I got caught doing that. The important thing to know about me is that I track down the worst of humanity and then turn them over to the authorities, whether the police or now the Church."

"I think it best to explain more about what or who you are if we are going to work together to find your answers," she said in a no-nonsense tone.

"Hmm, you probably would not believe me if I told you. I'm not sure what I am."

She shook her head no.

"I can do a better job telling you what I am not. I do not transform into anything, ever, although I do a great imitation of being an ass. Nor do I crave or drink human blood, and I don't make any blood sacrifices to anything, or pray to any pagan deity. I don't do magic of any sort. The Church is contracting me because I'm faster than humans, as you just saw, and my strength is also proportional to my speed. I heal extremely fast and I have lived a long time–" she started to interrupt. I held up my hand and continued quickly. "Before you ask, I don't know exactly how old I am in years because I spent a lot of my past life in a series of extended comas or hibernations. I won't tell you the approximate year of my birth until I get to know you better."

Joanna looked at me like I was a test subject or a monkey that had just spoken English. Winning her trust was going to take a while.

"Look, I know this is difficult to accept. Just keep working with me, talk to Michael, and then you can decide whether to stay and help me or head back to England."

That seemed to mollify her somewhat. "OK. A week to see how it goes. That you are here and working with Michael makes me feel better." She sounded skeptical, but it was a minor victory. Now I had to keep from being myself for a week. Should be doable.

She continued on with her run, and I went back to the house. I was not sure how this was going to work out.

"Winning friends and influencing people?" Michael asked when I got to the front door.

"Always my strong point," I answered. "And I hate it when people quote Carnegie, the daddy of self-help. Please tell me the Church does not promote that."

"Oh no, we have better authorities and mentors to follow. I thought you would appreciate a secular American's quotation on your ability, or inability, to interact professionally with female colleagues."

I just stared at him and his evil smirk. "There is so much wrong with that sentence I don't know where to begin."

I left him and his smirk on the stoop and went inside.

When Joanna came back in after changing, she was all business. She asked me some specific questions about my condition. I answered as best as I could without giving away too many details. She seemed stumped by what I was. Welcome to my world.

"I really need to put more thought into this. At the moment, I cannot come up with any myth or legend that quite fits you. Slow aging, fast healing, physical enhancements, but with no side effects other than long periods of sleep. I'm going back to England this weekend and I am going to look at some old Celtic manuscripts that I normally do not include in my research. Perhaps they may have some passages, but I am not optimistic."

"Thanks for seriously considering this issue. I have also put time into the search and found nothing, either."

We finished early for the day so she could get to the airport. She no longer seemed to hate me but was quietly contemplating the new riddle I had given her. Or maybe she felt more trusted, as I had given her one of my secrets. Just as she was leaving, she stopped and turned around.

"You have told me a bit about your status. I am sure there is a lot more that you are not telling me, and I think I understand why. But something you have not mentioned is how you feel. So Senecus, how do you feel?"

I was quite surprised, and completely unprepared for the question. I did something unusual and told the truth. "I feel quite old in my mind. Most days, my life feels washed out. I manage my money, which is beyond boring, change my identity every so often, and try to catch bad guys. Beyond that, I enjoy reading and sometimes traveling. But mostly, what I feel is empty and guilty. I have lived this long life yet feel as if I have not contributed enough or lived to my fullest."

"That sounds lonely. I hope we can find your answers and you come to find your purpose."

"Thank you. I hope so as well." And then she was gone. She was going back to a busy weekend with a trip to Wales with the extended family, but I think she would probably rather of had a quiet stay at home instead. As the favorite aunt, she seemed to end up with the kids, and the parents were happy to oblige.

Chapter Six

I spent my usual weekend doing mundane things and staying outside as much as possible. I was supposed to meet up with friends, but a last-minute business trip had come up to prevent it. Meanwhile, I had to admit I was looking forward to the next week at the cottage.

My closest friends, at least in this life's iteration, were three people. Thomas was an avowed extrovert, probably too handsome, and was extremely popular for his wit and yet propensity for kindness. A devastating combination that made him famous in Amsterdam and rarely without a date. He likely had dated half the eligible male population in the city. He spent his days running one of the busiest airports in the world, so he deserved his fun. I sometimes accompanied him on a round of his favorite bars and he either already knew everyone or they became friends that evening. I was his quiet and mysterious straight wingman. Not that he ever needed one, but it was nice of him to take me socializing. Somehow, all his gay friends immediately knew I was straight as soon as we met. Since there was no flirting or competing, those that weren't actively prowling would sit and drink and provide fascinating and lively conversation. I was a listener and became attuned to the community of people Thomas interacted with. Eventually, that would lead me on to another hunting expedition.

The other two friends I had met through Thomas. Katherine, but we called her Kate, or Kat when drunk, and her partner Anna. Kate was a whirlwind of activity, a managing director of an international corporation. Then she came home and would move furniture around, paint a room, then take a ten-kilometer run. She did it all while looking gorgeous. Anna was a quiet beauty and a popular pediatrician in the community. She was kind and thoughtful and spent her time outside of the clinic in their small garden or in the kitchen. They made a wonderful couple and were still deciding about whether to have kids. Thomas teased them mercilessly about how that would screw up their lives, but I wisely kept quiet. I firmly believed they would be great parents, but from experience I knew there were certain topics that I had best leave alone.

We met for dinner every few weeks and occasionally for lunch if we could work it into our schedules and I was in the country. I interacted well with them and they sensed I was not a threat; they teased me about setting me up with one of their several female friends, but it never happened. Perhaps they thought I was asexual. I was not, of course, but lately that was an apt label. We made a handsome foursome when out on the town.

Because of the late cancellation by Thomas for the weekend dinner meet, we moved it to Tuesday night of the coming week. It was while I was thinking of my friends that I finally decided on my next course of action. I needed to approach it carefully, but I would ask Joanna to dinner with the group. A safe group social activity might continue improving our working relationship.

When Joanna returned to the cottage on Monday morning, she was looking rather frazzled. I said nothing other than to offer her caffeine. I was learning to not poke the bear. She looked grateful as I gave her the cup and did not say a word. My tea making skills must have been adequate, as she never complained. I nodded toward the garden, and she followed me out.

Since we had paused for tea and walked outside to the garden before getting down to work, I took the plunge and broach the dinner subject. "I wanted to thank you again for your effort," I said. "I know this may not be the most exciting project you have worked on, but it is helping me."

"I am not sure how much it is helping you, as we seem to find more questions than answers," she replied.

"But I can work with questions as well. I want to ask you something, knowing you may not accept, for whatever reason."

"Go on," she said, looking at me inquiringly.

"I have a small but wonderful group of friends I try to meet every few weeks. We are meeting on Tuesday for dinner. I would be honored if you would come with me tomorrow night."

She looked at me, then away. "I don't want to intrude on your plans," she said. I really could not tell if she wanted to go or not.

"No intrusion at all. They are much nicer than I am, much funnier, and are always looking for a chance to embarrass me."

She paused and finally said, "I'd love to go."

"Great. We can leave from here or I can pick you up at your place in Den Haag. Of course, that would be the Hague since you are British. Let me know if you need time to change beforehand. We are an informal bunch, so all you need to bring is a sense of humor."

"I could use some laughs, especially at your expense. And since it's meeting new people, I'd rather change first, so a pickup from my place would be great. You can leave the attitude at home; I know it's Den Haag."

"Done. I'll pick you up around six tomorrow evening. Just text me the address for my GPS. Your ride shall appear, sans attitude."

We had an abbreviated morning session because I could tell she was exhausted. I suggested an early adjournment in the afternoon, which she gratefully accepted. Then, to make up for it, we had another long bout of information download and constant questions on Tuesday. Michael was missing in action and I presumed for important Church stuff. We finished a little early so Joanna could get back to her place by four to miss traffic and change clothes.

I drove back to Woerden, left my jeans on but changed shirts and put on a casual wool blazer. I suppose I would never get over my need to keep something wool around. The days were quite warm, but nights, even in May, were still cool. I drove south and got on the A-12. Luckily, our group was meeting this time in Utrecht for dinner, so I would not have to fight Amsterdam traffic. Just a back and forth on the highway. It was usually easy unless the farm tractor crowd was protesting another dairy cow tax.

I arrived at the address Joanna had texted, a nice section of row houses near to the city center. I parked, got out, and knocked on the door. Joanna came out wearing a simple black dress. A stunningly simple black dress. Damn, I needed a larger dose of suppression. I opened the car door for her. She didn't bristle at the gesture, so I had not screwed up yet. I got in and off we went. I put on some of my Americana music and we made occasional small talk on the forty-five-minute ride to the restaurant. She seemed more relaxed than during our day sessions, so I stayed fairly quiet to keep from ruining the mood.

Thomas grinned and looked ecstatic when we walked into the restaurant. "Welcome to our gathering, Joanna," he gushed. He had stood up as we came to the table.

"Just call me Jo," she said.

"Can I call you Jo?" I asked.

"Sure, as long as you behave yourself," she answered.

Kate and Anna smiled but were checking Jo out surreptitiously but meticulously in the way only women can. The three of them traded a round of "nice to meet you" as we all settled in.

"What brings you to our fair but soaked land?" Thomas asked.

"Jo is a research librarian, and we are collaborating on some areas of common interest," I answered for her instead.

"And those interests are?" Thomas asked.

"Folklore," I answered for her again.

Jo looked at me, and I could tell Anna was looking embarrassed. Kate hit me with a double dose of dagger eyes. Thomas, doing his best guy imitation, was still clueless.

"And with that faux pas, I will shut the hell up the rest of the evening and let the smart people chat," I said. Then I leaned back and did precisely that. It was exactly the right thing to do. I had made my last screw up for the evening and did not plan another. The four of them proceeded into animated discussions on work, travel, and children during drinks and appetizers. I was not much of a borrel fan but nibbled more than usual, so I had a reason to keep my mouth shut.

"So, my dear friend," Thomas directed at me just before dinner arrived, "what do you think of our new besty, Jo?"

Damn him, I should have known that was coming. He had put me in similar positions at our bar outings. It was all in good humor.

"I think she has the finest mind I've met in a very long time," I replied.

Anna burbled out a delightful chuckle. Kate and Thomas looked at me like kestrels watching the dune hares. Jo looked completely surprised. Whether by the question or my answer, I wasn't sure.

I just shrugged and carried on my false love affair with the borrels. Old fried cheese and bitterballen couldn't possibly appeal to anyone, ever. Like kimchi or garum. I think that rather than an acquired taste, bad foods existed so that drunk people could dare each other to eat that crap.

Thomas grabbed my arm and said, "Excuse us, ladies, we need to go outside for a smoke." Which wasn't at all suspicious since neither of us smoked.

We got up and headed for the door to the side patio.

"Obvious, much?" I asked.

"Needs must," he replied. One of our games was to have conversations where the winner was the one to use the fewest words. Similar to the old contest of only answering a question with a question, but less fun.

Once outside, Thomas looked at me and grinned. "Does she know you've developed an attraction for her?" he asked.

"I really do not know," I said. "And my attraction, so far, is professional. For all I know, like any other two people, we may well have irrevocable differences that prevent any relationship."

He stepped closer and sniffed. "I've smelled that cologne before. I believe you are wearing a healthy dose of denial," he said.

"Smell whatever you want," I said. "After those borrels, I'll be happy to oblige you soon. But Jo and I have a work relationship and that's how it has to be."

Thomas just looked at me with a smirk. "Sure," was all he said, unbelievingly.

I had a thought. "Wait, why are you suddenly interested in my love life?" I asked. "Have you met someone?"

He literally gleamed. "Yes, and it's lovely. But too new to spoil with a conversation yet," he said.

"OK, but we soon need to have a boy's night so we can appropriately embarrass each other," I said.

"I'll hold you to it," he said.

We walked back to the table full of plates that had just arrived. Kate looked at us knowingly and winked. Anna had the excellent sense to just smile at us and then turn that same smile towards Jo.

I now realized Thomas had not only taken me outside to get the scoop, it had also let the girls get to have a talk. I was worried about the topics. But Jo looked completely at ease and was smiling, too, so whatever was happening, it was not going too badly for me. Hopefully, they had at least told Jo I was not a serial killer. Although, I guess I might be, but they did not know it.

Dinner progressed well. I polished off a mushroom risotto with a parmesan crust. The conversation went smoothly between bites, and I only interjected occasionally. Lesson learned. Wine was liberally poured, but everyone was mostly sober. Coffee went well afterwards as the conversation slowed, which was a good sign that everyone was comfortable. I had finally found the secret to a pleasant dinner party: shut the hell up and let the socially adept run things.

We said our goodbyes in front of the restaurant. Thomas was taking Anna and Kate home. Then I was sure he was off to an unspoken rendezvous. I walked with Jo back to my car. We had nearly an hour's drive for the trip back to Den Haag. More good music, or at least I thought so, and Jo did not seem to mind my musical choices.

"You have lovely friends and they care very much for you," she said.

"I think the world of them, too," I answered. "Which makes it harder to leave them, as I know I must do, eventually. As I leave everyone, or perhaps more accurately, that they leave me." It came out sadder than I expected, but that was probably because the evening had turned out so well.

She kindly said nothing but looked thoughtful, and maybe a little sad. "There are a lot of questions I have for you personally, but I gather this is not the right time or place," she said.

I nodded agreement and kept driving.

The rest of the ride was quiet as we both traveled along in our own heads. I pulled up to her house in the nice residential area that Michael had arranged for her. After parking, I stepped out, as did she, then she walked to the small gate fronting the tiny manicured yard.

"Goodnight, and thanks so much for including me tonight," she said.

"Goodnight to you and thank you for coming with me to meet my demonic friends," I joked.

She laughed, then took a step toward me, tilted her head up and kissed me quickly on the cheek.

I was shocked, so I did nothing. That meant I stood there like an idiot.

"Don't read too much into this," she said. "But I really had a lovely evening and wanted you to know how much I appreciated it. And that's the extent of my appreciation."

I smiled at her and then moved forward to her slowly, then turned my face slightly to the side so she wouldn't get the wrong idea and hugged her briefly. "Thank you for that," I replied. "I do hope we can be good friends and colleagues. I appreciate your gesture and I reciprocate the feeling."

She seemed happy and smiled as I stepped back to the car. I started it but waited for her to get in the door, then waved as I pulled away.

This evening had started a little rough but ended rather well. I was also feeling an attraction to her, but I was not sure what to do about it. For years, I had shied away from relationships with colleagues and close friends. I would need to be careful before going down that path. And of course, for all I knew, she was not interested in me in that way. With those thoughts, I drove back to Woerden

CHAPTER SEVEN

I had just lit the candles and settled down in my chair with a book when the bullet chinked through the window and passed just over my clavicle and through the meat of my upper trapezius muscle. Through my quickness and reflexes, I was already on the rug when the next two hit the empty chair. Damn, that was one of my favorite chairs.

I immediately figured out that from the trajectory of the shots where they came from. There was only one building high enough on that side of my building for someone to shoot into my apartment windows. My brain informed me that the rounds were probably 5.56 mm through a suppressor, based on the size of the hole in me and the lack of sound. I was dealing with a professional, so I would have to be fast. I was in the kitchen in a flash to grab plastic wrap to wind around under my arm and then around the top of the shoulder to slow the immediate blood loss. A second later, I was at my door and grabbed a knife I kept there, then ran down the steps to the outside entrance door, threw it open and ran to the right and into the alley. It ended at the open square, the kerkplein, with the church and old stone tower on the other side, across a hundred meters of open space.

This would be tricky if the shooter was still in position. I doubted they were still present, but it could be dangerous if there was a secondary spotter along for the hunt. They usually equipped the secondary with a suppressed machine pistol or short barrel rifle. It probably would not kill me, but it would chew me up good and prevent me from catching them.

I decided the shooter was already down from the tower. The front doors of the tower facing the square probably would not be the egress point. The right side of the massive building had a door; there was not one on the left side but there were windows. I chose door number one on the right as most stealthy assassins did not do window work. I do not know why, other than it could be noisy. But to get there, I had the hundred meters completely open to the church itself, then another fifty meters to the side door with only a couple of trees for cover. I also calculated that I had maybe five or six seconds to get there, and I needed to do so without being shot multiple more times.

But I had a big knife, some immortality, and a poor attitude after that hole in my shoulder. So, there wasn't much room left in my brain for logic. I began sprinting at a slight angle toward the corner of the building ahead. Every few steps I would push off harder with one foot or the other to jerk to one side, hoping that would throw off anyone looking to snipe me, knowing it would be less effective on a burst from a machine gun.

As I got near the corner of the building, it turned out it did not matter. I heard a car accelerate from behind the building and to the left, the exact opposite corner from where I was. My only chance was to go back left as fast as possible in case they were on the one-way ring road that circled the town; if they stayed on it, they would swing back to near my location. But if they were smart and turned off to go straight west out of town, I would never get close.

I started running again to the left and got into an alley that emptied on the ring road. No cars went by. As I made it to the end of the alley on the road itself, there were still no cars nor sign of one approaching. The car must have gone west and out of town. No leads on a vehicle then.

I jogged back to my apartment door and went upstairs to take care of my wound. Nothing vital hit, so I would mostly heal by the morning, and then the area would be sore for a couple of days. I plucked off the plastic wrap, doused the area with alcohol as it always pays to be safe just in case, and taped gauze pads front and back. I didn't worry about cleaning the chair, as it would have to be reupholstered.

I went back over what had happened tonight and how stupid I had been. Rushing out my door, they could have ambushed me with either machine gun or shotgun; running across the open kerkplein was stupid if there had been two snipers. Relying on my immortality was going to get me killed. Ironically, only the shooter's acute sense of self-preservation had saved me. I believe there was a lesson in there somewhere. I was also lucky that I lived in such an old building that still had many of the original ancient windows. The glass sagged in most frames and refracted the image slightly, just enough to throw off a hundred-meter shot by a couple of inches. I realized how lucky I was, and how sometimes that was better than smart, which I had not been so far this evening.

The last thing I did was walk back over the kerkplein to the old tower on the front of the church. They had built it partially with stones from the Roman garrison where I was once stationed. The watchtower where I fell into the river was barely a hundred meters from here. I knew from years of observation that the keepers of the tower had a key in a secret place along the wall. I found it and opened the tower door, then sprinted up the narrow winding stairs until I got to the belfry. There was a wooden ladder up one more story, where an exterior door opened onto an observation platform that ran along all four sides of the tower. I looked for any evidence of the shooter on the belfry floor first, such as shell casings, but there were none. They were professional and left no evidence. I went up the ladder and onto the outdoor platform.

There was a marvelous view of my apartment windows from here, but again, no evidence remained. What was lurking, however, was a smell that I last encountered in Utrecht. The sickly- sweet burned spice smell was here, but faint, and slightly different from what I remembered. Only my enhanced sense of smell allowed me to pick it up. OK, there must be some connection between the jinn and the shooter. Either they hung out together, lived together, or worked together. That brought up a whole new series of questions. I would get Monk to do some searches and present it to Michael so his vast organization could start looking for connections.

I walked back to my apartment and jotted down some things on my to-do list. I also made a decision that would likely change my life. It was time to put a little faith in my colleagues. I sat on the sofa with my laptop and began putting some of my life story into writing. They might use it against me, but I had to try something different in my life. Perhaps new allies and friends were the right start. I passed the evening typing, deleting, and editing. While writing, my thoughts went off on several tangents as well. By morning, I had my highly selective memoir summarized. I had intentionally withheld almost all of the times I had lived in America. I read it over and then printed it to take to the cottage.

I had enlisted in the Legion by my given name. Seneca Marcus Aquila, but I usually went by Senecus. They sent me to the Ninth Legion, already stationed for some years in Britannia. It was not a prime assignment, but I had little choice. Weather there was like the Netherlands, but even colder. The native tribes were not always troublesome. However, when the Druids whipped up the population into a frenzy, things got very interesting. And several of us got very dead.

Most of us were relieved when the order came to march, sail, and march again to the south to a new posting, we welcomed the change. At least we were back on the continent. The Limes Germanica, some of which was in old

Holland, were more established and the tribes were more civilized most of the time. Which made them more dangerous in other ways, as their political machinations were always a threat. Daily patrols were easier and less deadly, but when war came, like the Batavus uprising, they played for keeps. That made the usual small raids almost pleasant.

I wondered about the stories told about the Ninth after my change and loss of years spent comatose. The past few years, I found it humorous that an entire mythology had grown up around the mysterious disappearance of the Ninth before 300 AD, somewhere in present day Scotland. Meanwhile, the truth was so mundane it had gotten lost in history; we moved on to the next posting. Direct evidence from archaeology showing the Ninth was on the Limes in Holland after the supposed disappearance in Scotland did not stop the books and movies about "what really happened to the Ninth Legion in Britain".

The real mystery for me was what happened to the Ninth after it served in Holland. When I became more cognizant many years later after my change, the Ninth was gone, as was all of Rome from these parts. I assumed the empire had posted them elsewhere since most Legions moved around after some years in a region. Or perhaps they got caught up in the innumerable battles against the ever-larger barbarian armies from the East and were obliterated. My Leiden days of study shed little light on the modest effort I had once made to look at the Ninth's history. My conclusion that the Legion had moved on without records of the new posting might not be valid. That was a question I would follow up with Michael and my new librarian.

Although the mystery was interesting, daily life in the Legion was not. Dig, carry stuff, weapons drill, build stuff, dig, repair stuff, weapons drill, march, dig, build, drill, march, and so on. Most of the time it was not exciting, but it was normally busy enough to keep us out of trouble. Vices were common enough for most soldiers and the camp followers, with plenty of drinking, gambling and whoring. I guess the Legion had evolved into college fraternities, without all the work, or ethics.

We marched along the river that ran through Woerden to outposts stationed on the south side of the river or rowed along it in longboats. For me, getting out of tedious duty to row on the river for patrols was a pleasant change of pace. When time allowed, we often diverted up the creeks and marshes for waterfowl hunting, which helped relieve our boring diets. The longboats were fast enough that we could hunt and still make up time to not be too late to the next outpost. I thought about some boats unearthed in Woerden and other towns and wondered if I had sat in any of those actual boats. It did not matter, but perhaps I should have carved my name in them and then I could have checked at the museum.

Rowing was hard work, but the muscles used differed from those exhausted by digging and marching. I suppose it was an early version of cross fit. The boat patrols also let me observe my favorite bird, the kingfisher, in full action. After a long and distinctive trilling call, they would dive deep and come out of the water with small fish. They looked more like a songbird with brilliant multicolor feathers, so seeing them dive into the water struck me as funny. A tarted-up land bird that was really a cold-blooded killer of fish in disguise.

I also thought about the men I served with. Quite a few, like me, were in the Legion, but not truly Roman. Like me, most of them had never seen Rome. As Rome expanded and the need for soldiers increased, we were recruited from the conquered lands. For those of us not of wealthy families, they promised us a bit of income and a plot of land after twenty-five years of service. Twenty years of labor and fighting, five years of relative coasting, and then an easier and better life. Find a woman, pop out some kids, then die in your fifties. But altogether better than what most of us could have looked forward to otherwise. Of course, many of us would die from disease; some from battle; and, worst of all, they would dismiss a percentage after injuries suffered from battle or work, without pay or benefits. It was a tough life with no guarantees unless you made the full twenty-five years. The Legion was Rome's way of staying safe while using up the excess population. Then the Industrial Revolution came along and perfected the system of using people up, even more effectively than the royal families working serfs to death in the Middle Ages.

Life in the Legion was hard, but it had given me a place to start a career. I was the fourth son of a poor citizen in Gaul. I did not have attractive prospects staying where I was. Although my father had gotten citizenship, it was only through his grandfather, a minor noble, who helped the Romans in the early days with provisions and scouting. Although it was probably from ratting out other minor nobles plotting insurrection against the Romans. But he, and then my grandfather, had lost all their money gambling on the river trade. Too many of their boats disappeared or were robbed. Culprits were likely the families of those my great-grandfather had delivered to the Romans. My father ended up working for a landowner for just enough to get by on food and shelter. So, it was off to the Legion for me. I had believed and expected it would be a hard life, but fair, with what I hoped was a nice retirement after my service.

But we had too few men, almost no supplies, and little good news from Rome. The northern frontier, the Limes Germanica, was close to another ending. Wouldn't be the first time but might be the last. The Empire was always ebbing and flowing on the frontiers. Our situation constantly changed based on the flow of politics and populations.

You could get vertigo from turning your head back and forth watching the tribes change allegiance away from us or each other. The only faster game was watching the Legions changing allegiance to new political risers in Rome. On any month, we might be on the verge of fighting three different tribes, at least one of those close allies, or even another Legion up the river or further east. Most of the time, the rumblings would die down and we would keep on with our rather mundane lives. But humans were perfecting the art of politics that would reverberate through the centuries and affect nations that formed later. Throw in terrible food and poor weather with the constantly changing political morasses and morale was not good this far north. Yet I still was optimistic everything would improve. Nothing could have prepared me for what happened instead.

I was on watch on a windy, cold, and sleety night, which was too often a typical evening in pre-Holland. My leather boots were sticking to the icy wood, and the wool uniform did little for the cold, as it just wasn't thick enough. Normally I would not have been on watch rotation, but we were so shorthanded there wasn't much choice. I sensed something behind me, then in the same second I felt an intense burning sensation on the right side of my neck. I quickly spun, pulling my sword as I did and sweeping it outward. There was something, a black shape, already ten feet away. Whatever it was, it was damn quick. As I came around with the sword, I felt myself losing control over my limbs and noticed blood spilling off my shoulder, and my momentum kept me spinning. Right on around and then off the watch station tower. I fell fifteen feet into the river below. Of course, ice had covered the river over, so I smacked hard onto that first. My weight broke it and I went into the water.

Somehow, I still had my sword and was flailing, even though my movements were slowing down. Something large was beside me squirming in the frigid water, so in my shocked state I reached out and grabbed with my left hand and felt something soft yet bristly. Perhaps gills? Meanwhile, I was reflexively stabbing at it with the sword in my right hand and slicing through flesh. The big shape threw me back and up, then my head hit the bottom of the ice. I gasped and took in water and lots of blood as there was little air trapped under the ice. I realized I was tangling with a damn big fish and that wasn't what had originally attacked me. The fish, what with sword wounds and me manhandling a gill, was losing blood faster than I was. The time between my neck wound and the killing of the fish in the river was only a few seconds. But that's all it took to drown in frigid water under the ice.

I could no longer move and couldn't breathe. I floated heavily under the ice as the current pushed me downstream and then against what I felt to be a mud bank. Everything went white in my vision and then blank after that.

Chapter Eight

I woke up with no idea of where I was and found myself jammed in a hollow spot under a mud bank of a river. I felt terrible, yet I was strong enough to pull myself out of the mud and onto the bank. It seemed like the same river I had fallen into, but now the weather was warm, and everything was green. Feeling terrible, I lay down for a while. I started walking upriver, but only made it a short distance before pain exploded all over my body. I started sweating, then it felt like a wagon had run my head over.

I woke up again in much the same condition as the previous time. But now a couple of mongrel dogs were barking and snapping at me. I was in a large, tangled mass of driftwood on a sandy beach. I scared off the mutts and sat down. The weather was cool now, more like fall. As before, I did not know where I was, and it did not matter as the pain and sweating returned. I blacked out again.

Once again, I awakened in what felt like the summertime. My clothes were gone. Based on the sound of the surf, I was still near the ocean but in the high dunes, well off the beach. I did not know if I had been sleepwalking or if storms had somehow transported me. No weapon, no clothes, and no money meant I could be in trouble. I built myself a shelter and waited for the next blackout. But I stayed awake, so the next morning I went scouting for clothes. I could see smoke in the distance and followed it to a village. I stayed hidden near the edge of the village until the night. It surprised me how well I could see. Despite not having eaten, I was also physically in good shape. I slipped through the village but could find nothing to steal that I needed. Near the last house there were some old garments hanging outside a house, so I grabbed those and ran. They did not smell very good or fit well, but at least I was no longer naked. There was a well-worn trail leading out of the village, so I followed it that night. Two hours later, I was outside another village. I waited until dawn, then entered the village. I hoped to discover where I was, and perhaps find out where the nearest Legion outpost was located.

I found a few farmers up early and asked them about the Legion in Latin. They did not understand. I tried the local dialect that I knew. They responded that there was no Legion and had not been for years. Their language seemed a version of what the locals had used in my former post. They asked if I was looking for work. I guessed they must think me a vagrant. I nodded my head yes to prolong the conversation, but they said there was nothing around here; however, a day inland there was plenty of farming and digging to be done. I thanked them and moved on. I started walking inland toward the rising sun.

I stayed mostly on the trails, surprised to see no roads in the area. I thought about what had happened to me, but I had no explanation. My hair and nails were not any longer, but I must have been asleep for a long time. I was hungry, but not starving. Everything seemed strange, and I needed to find someone in my Legion cohort to determine what was happening.

The next village was a half day walk inland. It was so small I did not even stop, as there was likely no chance of even finding anyone to ask about the Legion. By the evening, I had come to a large village or town. I waited outside until well after dark, then went in over a short wall to scout around. Again, my great night sight and physical strength were surprising but helpful. I grabbed some bread and another nicer shirt with no one noticing. I then went to the stables and climbed into the loft to spend the night.

Before dawn, I jumped down to take a short walk around. I came back to the stable, and a boy was just working on the horses. We had a brief conversation, and I found out he did not know of any Legion and that I was in the town of Alphen. But long ago, the Romans had named it Albaniana. It was a shocking revelation. If true, this was once a major Roman garrison. I left the stable to roam around. It was obviously no longer in Roman control, but I found where the old castellum had been. This changed things completely. I now needed a new life, and the Legion would not be a part of it. I asked around about work and was told there was plenty if I liked dirt. The larger of the local farms had begun major ditch digging efforts to drain marshy areas and build up fields. Since the Legion was all about digging, I thought I could be a productive laborer. I walked out per directions to the three largest farms and spent some time looking at each. I chose the one I thought was the best option, which meant they had the nicest barn, since that was likely where I would sleep.

The owner's son told me they could use me as a digger, and the first season's pay was food and a place in the barn. If I lasted past that, there would be some money passed to me, plus I could have a tiny patch of ground to grow a garden. I agreed, and an hour later I was digging a ditch along with three others. That was how I spent three more years. Decent food, hard work, and a dry place to stay. I needed little money since I had no expenses, but I purchased a waterproof leather pouch, a knife, and a leather wallet to put my coins in.

Then one morning I felt sweaty as a familiar pain coursed throughout my body. I knew these symptoms by now, so I was prepared for this next event. An old stone shed lay abandoned at the back of the farm, so I grabbed my things and went there. I climbed into it and basically fashioned a nest. In my pouch was a change of clothes, the knife, and my wallet. I had no way of knowing if I would wake up again or die in the old shed, but if I woke up, I would at least have a few things to start again. I passed out once again.

I woke up, and it was cold. Even my bones were cold. The old shed had fallen down, and there was snow on the ground. I eased myself out of the ruins and through the dead vines. At least I knew which way the town was. I put on the clothes and noticed they were smaller than before, or I was bigger. And the cold did not bother me nearly as much as it should have.

I trudged into town, repeated my past actions, and had a job as a ditch digger on a farm again. A few years later, there was another blackout, but again I had made the same prior preparations as before. Once awake, it was back to town, another farm job, then another blackout. My life had turned into a very annoying pattern.

The next time I woke up, I decided on a fresh course of action. If this was my life, I needed to make it better. I walked east to the next village, and found a job not only digging ditches but also doing farm work, and with real wages. Learning a little about a lot of things, from animal husbandry to carpentry to planting crops. I was so much stronger and faster by this point that I had to be careful not to let anyone know I was special. That was also when I first became a vigilante.

The local lord and his two sons had a penchant for riding their horses around and bullying the farmers and molesting the daughters. It was all great fun for them. They started showing up on the farm I was working, because the farmer had attractive daughters. One son had shown up as I was coming in from the fields and had pinned one of daughters in the barn and was about to abuse her. I ran up behind him, snatched him by the back of his neck, and flung him across the barn. He hit the wall hard enough to break most of his bones. Since it was dark and she was crying hysterically, the girl didn't even notice it was me. I grabbed his body, threw it on his horse, hopped on, and rode it to the big house where they lived. I waited a while until the house settled down for the evening, then went inside. No servants, nor the lord's wife, were there. I broke the necks of both the father and the other son. Then I hung the other son's body by the neck in the barn with a rope. I left a note I had written in blood below the body. It stated that he had killed and burned his family because they were witches.

I went back in the house, checked that there were no other people sleeping, then helped myself to everything of value that I could reasonably carry. When I got everything outside, I set the house on fire.

I was not proud of my actions, but all three had been preying on the local farmers and their families. No one had stopped them. My concern was that the local constable might trace the son's movements to my particular farm. Then the farmer and his sons would receive punishment and potentially be executed. Of course, I could have just left the one son hanging in the barn, but I saw this as a simple way to rid the area of a particular scourge. Even as a Legionnaire, what bothered me most was when men preyed upon women.

I carried my loot back to the farm and hid it. When I went into the barn, the girl had disappeared. The farmer was looking for me and asked me if I knew what had happened, or where the lord's son might be. I told him I had seen the son ride off quickly when I came in from the field. About then we noticed the glow in the sky from the east, the direction of the lord's house.

The farmer gave me a knowing look but said nothing. He continued to say nothing about what happened, but he always seemed grateful to have me around. Over time, I converted my stolen goods to coin. I now had enough to buy a place but did not view that as an excellent investment, since I'd black out again and wake up with someone else owning it. Something I had also noticed was that I was not aging. I needed to think about moving around more, as the blackouts were coming less frequently, and people would begin to notice if I stayed in one place too long. I was right about not buying a place, because a few years later, I blacked out again. Luckily, I had bought a much bigger wallet to keep all my coins.

Upon waking, I carried myself and heavy wallet eastward. I settled in Utrecht and became a stonemason. I worked on the cathedral there as it was always in a state of construction or repair. After that life ended in blackout, I went a little further east to Bilthoven and continued as a stonemason. A few years passed and then I went back to Utrecht to work on the Dom again, this time on the tower. I used that opportunity to build myself a nice little hiding place, just big enough for me, in the attic. I was getting smarter and always looking for a better place to spend my blackouts. As a stonemason, I worked on several crypts for wealthy families, and I realized those were excellent places to spend a blackout. Quiet, protected, and nobody would discover me if I had a hiding place staged in the crypt. That was my new failsafe. And that wallet was getting almost too heavy to carry around.

My vigilante exploits during this time were mild. A few of the worst criminals, guilty of murder or rape, went missing. Others, such as the wealthy who robbed the poor, fell off their horses at night and broke their legs. I spent most of my efforts getting the scumbags noticed by the law, made difficult as the legal system barely existed in those days. I was concerned about continuing to kill as the guilt lessened with each new death. Not a habit I wanted to get comfortable with.

I moved on, and my next stint was as a tree cutter and barn builder in Laren, not too far north of Bilthoven. I could build hiding places under the barns easily enough, so between the barns and the crypts, I had options. After some time in Laren, I invested some of those coins in a small place there as well. I had met a merchant's daughter in town, and we seemed well suited for each other. I was staying awake now for extended years, so I thought it could work out. We got married after a two-year courtship and she moved in. Over the next ten years, she got pregnant, but all ended in miscarriages. I assumed it was because of my nature, and I didn't really try much after that. Another ten years went by, and her hair had already started turning gray, but I did not look a day older than when we met. She suddenly became quite ill and then died. We had a happy twenty-two years together, but between the miscarriages and her death, I now knew the particular danger that affected my life. To prevent that heartbreak, I limited my female companionship to courtships, but no marriages and family, for many years afterward.

I sold the house and moved on. I continued building barns and moved north and west. Eventually, I ended up on the shores of the Zuider Zee and took up fishing. To me, it was a perfect way to learn to sail. That lasted a while until I accidentally became a Viking, and then a temporary German. Then I ended up on a crusade in the Mediterranean, had some brushes with the Spanish and French forces when they invaded Holland, and several other exploits in different places, including America.

Then I realized I had been awake a century with no coma episodes, then longer. I also was not aging, so I had to reorient my strategy and move within society, manufacture legal documents to change my identity while inheriting some wealth from my prior life. An upstanding gentleman of means, with occasional bouts of vigilantism. I had no problem removing certain people from society, especially those the law would not or could not touch. But I could touch them. Most were vicious criminals, but the worst were wealthy sociopaths. They had lethal accidents, and my means grew somewhat each time. But then I decided I had more than I would ever need. The wallet that had once been a simple leather coin bag had now become large enough to require a vault. All I needed for myself was keeping enough money at hand to use for an escape or large bribe in case I ever got caught, and to fund my next life. Perhaps it was just to soothe my conscience, but the excess wealth I came across ended up with the local Church when I thought they were honest enough to distribute it to the poor. If the local Church was not honest, then I delivered it directly at night to families I thought deserved it.

Although I had lived a very long life, I wasn't sure what might kill me. Based on what had happened in the past, I knew what would not kill me. Still, I'd decided not to venture into situations with large explosions or artillery rounds, as I believe greasy spots don't regenerate to human form. I had not been in a fire and had no plans to be. Drowning conditions for most people seemed to be survivable, as I could swim for miles even in cold water. Bad food still gave me a mild upset stomach, but pretty sure salmonellosis would not do me in. When shot or stabbed in the past, I healed in a day or two, but it still hurt. I had not taken a severe wound through the heart or brain yet and no desire to test it.

Age would get me at some point. It was very slow, but I aged about five years each century since the last blackout. I was guessing my physiological age at perhaps forty-five. Not sure if cancer would be an issue, or if something like that showed up how I'd go about getting treatment, or if it would even be effective. And filling out the health questionnaire might get me committed. Therefore, a lot of unknowns kept me from risks I suppose other nearly two-thousand-year-old men might take. Prudent living with low risks might net me another six centuries. Or an asteroid could show up and void that ticket to ride tomorrow. Some days I was hoping for the asteroid to come calling.

Chapter Nine

The next morning, I took the car rather than the bike to Meije as my shoulder was still tender. I was glad to see Jo, and although she smiled when I came inside, she didn't get up to greet me. Probably still a little unsure about the previous evening.

"Good morning, and thanks again for yesterday evening," I said, as I took my customary position by the teakettle.

"Good morning," she replied. Yep, still a little reserved.

"Have you seen Michael yet?" I asked. "I would like to meet with both of you this morning, if possible."

She looked surprised, as we had had no joint sessions yet. "He was here when I first came in, so I think he's around," she said. Jo was looking concerned as she read my mood but said nothing. I finished making our teas and handed Jo's to her but winced when I extended my left arm.

"Age catching up with you?" she asked.

"Nah, nothing a bulletproof vest wouldn't have prevented," I responded.

Now I really had her attention. "Are you serious?" she asked.

"Absolutely," I said. "I never lie prior to having tea."

She looked unsure whether to query me further or let me pick up the conversation.

I sipped my tea for a moment, then said, "Three hundred."

She looked at me. "You are being stranger than usual this morning. Three hundred what?"

"Three hundred is the magic number of the morning. My birth year, approximately," I said.

"I don't understand. Three hundred…"

"Now who's being old and repeating themselves? And the answer is AD. Although closer to 275 AD for the actual birth year. Can't be more precise because the calendars kept changing over the centuries."

She sat, stunned. Wanting to act like she didn't hear, or didn't believe, or that I was off my meds. That probably was not what she was thinking, but a few different expressions crossed her face, so I could have been right. "I don't want to believe that."

Michael stepped in from the patio. He stood for a second and then looked at us; I could tell he was wishing he had not come in.

"Should I enter and intervene or turn around and leave for a while?" he asked gently.

"Please come in and save this conversation that I have just begun but already botched," I said. Jo sat silently and watched both of us.

"What would be the topic that has so spiraled out of control?" I knew he was a smart guy.

"It is about secrets," I said. "Time for me to give some and maybe get some. I got a reminder last night life is not guaranteed, no matter how long it had gone on."

Michael was now completely on alert. "Something like a threat?" I assumed he was being cryptic with Jo there. I also realized since he came from outside, he probably didn't hear our earlier conversation.

"Yes, via a sniper at my apartment in Woerden," I said. "I assume not one of yours," I threw in, since we had already had some friendly sniper banter.

"Definitely not one of mine. They have better aim," he jested. Then he looked at Jo and asked, "Would it be better to have this conversation elsewhere?"

"Nah, this is just a side conversation and I'm done anyway, for now. We need to have a different conversation later though, as this might relate to your disappearing jinn," I said. "Getting shot reminded me to get on with some things I've been avoiding for a very long time. Things that both Jo and you need to know about. The conversation I have just started with Jo is that I was born around 275 AD, then reborn or changed around 300 AD."

Michael looked thoughtful but said nothing.

Jo was still trying to decide if I was serious or deranged. "Why do you think you were born near that date?" she asked.

"Because I served in the Ninth Legion, stationed on the Limes Germanicus," I answered. "Then a strange series of events turned me into something different from the thousands of other Legionnaires recruited from Gaul. This something that I am, is what I have been researching for years, and why I asked you all those tedious questions."

"Are you able to remember, or can you talk about how you changed?" Michael asked.

"Yes, but this will take some time." I pulled out the folder I had brought in with me. "This is a summarized version of my life. Not nearly complete, but there is plenty to understand my history."

Michael made a coffee and sat down. I looked a question at Jo, and she shook her head negatively.

"This could take hours to cover, but I can cover it in thirty minutes. The document will answer most of your questions. I will answer questions today, or again if needed, after you have reviewed the document." I then launched into my summary.

Thirty minutes later, I finished up. "So here I am, seventeen hundred years later, possibly full of nucleated red blood cells and protein from a fish, river mud microbes, and maybe a vampire bite. Somewhat taller and larger after my Rip Van Winkle episodes. Questions?"

"Remarkable," was all Michael said.

"I have so many questions I am not sure where to start," Jo said.

"I believe we can rule out any vampire influence," Michael said. "Other than the lifespan, you are not exhibiting any attributes, and we have centuries of study on that type of being. However, the rest of your condition does not conform to anything we normally deal with. Jo, do you have any ideas from the myths and legends side?"

"From my perspective, nothing really fits either," Jo said. "There are some things that have occurred in the old oral myths, including the Celtic manuscript I recently reviewed, that can impart a long life. However, I don't see any connections to Senecus. Perhaps this is a unique occurrence; otherwise, there may be contributing factors we are not considering because we don't even know about them."

"Well, that is about what I have been able to put together myself - mostly nothing. My question is, what will be the Church's response?"

Michael sighed and looked at Jo. "He just put you in a different security classification category. In fact, I am moving you up two more security classes and management levels anyway, based on what you have heard today. There will be paperwork for you to review and sign tomorrow. You are also now reassigned to my team indefinitely, as I don't think he has finished with his revelations." Then he looked at me. "I have no further input into your origin. For the present and future, we will continue on the current course as planned. Continue working with Jo, then we will begin your training to better prepare you for the contract work."

"Before I get all of us into purgatory any further, is your security clearance even high enough?" I asked Michael mockingly.

"It'll do. But be reasonable with your revelations since I don't have the budget to keep creating new departments or promote Jo any further. Yet I suppose I should wait until we hear the rest of what you are about to tell us."

Well, at least Jo was getting a prize out of this. Although I wondered if her life had just gotten more complicated because of me.

"The other matter I'd like to introduce is my hypothesis on how this might work from a physiological perspective. Before I get too deep into this, how much do you know about microbiology, virology, metabolics, and protein chemistry, either at the macro or molecular level?"

They looked at each other for a moment, then Michael said, "Lay out what you have discovered or have a hypothesis for, then we can stop you if it gets too technical."

"OK, here is the short version. I have a longer version, but I'll go through this first. I had lots of years to figure out how to study my condition. A few hundred years ago, there were lots of supernatural explanations for many things, as science was sorely lacking. Some stories and myths brushed on what I experienced, but nothing really came close to fully explaining it. Most material I reviewed was from Europe and western Asia, with little from east Asia or Africa. I did not look at North America or Australia."

"Just as well," Jo said. "Despite looking at those areas previously, I don't recall any close associations for what you have described."

"I thought so, since I've come up with nothing either. But I don't automatically claim that my condition is something supernatural in origin. Although there may be entities that truly are supernatural in constitution, I think it's likely that science hasn't yet developed the tools to provide a secular explanation for a number of those entities."

"That is our stance as well, at least below a certain level of entity," agreed Michael.

"My years of research into a wide range of scientific disciplines have pushed me in the direction of more secular explanations. When science had progressed enough, I began studying virology. Anything crazy on the science side without a ready explanation gets blamed on viruses, anyway. Then on to protein biochemistry and microbiology and a few other things. I learned enough to put together a partial theory with sizable holes still in it. Then, over the past few years, I dived into the microbiome. I have enough to propose a plausible theory, knowing that, like all theories, it may not be accurate. Especially since it lacks certain tests that I've been afraid to run."

"I don't think any of our researchers have worked across disciplines nearly as much as you have. You have an advantage I wished my people had, by being able to run research for decades," Michael said.

"Yeah, it certainly helps to have all the extra time," I said.

"Everything you have said makes logical sense, but I am unsure what steered you to the microbiome. How does that fit into your model?" Jo asked.

"I ended up at the microbiome because the traditional disciplines I studied didn't even partially explain my condition. However, most of those disciplines come together in the microbiome. Incredible numbers of bacteria, fungi, and yeast inhabit the gastrointestinal tract, doing things far beyond digestion of food. It's where most everything important to the body happens. The gut microbiome contains more total bacterial cells than there are cells in the rest of the human body. Think of it as a mass of alien cells living inside you, and without which you would quickly die, so it is extremely influential on you, the host. The research to date shows it is a major influencer on metabolism, it is the largest immune organ of the body, and it significantly affects brain chemistry and behavior. It determines who we are."

"I have limited knowledge of this area as it has not been a research focus of the Church," Michael said. "Can you explain that further?"

"Your guts contain a trillion cells that are not part of you, but act as a separate civilization. It influences your health and behavior to a great extent. That civilization outnumbers the number of our own cells. It is an incredibly important part of us, yet we know little about how it really works."

"OK, go ahead."

"I have a crazy hypothesis that it kept me alive during those long periods of sleep. As my body hibernated, a portion of the microbiome could have turned into something like a slime mold. Those have organization and directed movement, providing it the ability to leave my body looking for nourishment, hoovering up any bacteria, fungi, plant material or other critters it found. My resting body only needed minimal nutrients to stay alive, which was provided by the roving microbiome."

"Interesting," Michael said. "Please explain more about the slime molds. And why would your microbiome behave that way, compared to other people?"

"Slime molds are conglomerations of different cell types that combine and work together. They are unique because they cooperate as a single entity. Some cells become pseudopods, acting as feet so it can walk around finding food or a better environment. They are voracious feeders and eat anything, but mainly other bacteria, fungi, and yeast. Plenty of that stuff is around on any surface and easy to get to. It would not take much foraging to feed itself and a human body in stasis. The only other similar organism I can think of is the comb jelly. But I don't see how a marine creature lives in the intestines."

"Ah, I see the connection now. If the microbiome, or a portion of it, left the body and moved around to feed, it could maintain itself and the host nearly indefinitely," Jo said.

"Yes. Now the 'why' of that happening is conjecture, but what happens if an outside entity invades and takes over the microbiome?" I asked. "I think the microbiome is nearly unlimited in what it could become if it got smart. That is where it gets interesting. Imagine a virus that produces a sentient microbiome. Glial cells and a rudimentary nervous system would be easy for that mass of cells to construct. That new entity would have significant control over the host."

"Now that... that would explain quite a few things," Michael said. "I am not aware of the Church examining the microbiome as an origin of, or an instigator of some things we encounter. But it makes a certain sense."

"That could also be the basis for supernatural abilities that some humans exhibit," Jo said.

"I think so too," I said. "I know the idea of a smart fecal slime mold skittering around without a leash is not appetizing, and definitely not something you want to see going walkabout. But if it controls the host, at least one not in a coma, it directs the host to do its bidding instead. Giving the human host additional powers also improves the sentient microbiome's chances for survival."

"This makes even more sense, especially if we have been searching all these years for triggers in the wrong place. Or thinking too simply that a virus directly affects the human brain," Michael said.

"Yep, and even better, it is easily testable."

"Testable? How so?" Jo asked.

"I believe the Church may well have some living specimens to look at. And whole warehouses, mausoleums, or catacombs full of dead ones to pull samples from."

"Oh, yes," Michael exclaimed. "We could determine that rather quickly."

Jo sat quietly, but I could watch the gears turn in her head. "If true, this changes our understanding of mythology, as many of those creatures could have existed. And may continue to exist in some form. On a larger scale, this could change medicine and human development."

"Wait," Michael said. "I know this could progress into many tangents but let us test this first. Also, I need to put this perspective in front of the Church. I see an entirely new branch of our organization devoted to studying this if it proves out. Meanwhile, I need to make plans and budgets to get the Church moving. Do you have anything else to add?"

"Not really. But you will also have to figure out how to control it if it is true. Otherwise it may be used by some to create armies of superhumans. Good luck with that."

Michael sighed and got up. "Please excuse me, as I need to make some calls. I'm not sure when I'll be back," as he left through the back door.

Jo looked at me and seemed impressed for once. "In nearly ten years, I've never seen Michael so excited, or worried."

"His life, and the lives of many others, may have just gotten a lot more complicated. I think he sees that clearly."

"Before this discussion, you said someone shot you last night."

"Yes, a sniper ruined my favorite chair. I impeded one bullet to shield it, but alas, the other bullets have ended my leather lounger."

"Where are you injured?" she asked.

"Top of my left shoulder, but it isn't serious," I replied.

"May I see it?"

"Sure, I hear chicks dig scars." She laughed for the first time that day.

I carefully unbuttoned my shirt and pulled my left arm out of the sleeve to uncover my shoulder. She came over and sat beside me, looking at me like a scientist looks at a lab rat. She carefully reached out her hands and touched my shoulder, leaning in close to look carefully at the front and then the back.

"Amazing," she said. "No inflammation, no collateral muscle damage, and both the entry and exit wounds are already skinned over with minimal scar tissue. This looks like it happened months ago."

"Yep, my little critters working overtime to keep the jalopy running." She laughed again. I might as well enjoy her good mood now, as I had probably screwed up her life even though her paycheck was likely doubled since yesterday. She probably wouldn't be as happy tomorrow when she started the new security clearance paperwork. Or when she realized just what I'd gotten her into.

Michael came back in and paused before saying anything. He had a strange look on his face for a second. The one that said, "I can't leave you two kids alone for five minutes." Then he was back to all business as I pulled my shirt back on.

"I have sent this up the chain and need to postpone the rest of this week's activities," he said. "I had planned on starting your training, but that will have to wait for a time. I am leaving later today to begin some preliminary investigations. Jo, please stay here for now, but I may send for you in a few days. I suspect we will need you on the new team that will almost surely be formed. Let's take a break, then I need a side conversation with you, Senecus."

"Sure, seems like a good time for snacks."

Chapter Ten

We had moved outside to enjoy the weather. It was also more relaxing after the previous conversation inside.

"Senecus, as you were obviously a target last night, I need to address another event," Michael said. "We only have a basic history of your past. Are you aware that someone had previously targeted you for assassination?"

"No. I am sure I have really pissed off some people before, but I don't expect any of them survived to come back at me. Why do you think I am a target?"

"We have a record that you were on the train that crashed near Woerden some years ago."

"Yes, it was most unpleasant, especially for those mangled and killed." I thought about that vivid memory of a foggy morning sitting in a train car and then the world unraveling. Incredible forces throwing me around, loud sounds and screams assaulting my ears, flashes of light then high wind; altogether a frightening and confusing experience. Kind of like a high-speed bike accident with a series of flash bang grenades thrown in.

"That was not an accident, and you were the only person of interest on the train that day. No criminal investigation followed, as the evidence was too flimsy for the police, but we followed up further, once we realized a person of interest to us was involved in planning that event. He was also in the

Netherlands during the Second World War, and likely took notice of some of your activities. Apparently, he was willing to destroy a train because you were on it."

"That sounds unlikely. Some older German officer sabotaged a train nearly twenty years after the war because of me?"

"That is our information. And I never said he was German, nor does he exhibit all the typical attributes to be entirely human. We have indications he may be a dangerous entity."

"Damn, that sounds ominous."

"We agree with that within our group. A lot of analysis went into the investigation, including some quite recent developments. We also wonder if you might know him."

"I met and offed a lot of folks during that time. I need more specifics, whether a description or a name, or possibly which year of the war."

"It goes back a little further than that. The person we were tracking does not have a name that we know of, and we have only been able to get a general description. We have every reason to believe he was a colleague of yours in the Ninth Legion on the Limes Germanica."

Holy shit, now I really was speechless. I felt the world go dark for a moment as ancient memories oozed out of the old mud of my mind. Another Legionnaire of the Ninth alive? That seemed too unreal to me and was what finally came out of my mouth. "That must be impossible. It has to be too coincidental to be true. And you already knew I was in the Ninth before I told you today?"

"There were some indicators, but you confirmed it today. But it fits into our information on who may be behind the assassination attempt from last night. You mentioned something about a jinn connection?"

"Yes, when I went into the tower after the shooting last night, I picked up a very similar smell to that associated with the jinn. I doubt it is a coincidence."

"You may be right. Jinn are not assassins, but it could associate your shooter with him or his employer. How do you want to proceed?"

"I think I'll spend a few days tracking the jinn, see where he was or who he was with in Utrecht or before that. Should not take long."

"I agree. Consider it a Church assignment. Jo, until we need you for this other matter, it might be good for you to accompany Senecus."

We were both surprised by that. I was smart enough to keep silent and let Jo ask the questions. "What is my role in the exercise?" she asked.

"Accompany and observe, provide observations about jinn behavior, and gain field experience," Michael said. "And under no circumstance do you enter a known dangerous situation. Senecus, keep her out of danger. She can't heal like you can. Now I really need to leave to catch a plane. Call me if you have questions or if there are significant developments. I will text you the last address of the jinn and leave a file for Jo and you to review on your trip. Jo, I'd also like you to take Senecus' file and review for anything pertinent to your work regarding his origin questions. Good luck and stay out of trouble."

Jo and I agreed, and Michael left. We stayed in the garden.

"Jo, I would rather not work the rest of the afternoon, as my brain is tired. We can then get a fresh start in the morning to track the jinn. How do feel about a brief visit to Woerden today with the nice weather? There could also be ice cream involved."

"Should we not we stay and be productive?"

"I am confident that we can walk and talk and eat ice cream, all while being productive."

"Sure. But I need some time before we leave. Meet back here in a half hour?"

I stayed in the garden to revel in the weather. The morning fog had burned off, but large rainbows were out in the fields to the west. It had the makings of being one of those famous Dutch days. Beautiful sunlight on gorgeous clouds with emerald fields underneath. Sporadic deluges, sometimes with hail, from the clouds sailing over the fields. I would enjoy the sun while it was available. I watched the clouds slowly roll on across the greenest grass anywhere, at least outside of Ireland. But our dairy cows were bigger.

While waiting in the sun, I thought about the earlier conversation about an assassin and the war. The Great War, also known as the war to End All Wars, of course in due time became World War I. Obviously, people in the 1920s were overly optimistic. The Netherlands had the excellent sense to stay neutral during that ordeal. I had no dog in that fight, either, so I tried to stay out of it. Even during those days, I was not sure what it was all about, and it was even more illogical today.

When Germany began changing in the 1930s, it was gradual at first. As it sped up into national madness, most people just refused to believe, despite all the signs, that war was coming again. That changed by the end of the decade when Germany flexed some muscle and occupied other countries. But the Dutch were not too concerned. They left us alone last time, people said, and Hitler needs our farms. I was much less certain and had my US passport ready just in case.

Then damned if they didn't show up for a visit, and then outstayed their welcome. I waited before departing for the US. With my skill set, I thought I could still sneak out if necessary. The first couple of years were not too bad, and I guess the Germans needed the farms, and the Dutch were first or second cousins in a way. Some Dutch teenage boys and young men enlisted in the German Army. I think they wanted to believe the bizarre rhetoric or were just looking for fame and glory off the farm. All of them would eventually regret their decision. Not that many survived.

The Dutch Resistance began plans even before the Occupation with help from the British. They were earnest but outmatched. The Germans were entrenched, motivated, and skilled; plus, they already had experience with occupying and pacifying countries. I started contact with some in the Resistance by 1941. Of the eighteen people I met through those operations, exactly one was still alive in 1945. By 1942, I was active in a small way with gathering intelligence. I seemed to have a knack for getting in and out of most of their guarded zones intact. As a person of means and with no suspicious background, the Germans saw me as no threat. A good fit in their planned "world of better humanity" but I had no intention of participating. I knew enough about those types of humans over the centuries to realize I would kill them instead.

Castle De Haar, with buildings and grounds restored by one of the Rothschilds, was near to both Utrecht and Woerden. It became an informal base of operations for meetings of the Resistance and other activities. Typically, a contingent of German officers would have claimed the property. But a story circulated that the Dutch butler told a group of German officers that arrived to claim it that the Fuehrer had already spoken for it. They left without checking the story. It seemed a good omen, and the Germans did not move in, so I used it along with the Resistance when needed. It became a waystation to smuggle both Jews and downed pilots. Unfortunately for many of the pilots that crash landed in the area, the boggy ground resulted in gruesome outcomes. They thought they were hard landing on a firm field; most ended up embedded ten feet down in the peat bogs. But we rescued some and got them to safety.

By 1943, I was getting more hostile in response to the escalating German misbehavior. Stealing, raping, and murdering are not the signs of a welcome house guest. The problem for me was deciding how to respond. Stay passive or go on the offensive? I helped smuggle people when necessary and continued providing intelligence, but it did not seem to be enough. The Nazis still rounded lots of people up, and they disappeared without a trace. Their demands grew further as the war began draining Germany of resources. And as 1944 approached, the Occupation turned bad; the Resistance was aiding the Allies, even flooding the land to curtail the German tank and artillery movements. Germans don't respond well to lesser cousins misbehaving, so they began killing more people and then just starving the country. I unleashed myself.

I could take out isolated German soldiers and officers any time and any place. I loved that three-hundred-yard shot with a sniper rifle, watching that soldier about to do something bad crumple up and die. Meanwhile, the person being accosted would realize they were now free. That feeling to me was always worth it. But every time a German soldier was killed, they visited some terrible retaliation upon the local people, and it was even worse if an officer was wounded or killed.

So be it, I could adapt. The game was on and I wasn't playing for funsies. German officers that were already in either my book or the Underground's book of bad guys started showing up in gruesome accidents or suicided to death.

Over time, I was often responsible for the German officer eats-a-bullet scenario; multiple hangings from a rope thrown over ancient beams; several deaths from auto exhaust deep breathing exercises; and, ironically, gas oven asphyxiations. For the accident prone, lethal slips in the bathtub; alcohol poisoning (amazing what a funnel can do and works well to fill either the stomach or colon, and those with the newly pickled colons died faster); and occasional electrocutions from faulty wiring. Automobile accidents were common; a couple of drownings in the canal but only in heavily patrolled areas where the locals wouldn't get blamed, and I could arrange a witness; heart attacks and strokes via a few syringes of concoctions I carried around for those occasions; and once I even arranged for guard dogs to feast on a guard. I killed dozens and felt no remorse.

Drownings were fun as I'd jump in the canal, holding the officer just before the guard came around the corner. He would see the officer floundering in the freezing water but wouldn't see me holding onto his legs and dragging him under until he succumbed. The first trial was risky, as I thought the guard might jump in to save the officer. I realized after the first drowning that an unlisted man would not save an officer's life if it involved jumping into freezing water at night. Obviously, some things don't change even after twenty centuries.

I kept several German officer uniforms stashed in different places, but never in my house or apartments. I didn't speak any passable German but could usually get around well at night with no questions. An occasional foot soldier on guard duty, however, was found frozen to death with a flask in his hand. Autopsies were rare on the officers and not conducted on the enlisted men, so I had carte blanche to operate as long as I was careful.

I operated for three years and I was only shot once. Those Luger 9mm's do hurt at close range. Then that same Luger was used to put a bullet through the shooter's head, even if he was a little recalcitrant. Guns don't kill, but mad and shot up assholes like me sure do when I have a gun handy.

I had slipped into the quarters of this officer easily enough. I was just getting ready to put a rope around his neck from behind when he saw me in a mirror. He spun, drew his gun, and shot me through my upper arm as I was flinching to the side. Before he got off a second shot, I went into overdrive and grabbed his hand and put the gun to the side of his head. He did not plan to pull the trigger, but I insisted. I don't know how the guards explained two shots for that suicide, but I did not stay around to find out.

My body count was quite large by May 1945. Even though the war officially ended on May 5 in the Netherlands, a couple more might have gotten offed after that date. I didn't feel the need to adhere to the official end date with some of the worst offenders. I told myself they would elude the Allied authorities and go back home and torture puppies or something worse.

After I learned the full extent of what happened in the concentration camps, I wished I had removed a lot more of those officers. I hope my killing of officers may have saved some from atrocities. My long memory and experiences gave me an inkling of how bad the Nazis were, and how much worse they would have been if given more time.

Despite the hardships, the Netherlands survived and grew into the country it is today. The Dutch are extremely pragmatic people, but the hatred of the Germans is still palpable. And understandable. They deal with their feelings admirably, however. Every year, I try to be in Holland to take part in Remembrance and Liberation Days. The beautiful but solemn ceremony on May 4, for Remembrance Day, is the best way I have ever seen of acknowledging war without celebrating it. Everything closes in each city in the evening, silence is maintained, and solemn crowds march to cemeteries to lay wreaths. Then on May 5, Liberation Day, the people have a celebratory holiday to mark the end of the Nazis and a new beginning.

Jo came out to the garden and broke my memory trance.

"You seem to be lost in thought."

"Yes, just back over my days in the war, wondering where I might have met an old enemy."

"Anything show up?"

"No, just memories. I'm sure something will eventually bubble up. After the data dump I gave today, do you think I'm a freak?"

"No, not at all. But I am excited to have someone who actually lived during some periods I have studied. I plan to ask you hours of questions in the car."

"Oh great. So much for peace, quiet, and pleasant music. But you will pay for that afterward once the projects Michael assigns you build up."

"Maybe you are right, but I am going to be optimistic about all this. Besides, I already got a nice pay raise because of you."

"Finally, I'm good for something. With all that extra money, you can buy ice cream today."

I guided us toward the front door. I really was in the mood for ice cream; the weather was sunny and currently perfect. The big dark barge clouds laden with rain from the sea should hold off another hour or two.

Chapter Eleven

We got in the car and drove down to Woerden. It was only fifteen minutes away, across fields and hedgerows along the ditches.

"You really think Michael is going to get us, the Church that is, into a lot of work based on your hypothesis?"

"If it proves out, you will be too busy to have much time off for at least the next year."

"Why do you say that?"

"You are about to build a bureaucracy inside an existing bureaucracy, leading to political turmoil, infighting and budget competition. That won't happen easily or quickly. Meanwhile, you have the technical side feeding preliminary results back to both the administrative and theological groups. Expect a mess."

"How are you predicting all this? You must have spent some time in the Church hierarchy."

"No, just a very long record of dealing with governments, bureaucracies, scientific organizations, and religious bodies; all the unsavory groups of humanity."

She turned thoughtful and asked nothing else for the next few minutes. I took my parking spot in the underground garage. Almost just beneath the old Roman castellum. Some of the less important finds were displayed behind glass right there in the garage. I said nothing, but I noticed Jo glance at the case and then look away. We went up the stairs and across the same kerkplein I had sprinted across last night. Today it was full of sun, with children playing soccer and parents drinking beer. Saturday was market day and then it would be full of tents with bread, fruit and vegetables, cheese, and fresh stroopwafels, those wafers filled with caramel syrup. And my favorite South African chicken pies.

I pointed out that the brick pavers in the square had wide grey granite pavers placed in a straight line across the square and down a side street, where the line turned ninety degrees to the left.

"What are those for?" she asked.

"They mark the boundary for the old Roman garrison that stood here once. One that I spent time at, some time ago. Less than a hundred meters behind the old tower is the site of my metamorphosis in the river."

I could tell she was thinking and trying to imagine how it might have looked. "It has changed a lot since then, hasn't it?"

"Very much, and mostly for the better. Old Holland has turned out pretty well. It's sad to see the land and rivers changed so much, but with that came some of the best engineers in the world, and one of the top five countries in the world. I'm proud of what they have accomplished."

We continued through the square into town proper to my favorite Ijs or ice cream shop. Anything dairy the Dutch did exquisitely, including ice cream. I ordered some sort of chocolate orange concoction as it was early in the season and I was still experimenting. Jo got strawberry as they were fresh in season. We walked back over to Westdam Park, where I had first met Michael.

"I need to apologize to you in advance for a couple of things," I told her.

"Only two things? You think you have only offended me twice?"

"Uh, well, then I suppose I need a larger blanket apology to cover all things, from the past to the future. Plus, buying you ice cream as a start."

"You are right, the ice cream is just a start."

"Seriously though, I am sorry about making you a target, and twice over," I said. "As this initiative progresses in your organization, you will become a political target, and I wanted to warn you because Michael may be too nice to let you know."

"You really think that, don't you?" she asked. "Don't you think I can take care of myself? For the first part, I have been contending with arrogant assholes, mostly men, all over the world over the past ten years. I think I can handle things my own way."

"I am absolutely sure you can deal with that," I said. "What I am concerned about is the whole new crowd you are about to get thrown into, the politicians and the biological weapons experts."

She actually quit eating her ice cream. In some places, I believe that to be a sin.

"Oh my God."

"Yep." I was practicing my intelligent replies.

We sat a moment in contemplation and finished our treats.

"It really will come to that, won't it? If the microbiome theory is valid, then someone, either an ally or enemy, will try it. They'll build a police force or an army."

"Yep. Part two of my apology, for anyone counting, is you might become a target. Someone watching will notice you traveling with me and involved in tracking the jinn."

She paused. "I don't see as much of a threat there. If I'm riding around with you for a couple of days on a passive investigation, I doubt I'm in any more danger than any other of colleague or friend."

"You are probably right. I just wanted you to know that ahead of time. Do you have any firearms training or prior experience wearing body armor?"

"That would be a definite no to both. And I don't plan to for this trip."

"Right, it is much too soon for that. But the cottage has training areas for that kind of thing. You should consider some basic training in the future. Just to be prepared if anything unusual happens."

"Thanks for the advice. But for now, I'll stay in the office and library, where the only dangers are paper cuts and moldy books."

We walked back into the town. "Oh, I forgot to mention that this street used to be the river, before it was rerouted a few decades ago." To prove my point, we walked another block to an art store that had a rendition of the old town of Woerden in watercolor. "See, this entire length of street was a river, before they filled it in. In winters past, you could ice skate right through town."

"That must have been fun. I suppose with the climate warming, there will be less of that."

"A lot less the past decade. But the kids adapt and spend more time swimming in the warm months."

Then the rains flooded us out, and we ran to the parking garage. I dropped her back at the cottage, and we made plans to meet in the morning to trace our jinn.

I went back to my Woerden apartment, put new and better tape on those three new window holes, then visited my secret vault outside the apartment. It wasn't anything elaborate. Next to the Kazerne was a smaller building with a basement. They divided a portion of the basement off to give a few storage units for the building residents. The other part of the basement was a noisy disco for the designer drug crowd. Very annoying unless you needed noise to cover someone's screams. The back of the unit was all floor-to-ceiling heavy duty metal lockers. But behind that, I had spent some months cutting the concrete wall and digging out a cavity. Then fashioning a concrete slab to fit back over the cutout. It would never pass close inspection but looked like a plumbing or electrical access. I pulled out a few weapons in case we ran into anything on the trip. I had already picked up a box with some traveling food and water, and my luggage bag from the apartment. Not that I was expecting trouble, but centuries of survival had taught me to be prepared. I included a knife I could strap on my lower leg, and the rest of the items went into the car.

I called Monk to give him enough information to trace the jinn, beginning with the Utrecht address and name Michael had texted me. He should have me any information by the morning. I also called Thomas about a boys' night out sometime. He did not pick up, so I left him a message that I was on travel status for business for the next few days. If that changed, I would call him back and arrange for that night out.

I was back at the Meije cottage the next morning to pick up Jo. We talked briefly over our morning tea. She told me that Michael was in Italy but would be back in a few days. She grabbed her bag from the back of the house, then I took it and put into the back of the car. Then we were off to our first stop in Utrecht. The particular area we needed to check was within ten blocks of the train station, so I parked there and then we walked over. My least favorite part of traveling by car in the Netherlands was the chronic lack of parking. Most trips were just easier by train.

"What do you plan to do when we get there, and what do you want me to do?"

"I really don't know yet. Most investigations, probably ninety percent, are a waste of time. You go look things over, think about what you are seeing, then try to put things together. Sometimes you get lucky and see something that clicks, or unexpectedly, a person walks up and gives you pertinent in-formation. Mostly you get absolutely nothing. But if you don't go looking, you definitely won't find anything. Mainly, I want you to just notice anything unusual. When I'm in my zone, I miss nuances."

Another nice morning, so it was a pleasant walk, and early enough to miss most of the tourists and students on the sidewalks. We made it to the seedier side of town, with old row houses interspersed with some ugly concrete concoctions. The first address was just ahead. It was an old dwelling that, like many others, had been cut into ten tiny apartments. The exterior had its share of graffiti.

"What do we do now?" Jo asked.

"I'm still not sure. Act as if we are walking through, look into a couple of shop windows, and see if anyone wants to chat."

Twenty minutes later, we had covered the street and had no conversation in the three little shops we had entered. Cigarette marts, I called them. A small selection of fruits and vegetables, some drinks, lots of cigarettes and vapes, and newspapers in Arabic. We stood out a little in the shops. And nobody was interested in talking to us. Outside after the last one, I decided there was no point in continuing to walk around this area.

"Jo, I have little so far. I believe one of the shop owners was carrying a gun. All three looked tense. That was about all I picked up. What did you get?"

"Have you noticed the people on this block? Watch them walk past each other. No eye contact with anyone. In fact, they turn their heads or look down. Even when they are sitting on the bench together, they are not talking. The younger ones are not even looking at their phones or texting. They are subdued, afraid."

"You are right. Sort of reminds me of a herd of deer when there is a predator around."

"Did you notice the graffiti on the buildings? The building with the jinn address has a different color paint and symbols than all the other graffiti scattered around." She took some photographs with her phone.

I checked back and forth, looking at all the buildings in sight. "Right again. Not sure what it means, but you are quite good at observing."

"Something is wrong here. Likely they will not talk to us about it."

We walked back to the station and got in the car. "Next stop, northwest Amsterdam area, near the fair town of Sloterdijk. A lovely valley of faceless concrete and transient populations."

"It sounds lovely. What else is it known for?"

"Nothing, absolutely nothing."

I wove around Utrecht to get to the A2 highway north toward Amsterdam. I hoped traffic was light, or an hour's drive could turn into two. Monk had sent me a couple of addresses and an agenda of what he had found on the jinn. Appended was a brief note that said, "whoever this guy is, he did not conceal his trail".

We spent the next hour making small talk about America. She had been on a brief visit for business, and one of her sisters had vacationed there. Like a lot of Europeans, she knew it from television and movies, so most of that was really only a facade. But as with all things American, it was always difficult to determine between facade and reality, anyway. I talked a lot about culture, politics, and food. Then we argued good-naturedly about which food was worse, American or British. Chitlins versus blood pudding. We decided it was a tie.

Sloterdijk was just as fetching as the last time I drove through it. I put the address Monk had forwarded me into the GPS. Five minutes later, I pulled up to a very large concrete box near the train station. I felt it was an empty gesture, but I parked, then we walked to the apartment building. More concrete and asphalt surrounded it. A block over by the station had a few weary small stores. There were very few people out and no graffiti in sight. We went to the building first, through a door and into a bright orange lobby. I suppose they were going for bright and cheery. They missed, as the orange carpet and wallpaper were heavily soiled and threadbare. There was a bored attendant on duty behind a desk. I pulled up a grainy photo of the jinn that

Monk had sent to my phone. I showed it to the attendant and asked if he had seen this guy around a few weeks ago. He glanced at it, thought for a second, then looked again.

"He looks like a lot of guys that come through here. They don't stay long. But no, I don't recognize him."

"Thanks." I actually meant it, as he had looked at the photo but obviously did not know the person. "Anything unusual happening around here the past few weeks?"

"Man, you'd have to be a lot more specific than that. This entire area is weird, but no more so lately than any other time."

"Jo, anything you would like to ask?"

"No, I don't think there is anything here. Let's just go."

We walked out of the building and made our way over to the shops. They were just as lackluster in appearance and attitude as the apartment building. Nobody working at those places knew the person in the photo, either.

"How did you get a photo?" Jo asked. "I don't remember Michael sending one out."

"Friends in low places, the kind that find information for money. Our jinn did not conceal his movements, and cameras are everywhere."

It was time to leave with no leads in sight. We went back to the car and were both happy to head north.

"Wow, now I really don't want to die. I worry I would go to hell and it would be Sloterdijk."

"Yes, and it would be the ring of hell known as tedium."

The A10 was nearby, so I took it north across the water, then got off at Zaandam to drive near the windmill park. Might as well practice my tour guide chops on the drive. Jo seemed suitably impressed, and I drove north again. The next destination was Den Helder, where Monk had picked up our jinn getting off the ferry from Texel. He had spent no time in Den Helder, but we would take the ferry across and continue to the last address.

We spent another hour in the car, this time discussing things we liked about the UK. Jo settled on single malt scotch. She was a real connoisseur. I detested the stuff. I did not win any points when she asked me what I thought of scotch.

"I wouldn't pour that stuff on an injured goat to sterilize a wound."

Just to antagonize me, she described all the different peat flavors and the nuances between them. At one point, I contemplated driving off into a canal, but my fear of a Sloterdijk-like hell saved us. I told Jo that my choice of a great UK product was cider, especially the cloudy variety. She just sniffed and said I had an immature palate. We both laughed at that.

We arrived at the ferry but had to wait an hour before the next departure to Texel. We walked around the area for a while. There was a naval museum nearby, so we circled the grounds. Then back in the car and on the ferry. It was a pleasant day, so we left the car and went up to enjoy the sun and wind. We stopped in the bar on the way up. I bought Jo a bad bottled cider, and she bought me a cheap scotch. We laughed and traded drinks. They were bad enough that neither of us finished them. We went back to the car as the ferry neared the island, then drove onto the island of Texel. There was a very cheap hotel on the beach side where Monk had traced a debit card used by the jinn for one night's lodging.

The old single-story inn had seen better days. I parked, and we went in to the dingy but clean lobby. An older lady cheerfully greeted us. I took out my phone and asked her if she had seen the person. She immediately recognized him.

"We get a lot of people stumbling through here this time of year. They drink on the beach and barely have enough money for a night here. Many drink away all their money and sleep in the dunes. Then they will pool their money to rent a room, and I'll have ten people in that room taking showers. But this one was different, as he said little. But I remember him because he was sober but came in with his pants wet and muddy, as if he just walked in from the tide. He made a real mess of my floor, but he did not seem to notice. He carried a lot of cash but used a card to pay. It was only for one night and he did not check out. I never saw him again."

I thanked the lady, then we walked out.

"Well, I guess this is where he entered the Netherlands," I said. I was being an obvious mansplainer. Jo just looked at me sideways.

"Freighter from the Middle East?" Jo asked.

"That would be my guess as well."

"He gets off a big boat, takes a small boat in, wades ashore, stays in crappy places on his way to Utrecht. Does not cover his tracks. Then starts up a lot of trouble, and when cornered by the Church, completely disappears. That seems odd from my research on the jinn."

"I know little about them, but that is really odd for just about anyone. This is not logical. Either we are missing something simple or something bigger is cooking that we don't know about."

We were both stumped. The day was getting late and the last ferry before dark would leave soon.

"Jo, we are both prepared to stay overnight. What about doing it here and catching the morning ferry?"

"That sounds fine if we can get a place to stay."

"Should be easy to do since the season is still early, and it is a weeknight."

We both pulled out our phones and started searching. We settled on a small but nice, nearly beachfront place just a few minutes away. They had a vacancy and a small restaurant. I drove us over and we checked in. We had a light dinner after all the car riding. Jo suggested we take a long walk on the beach since the sun was still up. It surprised her that the beach was so nice. "I never gave it much thought but assumed the Netherlands would not have good beaches."

"We keep it a secret as much as possible. Keeps fewer tourists from coming over."

"I'm a huge fan of beaches. I've always enjoyed them. The beaches in Greece are the best. Have you ever been?"

"Not exactly." I said nothing else, as I had a sharp pang from an ancient memory of a Middle Eastern coastline.

"You don't seem to be a beach person."

"I can be, sometimes. When I am relaxed, I find it very soothing. Something about lying in the sun, blown by the wind and listening to the surf for days at a time is great."

"But not today?"

"No, too much on my mind. I cannot get over the feeling there is a play, or a con, going on that I can't see."

"Well, you may not dampen my beach mood. I rarely get to visit a nice bit of sand. Either act like you are enjoying yourself or give me a story about a pleasant time you had on a beach somewhere."

I thought about it but could not come up with a pleasant story. But I remembered a funny story about my fishing buddies, Peter and Paul. They and I chased an enormous fish across shallow sand flats, trying to catch it with our bare hands, until it got away. It seemed to do the trick and kept Jo entertained. I did not tell her they were long dead, and they were with me when I got hijacked to be a Viking.

I was thinking about those days when an incredibly strong rubber hose wrapped around my neck and dropped me on my ass. I was being dragged towards the surf, and I reached up and grabbed it with both hands, yet I couldn't budge it. Not a rubber hose, but a damned big tentacle, rubbery but strong as a steel cable. Jo, to her credit, didn't scream or run away, but jumped on me and tried to grab what was around my neck. Her extra weight slowed it pulling me across the sand, and apparently the other end of the tentacle was not amused. A second one came snaking out of the water. My mind cleared as I got mad, so I reached down and unsheathed my large knife from the leg scabbard. I sawed the tentacle as hard and as fast as I could before the second got there. The knife parted the tentacle, but the large suckers still held it around my neck. But I could breathe, so as the second one came in, I pushed Jo behind me, let it wrap around my waist, then I cut it off as well.

There was a thrashing in the surf, and I could just make out a blob of something that appeared to have two large, dark eyes. It disappeared as the remains of the two tentacles whipped back into the ocean. Fantastic, a kraken attack on a nice island beach. I was possibly not the best date around. We stood together, looking at the ocean, ready for another attack.

"Are you normally this popular with the wildlife?" Jo asked.

"What, you don't like to wear your sushi?" I asked, as I worked the tentacle off my neck. Those suckers hurt when they popped off. I dropped it at her feet, beside the other portion that had fallen from my waist. Suckers did not stick to clothing very well.

"Great, now we get to go back to the hotel, with you sporting those bloody hickeys all over your neck. I may die of embarrassment."

I laughed. "I guess that's better than dying of tentacle envy."

"Seriously though, what was that, and why was it after you?"

"I don't know the answer to either question. Maybe a giant squid, but never heard of a beach attack. I don't think I've ever had anything in the ocean mad at me before."

"Well, you've done rightly pissed something off."

We headed back after the impromptu adventure. It was dark by the time we got back to the hotel. The bar was open, so she got her fine scotch, and I settled for a rum, as they did not have cider. My neck was already better as we talked about nothing for a few minutes. We said goodnight and headed to our rooms.

As I sat in the room, I tried to make sense of the day. First, why would some random sea monster take a shot at me? It made no sense. Also, it seemed there were a lot of hidden curtains around this particular jinn. Last, I had to admit to myself that I had been enjoying a pleasant day traveling with Jo. And that I was really attracted to her. All the usual reasons, of course; great mind, sense of humor, physically attractive. But I could not go there. Too many problems on my side, plus the one where she had shown no attraction toward me. To begin with, I did not date coworkers or colleagues. Nor could I devote myself to another human more than a few months or years. The mental anguish from the eventual loss was too great. Flashes of the last time I fell for someone came rushing back.

Chapter Twelve

It began with an aimless wander, morphed into a supernatural love story, and ended with an atrocity. It all happened long ago in the New World. My first trip to America started, unlikely enough, in France and Spain.

I found solace, companionship, isolation, worldly gossip, and damn good walking trails on the Camino de Santiago. My first time was by accident after returning from the Mediterranean, post-Crusade. Afterwards, I did it every few decades to ensure I met no one twice that would recognize me. It would not have been wise for my lack of aging to be a topic of conversation for such a group of worldly and educated men. Then I realized I could go on back-to-back jaunts as that wouldn't raise any suspicions as long as I took a few decades off every ten years or so.

Since I could walk for hours, didn't need regular meals, and was not much affected by the weather, I rather enjoyed the long hike. Many people from many countries made the journey. Almost like an early global internet. But without cable fees, download slowdowns, and crazy right-wing social media users. Not that there weren't plenty of crazies around at every point of history, they just weren't relevant until modern technology gave us the same stupid politician or celebrity on every channel and website. The Camino was an excellent mixer for all people. I quite enjoyed the long walks, conversations, and occasional debates on Christ's resurrection or whether France or Italy had better food.

I also enjoyed the Lake District and Snowdonia treks in later years, but those were not the same. The scenery was good, the weather sporadic, but I missed the people that walked the Camino.

On the Camino, I heard about a plague in the Middle East, sometime in the mid 1700s. The disease's last known progress was Greece, or Venice; there were conflicting reports. Which plague it was and when it might arrive in Europe was unknown. Overall, the plague made everybody crazy. The anticipation, the arrival, and the aftermath were all terrible in their manner of hysteria. I wouldn't die from the plague but when entire cities and regions went insane for months, bad things happened. Entire cities could burn down. I decided this was an excellent time for an overseas adventure. Reports of the New World were interesting, and it seemed the weather was less hot than Africa.

Finding a ship in Amsterdam was easy but finding the right one that was going to the right place in the New World was difficult. I stayed away from excessively dirty or clean boats. The dirty ones spoke for themselves, and the clean ones usually had an obsessive-compulsive captain and crew. I found what was a suitable compromise, after two weeks of searching. The boat had sailed in from England and was bound for Charleston. It was close enough in both the destination and mid-range dirty quotient that I made my decision.

Many reasons had led me to hop on a ship to America. Besides the threat of plague, daily life and business in Holland had gotten somewhat rigid. I also felt a vague unease, something I later determined was "immortal depression". I thought a change could rejuvenate my fondness for life. For those reasons, I found myself on the boat for Charleston, South Carolina, to discover the New World. The continent was new to a lot of Europeans. Not so new to the people that had lived there for over twenty thousand years. I always thought the archaeologists had highly underestimated the timeline of when the continent was populated. Clovis dates never made sense to me, and now older, accurate dates were in use. At least until the next discovery pushing it back farther.

The trip had seemed like a good idea. But I discovered that in Charleston there was a small class of the wealthy, a small market class, a large indentured servant class, and huge numbers of Africans. The first three groups were all white. The last was all slaves. I detested the arrangement and the sanctimonious wealthy using their version of the Church to justify it all. If I stayed long here, then a lot of accidents would befall Charleston's elites.

The countryside was pleasant enough and reminded me of an exotic Dutch lowland, but much too semi-tropical. Damn, the bugs were relentless, plentiful, and insatiable. Add heat, humidity, storms, slavery, and stir until everyone went insane. I decided a long jaunt away from that town was the best idea.

I made my escape by walking to the northwest. I had a horse but rarely rode it. Marching came naturally to me. I had heard of a town called Pendleton in the upcountry that had fewer bugs. It took me quite a few days to get there. The journey gave me the pleasure of sampling several terrible roadhouses and log buildings called inns that mostly catered to bedbugs. Otherwise, it was a most pleasant journey.

The land was a patchwork of languid, slow creeks with extensive green fields full of dark laborers. Rice, at first, then as the land slowly heightened, there were many but smaller fields of tobacco and maize. Cotton, too, but very little, as other inventions had yet to come to spur its growth and fuel the eventual destruction of the South. In fifty years, these fields would become huge and filled with pink blossoms in the spring and bolls bursting white in the fall. Intrinsically linked were the unimaginable numbers of the enslaved spending their lives in the cotton cycle. Raw cotton was needed for the cotton gins, whether in the northern US or England. Only a terrible civil war would break the cycle.

I kept moving and felt like I was on the march again. At least this time, I was without the close quarters of five thousand sweaty men marching along together in Gaul. Eventually, the rivers narrowed and sped over wide falls. Then I kept on further until the rivers narrowed again and became more like rocky creeks. Finally, the nights became cooler, the days less so, but better than Charleston.

Pendleton was not a terrible place, but it was just a small town completely dominated by the plantation class I had left in Charleston. Some of the same men and families, actually. The town was laid out well with a square and the roads, though poor, radiated out to the important people, which, of course, were the plantation owners. They already had entrenched the practice and business of slavery there, and it was just as repugnant as Charleston. Other than the plantations, there was not much there yet. I kept traveling.

From Pendleton, I could see a mountain range to the north. It was very green and attractive. I heard the area was still relatively wild. Tribes of natives were farming and hunting the region, and there was no slave trade. The early settlers had taken Native American slaves for a time, but that had not worked out, and now there was a better alternative. I knew then it was my new destination. Because of the type of trip, I thoroughly outfitted myself with a musket, accessories such as a long knife and hatchet, and all the provisions the horse could carry. I had seen a couple of natives pass through Pendleton, and the concept of a barbarian tribe on a new continent intrigued me.

My meaning of that term was not what current connotation implies. Barbarian tribes were autonomous political and martial entities outside of some Roman rules and control. Some got Roman citizenship, like my family, especially if they had gold and were inclined to sell out a competing warlord.

I assumed the natives in America had also developed their own political affiliations and territories.

It was supposed to be just a camping trip in the Appalachian Mountains. Spawning a new tribe, a revolution, and love stories were all thoughts beyond my comprehension. I went upriver, crossed the upper Savannah River at a ford, and started my adventure.

The trail system was well used. Trails passed over creeks, springs, and followed along water or ridge lines. Sometimes one went straight up over mountains or ridges, as they were created before horses were available. I didn't know it, but the mountains generally formed parallel ridges running from southwest to northeast. Therefore, the trail in this direction was more meandering. But that explained why the trails I crossed running northeast looked even more used and seemed straighter. The trees were magnificent and more plentiful than in Europe. Great forests there were mostly gone as human needs increased for ships and housing, bridges and firewood. Old-growth forests here were tall thick pines, massive chestnuts producing more mast than the animals could eat, and the more familiar oaks, maples, and beeches. As I rode, I considered that as more Europeans came over, this forest, too, was doomed. The only treeless patches were where farmlets were developing, or on the high bald elevations above two thousand meters.

I eventually came to a wide river valley with cleared land along the flat portion and planted with a great expanse of maize. It was thick and lush and giving off that warm sweet smell that only corn fields exhaled in the summer. I also saw a village built around a large mound near the river. I had clearly found the natives, and they looked well fed and prosperous. Now for the tricky part. I had met several times with the Old-World tribes; hell, I was part of one tribe that the Romans had "civilized" in Gaul. But these people looked very different. I had once come across an injured kestrel in a brush pile in Gaul and had thought to take it for its feathers. But once I crawled in to grab it, I looked into its piercing golden eyes and saw no fear there, but a strength so great as to be almost arrogant. I left it alive there as I realized I had no right to take such a magnificent animal for my purposes. It belonged to another world and possibly a higher purpose. These people reminded me very much of that regal bird so many years ago.

Nearing the village, I saw timbers formed a palisade wall, and the houses were wood with what looked like some form of thatched roofing. A small group came out. They clad themselves in leather and cotton clothing, but with the midday heat clothes weren't abundant. Most had tattoos like I hadn't seen before. They were of average to tall height and well built. With that look of strength, they were a formidable people indeed.

We struggled through the typical "we can't communicate" nonsense and devolved into a lot of hand signals. I think the words were zero percent successful, the hands maybe fifty percent. I was passing by and needed nothing, nor wished to visit their village, and they seemed good with that course. They had been exposed to white men before, and as I wasn't a threat, they were polite but not friendly. We made some more gestures and then I kept riding. I thought they did not know how bad it would get in the next few decades. Looking back later, I don't know how many of those people survived the wars or the misery afterward. Various factions of white men and enemy tribes destroyed all the towns in the following years, and eventually much of the Cherokee people were force marched to Oklahoma.

I followed the trail as it gained elevation, finally rising into higher mountains. Fewer pines and more hardwoods. The creeks were running fast and rocky. I saw smoke ahead after four more days of slow riding. The natives had cleared a cove for a small settlement with houses and several small fields, lush with maize, beans, and three kinds of pumpkins. A couple of guys walked out and we exchanged the same useless communication efforts as in the previous town.

And then I saw her, and the world changed. Native and beautiful. But that was not what caught my attention. To me, she was literally glowing right through her golden skin. This was new. She walked right up, staring into my eyes, smiled, and held out her hand with the palm up. Her other hand she put on my chest. I stood there stupidly as I felt her energy through her hand. She said something, and the men went away. Her hand left my chest to take my hand, and she led me to a pool by the stream. She gestured for me to sit by the stream and I washed off the trail grime. She sat beside me and we looked at each other and then both smiled. I decided I was home for a while.

We stayed together that night, then for quite a few years thereafter. I stayed in that village with her and learned the language. The other villagers deferred to her, and so they accepted me in the group. Since I was a good and tireless worker, there wasn't much dissent, plus I soon realized she ran things. Her name was Uwoduhi, but she used Hia as her nickname. I moved my things into her dwelling, and my horse became the village adoptee. The village was small but part of a group of villages near a much larger town, similar to the very first town I had seen, with a palisade wall built around a large mound on a river. Our small settlement was so fertile there was constant travel to the town for trade. We spent our first year together there in her village.

That fall, Hia told me we must leave the next spring as our destiny was to be elsewhere. Based on many things I had seen and heard, I gathered she was a holy woman of her tribe and revered throughout the area, so I assumed this was normal for her position. In what I guessed to be March, before the warmth had returned to the mountains, we packed up the horse and headed southwest. Her village was not happy to see her go, but they had no hold over her. It surprised me that none of them went with us.

For two weeks, we journeyed among well-traveled paths and through several villages. Then, after two days on a single narrower path without villages, we crested a pass and arrived at a pleasant valley with a large creek and floodplains. She told me this was where we would settle. The valley ran north-to-south, with the creek closer to the western ridgeline. On a small hill on the eastern side of the large creek, we began setting up our home and farm.

Mountains that kept out most traffic encircled the fertile valley. Plus, there was only one village south of us, so visitors were infrequent. Beyond the southern village were unsettled hunting grounds that provided a barrier between another great tribe further south along the Etoho River. We started with a typical hut and then I began building a log cabin. We worked tirelessly during the days and bundled up together at night. I hadn't previously met anyone that could keep up with me physically, but she could work with me all day. I knew she was different and began wondering just how much alike we may be in certain ways.

One pleasant morning, we walked out to the creek as it played along the fields in the sunlight. The crops were doing well, as always, and the birds were making lots of noise. A pair of kingfishers were chittering up and down the creek. It was fitting, as she had nicknamed me for them. I was her great kingfisher.

"Darling," she said, "I must tell you of what you already guess. This will not be easy to tell you, but I must. I also think and sense that you are more than what you seem as well, so perhaps this is a time for truths."

"Yes, my dear. I do have questions, but I never asked, as our life has been so good together. I didn't want to risk any chance of it ending."

"The nature of life and its endless circle require endings. But not yet for us. Changes must come first and then someday our ending will follow." I wasn't completely following but let her continue. "I am of the people but separate. Our great tribe came from the far north and settled this land long ago. A small portion of the tribe, my people, trace back many, many years even beyond that. My people, the small tribe, are called the Nunehi. We carry a special gift, which the ability to bring life and fertility to the people. These are things you have already witnessed. To wield these responsibilities, the spirits gave us powers that make us more than human." She paused and looked at me.

"I don't know your tribe, of course, but have observed everything you've said. As you guess, I am not truly human, either. But what makes you different?"

She smiled sweetly and then quickly became a hawk standing atop her pile of clothes. Damn, I was expecting something dramatic, but not quite that. Despite my long life, I had encountered nothing like this. I should have been worried, but this was my Hia. And she was not the only one with a secret.

Then she turned human again, standing naked in the sun. "Now you know why I sometimes take long walks alone and how I know what is happening on the other side of the surrounding mountains." I was listening, but still admiring her. "Well, I see some things never change and I had best get dressed before you can hear me speaking further."

Yes, she definitely knew me. She finished dressing, and we sat by the water.

"I truly do not know how that works or why," I said. "It does not matter to me, either. But how does that explain your ability to enhance all the surrounding life?"

"We don't know either. Within our group, we can change into animal form and also improve life around us. It is just the way we are and, according to the stories, we have been that way since the beginning. We are shapeshifters that bring life and fertility to the world. Other shapeshifters try to counteract us, and sometimes kill us."

"I hear and am at peace with all that you say. Once you hear my strange origin story, you will understand how easily I can accept it. But who are these threats you mention?"

"Another group in the tribe can also change into animal form but they are mad and sow chaos and harm among the people. They are the Uya. Perhaps since they do evil and diminish life, we were created to counteract them. At least one of our origin stories claims that. We are mortal enemies, and my people have developed weapons to battle them. I will also teach you and our coming children how to combat them. There are not any in this valley or nearby, as most have moved north toward the lakes or stayed to the west. They are not a threat now, so my end is likely to be from the natural course of life in the next years."

"Now you have also spoken of endings, and I fear you are about to change our story of happiness."

She smiled sadly and looked away. "Yes. My time is not near, but will come someday, and then I must die. For that is the sacred circle of birth and death; to bring forth life requires that I must die. Each touch of life I bring to the world also takes from my body. I know I don't look like I'm aging or that I'm ever ill, but someday all the cost from those touches will quickly overcome me. Life requires life. We live much longer than the rest of the people and stay young, then one season we age quickly and always die during the first winter moon."

I was both relieved that she wasn't soon to leave me, but I was also overcome with despair for the future. I had known she was special since the day we met and every day since, but the thought of her ending unbalanced me.

"I knew something of what you could do, but not your true nature and what it cost you. What do we do now?"

"We keep doing what we are doing. We will have a good life and many children. Then we will move on, as our lack of aging will cause unrest among some of my people in the south village. We Nunehi live and work among the people, but even they become troubled by our presence over many years, so to be less obvious, we move every generation. People like your kind are moving into the country east of us. Your people would be even more troubled if they see both my and your nature. And our prophecies tell of our near destruction by your people. So, we must teach our children well as they will become a new tribe that will weather the coming storm."

"My nature? What do you know of me?"

"Only that you, too, are special. But not like me. I do not sense that you can shift, but your life force is constant, and you don't lose your energy, or perhaps you regenerate quickly. When I first saw you that day, your skin was like shimmering silver and I knew you were the one. Like us but not like us, strong and unbending yet not evil. Our lives were destined to be blended to produce wonderful children that could save our tribe. They will live on to teach, shepherd, and protect our people and live in these mountains until the dark path of the Milky Way claims this world."

"I will tell you of my people and my origin story, then you can judge if you made a wise choice in me." With that, we sat in the sunlight and I recounted my tale and what I had discovered or hypothesized about my origin. She did not seem at all afraid or awed by it but was surprised at the sheer time I had been around.

"You have not told me anything to make me doubt my choice. Time and your actions have cleansed any chance that the original creature passed its evil nature to you. And we all carry some evil as that also is part of life. Truly, you were the one I was to find."

As Hia predicted, our life was idyllic and plentiful. Within months, she was already showing her pregnancy, but still worked as much as I did. Then she bore a son with little help from me and was breastfeeding and then up working the next day. From everything I had previously experienced, I knew this was anything but normal. But the baby looked, cried, and leaked very much like a human baby, so it eased my misgivings.

We stayed on that land, and each year the fields grew more fertile. It seemed like the crops yielded better each year, and our crop of children grew almost yearly. Son, daughter, son, daughter, until we had five of each. All were inordinately healthy the day they were born and survived childhood with no issues. Again, I knew that was unusual.

The children helped expand our holdings in the valley, and we traded often with the village to the south, and a further one to the northwest. Farming, hunting, raising animals, playing with children, and schooling occupied us constantly. We grew our food, tended animals, and hiked to the ridges to the west to visit the caves and draw inside them. We were careful not to intrude on the drawings and carvings already there. Clothing we sometimes made from animal hides but usually traded for cloth from the larger northwest village, or the few times I traveled back east to the white towns to get books.

Our school was more of an advanced class on successful living in the wild; everything from game tracking to edible plant identification, proper planting techniques for maize to learning English. Language and history lessons were why I traveled back east occasionally to trade for a few volumes. Altogether my life with my family was a welcome change from my former life. All the while I appreciated everything about my wife, from her golden skin that seemed to glow and the incredible luck she had with every living thing she touched. I also observed that others did not notice her differences, but all were affected by her presence. My perfect life continued. Although we heard rumblings about unrest to the east and north, we were far enough away and insulated in the mountains to be away from any violence.

Chapter Thirteen

The years passed, and our ten children grew rapidly. Our eldest, now a young man, was set to leave and strike out on his own. Despite all the hard work and children, neither Hia nor I had aged. It was the year of our eldest son's eighteenth birthday that we discussed changes.

We had been out walking and discussing the next chapter of our life. She strongly felt we should move north to a major village I had not visited. She and I could blend in there without too much notice, and the children would have more exposure to the people and culture there. We told the children of our plans and began preparations.

The summer went by quickly and around August it was time to leave. We had buyers for the crops already harvested and for crops left in the field. A family from the southern village was moving up and taking over the farm site. While the weather was still warm, we packed up what we needed for our new life. With our small band in tow, and each leading a laden horse, we left the Brasstown Valley.

The journey north was slow but pleasant. The children were all old enough to keep out of trouble other than harmless fun, like splashing each other when we crossed streams. There were many villages, and they were happy to take us in for a night. We made it to our destination town, Cowee. It was a large town on a river with prominent floodplains, again with a large mound in the middle of town. From what I gathered, the mounds in the region were here long before the current people arrived, so these sites were much older than they seemed.

We settled in easily, as the townspeople recognized and welcomed Hia. I got lots of curious glances but fit in, as I don't think anyone wanted to offend Hia. The kids all acclimated and seemed to enjoy having dozens of other children to play with. After the first year, our eldest son moved on to the north and east and began a family of his own. I asked Hia if our children were to be like her or I. She told me that often the offspring of shifters would become shifters, but she was not sure about our children as I was not a shifter. Usually, about half the children would have the gift; more girls than boys would be shifters. She had decided our eldest was not a shifter. However, he was special in that he was a born leader, and everyone seemed to like and respect him. He was more extroverted than our other children from an early age. I often wished later that we had kept him with us longer. But fate has a way of making things happen, regardless of our desires.

Just before our eldest left, Hia told all the children of their heritage. They seemed quite excited, and some looked doubtful, but when Hia changed to a hawk, there was no doubt. She told them that some of them would develop the gift, but only time would tell. It typically happened the first time when they were approximately twenty years old but could happen earlier under some circumstances. She also told them about the Uya, and that they were bitter enemies. To my surprise, she then told us how to bind and cleanse the bad Uya, removing from them the ability to shift. However, the process also rendered most of the Uya insane, so they would have to be watched over or banished afterward. It was not a decision to be entered lightly, as the people did not imprison anyone. I understood then that the people killed most of them once they went insane.

For the next two weeks, Hia instructed us on how to prepare the binding and cleansing potions. We went into the deep woods to gather ingredients. We refined the binding potion from a rare salamander from high mountain springs, a toad, and two mushrooms, both fairly common. The cleansing potion had the salamander, toad, and mushroom extract. Plus, several herbs and plants, tobacco, and a strong reduction from the poison ivy vine. They could administer the binding potion through food or water but was best used through skin contact over much of the body or put in the bloodstream. Splashing a jug of the binder on a shifter while they were bathing or hitting them with an arrow dipped in the binder were the two recommended methods. The binder acted fast enough so they could not change out of human form.

Once incapacitated by the binder, plus also physically bound, the cleansing potion was given by mouth for three full days with no other sustenance. The effects were severe nausea and diarrhea, which would be unfortunate for everyone involved. It was best that no one be in contact with the fluids exiting the shifter. After three days, the now incapacitated shifter could go on broth for a week and then back to normal food.

Many years later at a university, I pieced together that the binding potion was a potent mix of hallucinogens and neurotoxins. The cleansing potion also had stimulants and poisons from tobacco, including nicotine. I did not know what effect the herbs rendered. Poison ivy extract would inflame and strip the lining from the gastrointestinal tract. The binder trapped the shifter in human form, with the brain too addled to shift. The cleanser kept adding to that effect, plus the nicotine and other plants and mushrooms poisoned the gut flora and body cells. Meanwhile, the poison ivy stripped the gut lining, including any attached microbes. That was my first inkling of the role of the microbiome in supernatural beings.

Altogether, the potions were an impressive way to render a bad shifter impotent. The only downside was then taking care of the resulting insane human or killing them. We gathered all the ingredients and carefully made the potions. Then remade them again so all our kids knew the recipes and the precautions to take. There was no one to try them on, which was a blessing. We buried all the potions in a marked location in case the Uya moved back into the area.

We spent a few very pleasant years in Cowee town. Our eldest son and his family were doing well to the east, and two daughters and the second oldest son were also finding partners and beginning families. Both girls and the boy were showing some signs of shifting ability, so Hia was coaching them on options for their lives of service. Our eldest was involved with the settler towns and had the people's respect there. He showed signs of becoming a politician on the frontier. There were also lots of rumblings from the settlers, the British governor and his armies further to the east, and other Native American tribes in our area. People were acting like people.

By 1770, it was becoming dangerous, and then groups of men in the west and central portions of North Carolina finally rebelled against the British government and Governor Tryon. The Regulators were organized enough, or actually naïve enough, to think they could take on the British and win. I knew the British army was not invincible, but they were experienced. The battle at Alamance in 1771 went poorly for the Regulators and they were defeated, many of them captured. They pardoned and sent almost all the men home, but Tryon needed to make an example. He hung several of the leaders at the Hillsborough courthouse. One of them was our son.

I was in Cowee when I heard the news. I immediately started packing to go pay Tryon a visit. Hia stopped me. She had been crying because she somehow already knew our son was dead.

"This is not the time for vengeance. That will come later. Now we prepare our family and people for the coming storms."

"You are right. Let us prepare as best we can." I had to let the hate melt back down into a low simmer. But I would have my vengeance.

We gathered our family together, which took some days as the older children were spread around towns with their own families. The gathering was somber as we mourned our loss. It was just the beginning of the dark times. We spent the next two weeks discussing how to plan for the future. Later that season, we had further talks with Hia's Nunehi people to discuss the future. They were also alarmed and felt things would worsen.

That fall, I was working on our dwelling, preparing for the upcoming winter. My youngest daughter, Rae, ran into the village to find me.

"Mother has fallen in the field and can't get up. Please come quickly," she said, with worry in her voice.

What the hell? Hia was as strong as I was, and I could not imagine her ever being injured. I ran with Rae to the field nearest the river. Two of the villagers were sitting with Hia. She looked different and seemed to have difficulty sitting up. I kneeled by her and held her around her shoulders.

"My love, my turn has come, and the change now comes quickly for me."

"No. You are too young for this." I refused to believe that she was dying.

"Ah, I was already old for my kind when we met. I had not married because I knew I was waiting for you. But we had our time together and have made a family, an important family to guide our people. Now I wait for the winter moon. But you must continue to guide our children to assist the people."

I just looked at her in disbelief. I then noticed the strands of gray in her hair and the lines in her face. None of that had been there yesterday. She was going to go through old age in three months. I selfishly then thought of myself. If I survived long enough, my old age would be two hundred years of pain and deterioration. But thinking of it that way made me see Hia was lucky, if only that she was going to be spared the worst of a long aging process. I knew it would not make accepting it any easier, as she would be gone so fast.

I picked her up and carried her back to our place. We talked and made small jokes, but both of us were sad for different reasons. She was going to miss all that was happening with her family, and I was going to miss her.

Hia died just over two months later on the night of the full winter moon. All the family gathered to see her off. In the morning, I carried her emaciated body for two days and laid her to rest on the tallest mountain for a hundred miles around. I placed her on the bald in a thicket of fire azaleas I knew would be brilliant orange in a few months. Then I sat on the freezing mountain and tried to think what I would do for the next few hundred years by myself. My thoughts turned dark, and that day started many years of dark thoughts and sometimes actions.

I walked back to Cowee and continued life there with my youngest children. My life was no longer happy, but I stayed until Rae, the youngest, was a teenager and ready to leave to lead her own life. I said my goodbyes to her and all the rest when they came for a last visit, after I announced I was leaving. I gave them with most of my wealth and advice on how to buy land and live as white people outside the Cherokee villages. They would be safer that way when the white armies came to destroy the villages.

I gave our dwelling to Rae and started walking east, backtracking my route from a couple of decades previously. The Revolutionary War was just underway, but it had no effect on either my trek or finding passage on a ship back to Europe. Charleston still had plenty of loyalists, so I just had to act like one of them. I had plenty of gold, both leftover coins plus plenty of nuggets collected from the mountain streams. I bought new clothes and then departed the New World, wondering if I would ever come back. As I left, I was ashamed of abandoning my family, but it seemed the only way to deal with my grief. America had given me much, but it had also taken a lot from me.

A few years later, I was in London and had set up at a decent inn. I was planning a visit to an old acquaintance. For two weeks, I had watched his house and learned his regular habits. I then made travel arrangements by booking a ship to Amsterdam for the following day. But that evening I crept out of the inn after midnight.

I went to a pleasant house that was now dark for the evening. I climbed the wall surrounding it and then up to the second story of the house. The windows were unlocked. I entered quietly and then went downstairs to find the servants' quarters. Before they knew what was happening, I subdued them and tied them up in their rooms. The target was the only other person left in the house, as his daughter was out visiting other family. I walked back upstairs and entered the room of Governor Tryon. I had almost forgiven him for hanging my son, but then I found accounts of his atrocities in New York during the War, after he left North Carolina. That made me quite unhappy with myself, because if I had killed him in 1771, he would not have been alive to commit those actions. But now he would pay for everything.

I woke him. He yelled when he saw me. A sock roughly stuffed in his mouth stopped that noise. I tied him to a chair and pulled it over to the fireplace, which I started up for light and heat. Several candles added light. I introduced myself as a Dutch resident, formerly a resident of North Carolina, during his governorship. I then told him the name of my son. It took him a minute, but then he realized whose name I said, and the relationship. Now he showed genuine fear. As I readied my tools, I told him about my son and our life in the mountains. As I finished my monologue, I slid a razor-sharp knife into the skin of his foot. He screamed through the sock in his mouth. He screamed a lot more when I used the knife, with the aid of the light, to skin both of his feet, then started working up the shins. I also isolated and pulled out a few veins, as I knew the nerves ran along the blood vessels. He began passing out and was shivering, either from shock or hypothermia, as I removed his skin. I needed to move to phase two before I lost him.

I slid the knife into his gut, from below the navel to the breastbone. Carefully, I began pulling out the intestines. It would not be good to pull too fast; it could break them, and the smell would be awful, or the mesentery veins would open and he would die too fast from blood loss. Once I had nearly twenty feet spooled out, I started wrapping them around his neck, then working up the head until his face was completely covered. I had heard soldiers talk about strangling someone with their intestines. It simply can't be done because intestines do not have the tensile strength to be wrapped tight enough around the neck to cut off blood flow without tearing. But they can smother someone when applied correctly. It took Tryon about three minutes to cease breathing. I washed up for the next few minutes, then left him there as he was while I walked from the house and back to the inn.

The next morning, I went to the dock and boarded my ship. I read the next week that former Governor Tryon had died of a sudden illness in London. Yeah, it was pretty sudden, not being able to breathe through your own guts.

It was the worst thing I had ever done outside the battlefield, but I felt it was justified in his case. But the guilt haunted me and has still prevented me from torturing anyone since that time. At one time, I thought about going back and kill his daughter, but I knew I could not do it. She died an ignominious death when she fell out a window and impaled herself on a fence. It was certainly something that I could have staged, but I did not do it. It was not my place to wreak vengeance on the offspring of an evil man.

Chapter Fourteen

I met Jo at the restaurant for breakfast. She ate while I drank several coffees.

"You appear to have had a rough night. I slept soundly with the surf. Are you still thinking about the jinn?"

"Ah, no. That conundrum will be for the ride home. Last night was thinking about some of my past, both good and bad."

"Is there anything you would like to talk about?"

"Not right now. Just trying to work out some things in my head."

"OK, I will be available if you need a conversation."

"Thanks. Now just five more coffees and I'll be good."

We checked out, threw the bags in the car, and headed to catch the ferry. We made the quick trip to Den Helder, and then had nearly three hours to the cottage.

"I thought you had lots of questions for me about my past."

"I do. Should I list out all my questions at once, then go through them, or ask and you answer one at a time?" she asked.

"I appreciate your logic, and I'll be happy to accommodate either way."

"Well, you told your friends I had a great mind."

"It is true, but it also would have been impolite at the time to mention your great ass."

There was a second of shocked silence, followed by a roundhouse right to my upper arm. I suppose that was a bridge too far. "Ouch. That could have caused me to wreck and kill us both."

"No, I'd be dead, and you would walk away."

"OK, now that you say it that way, I see the positive. But then I'd have to buy another car." I mostly dodged the next punch.

I typically would not have said that, but the previous night I had decided to treat Jo like a guy friend. Maybe that would keep me thinking of her like a buddy, or possibly drive her away with stupid guy humor. It was weak, but I needed to set up some kind of barrier. Thinking of Hia had convinced me of that.

"I have some questions, as it seems you were in England with the Ninth Legion. Do you remember any specific people that made it into the history books, or any noteworthy events during your stint there?"

I gave her the background of the place and time of my posting. Not much happened there on my watch. Skirmishes, bad weather, and no famous people visited I knew about. It was boring, but she seemed entertained. She also asked about building techniques and weapons, and I could give her much more information on those topics. The rest of the trip sent smoothly.

I parked at the cottage. We walked together to the study and met Michael. He looked tired, but excited.

"Coffee or tea, anyone?" I stepped over to the sideboard. Both asked for coffee, so I spared no expense in effort by dropping a capsule into the machine. I made all three of us a cup and handed them out as I sat down with them at the table.

Michael led off the conversation. "I have, with help from many others, been able to start up a new Center to study what we have talked about previously. Within that Center there is a Technical Group that includes both a Resource Team and a Research Team. I am glad to offer Jo the leadership of the Research Team. We have identified another scientist to head the Resource Team. Jo, do you think you will be interested in that posting? It comes with all the typical benefits, about twice your current pay, but will require some time in Italy."

"Yes, I think so. I may need more details, but I am ready to see where this project goes."

"Good. Your department and the other will act together to study this issue and determine policy recommendations to be forwarded to the highest levels of administration. Senecus, I think I know the answer, but would you consider a position at the Center, either officially or as a consultant? I could even offer the chair of the Technical Group."

"Go with what you know, Michael, which means no thanks," I answered.

"I thought not but wanted to ask. I really cannot say any more about the Center or its activities, and certainly cannot in the future either, for security reasons, but you should know that the preliminary work has been extremely promising."

"I understand and it is alright with me. If I am not on the team, then I don't play in the game. Which gives me time to deal with some other pressing issues. Glad it is starting well. I had some more thoughts on your project if you'd like to hear them. But I think we need to discuss our jinn trip first."

"Absolutely, go ahead."

"Jo, you were better at picking up details than I was. What were your observations?"

Jo went through the summary of our trip. She ended with, "Perhaps the only real physical evidence of the jinn's passage was the graffiti in Utrecht. I have a rough translation of two of the symbols painted there. 'The end is near' and 'those from high' are what I have so far."

"What were your impressions?" Michael asked me.

"Basically, what Jo said. My paranoid self says there is something else going on, especially as this is not normal jinn behavior, from what little I know of them. It seems like the purpose was random chaos, but then..." My mind was on overdrive as a partial memory came back to me, then another strong one. "Damn. I missed it. It was there the whole time, but I didn't put it together. Michael, do you remember a couple of kids that were found murdered recently, in the Amsterdam area?"

"Yes, only because murders are so rare here. Why do you ask?"

"Our jinn, or someone he was working for or with, was involved with the drug dealer that was responsible for the deaths."

"I assume we will need a new investigation to catch the dealer and prevent more deaths."

"Uh, well, I don't think you need any new investigation. You might have noticed there have been no recent deaths in the area."

Michael looked at me and the boa constrictor face was back. Jo was also observing me. He finally relaxed, as he must have made an internal decision. "Can I then trust that the matter has been handled and will not require any further response or effort?"

"Yes."

Michael looked satisfied, but Jo did not. I was certain there would be a follow up conversation later with her. I decided it was in my best interest to change the topic.

"Jo, the graffiti symbols that you found. Is there any historical precedent for them, or are those just the rants of a scared population?"

"Those are mostly general concepts. They have been used before in some cities. At least twice, in the Middle Ages around the Mediterranean, records show those symbols painted in towns before plague outbreaks."

"Thanks," I said. "I assume we should be safe from the plague here. But that seems odd. Is it possible that the jinn was providing a warning?"

"Not enough information," Michael said. "All that we can do is keep watching and gathering more data."

"I'll have to agree. Michael, I had a couple of things for you regarding all the topics we've gotten into on the science issues."

"Go ahead."

"I'm concerned about what could happen if the Center progresses in certain areas. I don't think you need thousands of me running around if the technology gets out. The Center could prove the incubator for a large-scale controlled release, whether intentional or accidental. And we both know somebody is going to try it."

"That problem will have to be considered and tight controls maintained on the information," Michael said. "Beyond the research needed and scientific study, I believe there will be an enormous ethical dilemma before even considering further testing."

I thought it best to be quiet and not add anything to the conversation. I had already long considered many of the problems associated with replicating my condition. Yet I had been harvesting material from myself with my medical supplies. I had enough material to turn several people if needed. I just hoped it never happened.

"Another issue is the medical advantages the technology could unlock. It seems obvious humans could benefit from it, but I'm worried about seven billion people living for thousands of years."

"I agree, and that research will need to be controlled as well. I hope we can produce something that works for human illness, but I know the dangers with such lifespans. We've already considered adding medical staff to the Center, but we will need a larger budget."

"It is not over yet," I said. "You might need additional medical teams."

"Oh, what's next, and how much it likely to cost me?" he asked.

"Staff will need to determine if there are any neurons or glia cells present in the microbiome of the infected. I suspect, as I mentioned before, there could be nervous tissue present. If it is 'smart', you will have ethical questions since it's a sentient creature. A trillion-cell slime mold with an IQ of one hundred and sixty controlling a human host is both a marvel and a problem."

"I think all of this is an extraordinary leap in an entirely new area," Jo said. "What are the next steps for us?" She was looking at Michael as she asked the question.

"Getting the Center functional as fast as possible, then assigning these issues to the right people and departments," Michael said. "Jo, you will get your share of this, probably sooner than you expect. I think it is time for a break. I need to make some more calls. I should be back in a few minutes."

Great, just long enough to get blistered by Jo. I went to make tea, and she was already beside me. "What happened to that drug dealer killing kids in Amsterdam? How do you know there was a connection with the jinn?"

"Second question first. While sitting here today, I finally remembered a certain odd smell I caught on the drug dealer. It was the same or similar to the jinn's scent in Utrecht and lingered in the tower where my would-be assassin shot at me. I believe all those incidents are connected. My enhanced sense of smell is very attuned to that sort of thing. Unfortunately, I didn't put that together until now."

"OK, that explains the second question. Now the first question - what happened to the dealer?"

There was no getting out of this. "I took care of him."

"Oh my God, you killed him, didn't you?"

"Yes. I reported him to the police, and they did nothing."

"But why did you kill him? There must have been another way."

"I caught him with the third dead kid. Mercy was not an option."

"You say that so matter-of-factly. How many people have you killed?"

"Probably a few hundred." She looked stricken. "But very few since the Second World War."

It was the wrong thing to say. Her face was red, and she stomped off to the back and through the door. She was mad and disappointed, and she was going to feel those emotions for a while. There was also the chance that she would never get over my killing habit. From her point of view, she had just been riding around the countryside and bantering with a mass murderer. Well, I had wanted a barrier to romance, and now I had one.

Michael came back a few minutes later. Whether he had heard something or just noticed my attitude, he knew something was wrong.

"I assume Jo is not pleased with your actions?"

"Yeah, you might say that. Maybe the realization she has been cooped up with a killer the past two days didn't help."

"What do you plan to do?"

"Nothing at all for a while. She needs to process everything, then decide how or if we continue as friends or colleagues."

"Eminently sensible. I will also have some time the next week to talk to her. I'll also encourage her to read your life summary and discuss it with me."

"Do you think that will help? It just has more evidence of my killing nature in it."

"Everything needs context. For most of your life, what you did was within societal norms, but not now. However, I'm concerned with a different aspect of this. In recent years, how do you feel after you have killed someone?"

"Well, I feel nothing. Afterwards, if I think about it, I can get a mild sense of satisfaction knowing that a murderer or rapist is no longer hurting others."

"OK, so no sense of exhilaration, gratification, or sexual impulse?"

"All those would be a definite no."

"Then, as we both already know, you are not a psychopath or sociopath."

"I would agree."

"But you also don't feel any grief, remorse, or pain afterward?"

"No, not at all."

"Don't you think that is odd?"

"Not really. I just took out the garbage. No reason to feel guilty about that."

"When you were a soldier and were involved in battles, before you turned, how did you feel afterward if you killed or wounded men?"

"Before the battle, I'd be nervous. During the battle, it was all adrenaline, fight like hell or get killed. Just after, I'd be tired but would feel slightly elated, mainly because I had survived. Then the next two days would be bad. I'd feel sick and would not eat much."

"And now you kill and feel nothing. Yet any time a life is taken, there is always a spiritual cost. You used to feel that after a battle."

"I, uh, guess you are right. But not feeling guilt or remorse is a good thing. It lets me kill when necessary."

"Perhaps, but that stain on your soul still occurs after every kill. You don't notice it, possibly because that is your coping mechanism, and it gets repressed to a deeper level. But it is still there. In your case, there are many 'still there's' lurking in your psyche."

"OK, I see where you are going. All of that weight on my soul from killing seeps back out like depression or other negative feelings."

"Likely, and I think that is where I can help by having these kinds of conversations. You really don't have anyone else to speak with. We can also direct your violent impulses toward non-humans that are harming others. They don't leave nearly the mark on your soul that human deaths do, and sometimes they need to be killed for the good of humanity. Regardless, if you continue to kill, you will need some outlet to relieve the angst that you don't even consciously notice anymore."

"Alright, I think I understand. From that standpoint, it makes sense. Probably the best course is to stop killing."

"That would be preferable, but it may be more difficult than that. Sometimes your work, especially with us, will require you to make quick and lethal decisions. All I can counsel is to forego lethality as a first choice, but sometimes where you are protecting yourself or those you care for, take whatever action is necessary."

"In that context, killing the drug dealer was not valid. As with the jinn encounter, deadly force was unnecessary to fix the situation."

"Good, I'm glad you understand. I'll move on to other discussions as I don't think Jo will be back today."

I nodded agreement. I doubt there would be any contact for some time.

"From your description of your origin plus other factors, I have to consider that you are outside of the Church's purview."

"Uh, you may need to explain that."

"Your existence defies all odds, as far as everything we know about or deal with. In our experience, that is best explained by an intervention."

"Divine?" I asked sarcastically.

"Possibly."

"You are serious?"

"Yes. If true, that may place your fate and destiny outside of or above the Church. I just don't know yet."

"I have a bad feeling about where this is going," I said. "Just to let you know, I was never baptized."

"Weren't you?" That should have been a question, but he said it more like a statement.

Crap, I guess I sort of had been. "I'm confident the dark shape on that night in 300 AD was not John the Baptist."

"Certainly not," Michael replied. "Perhaps that entity will never materialize. But divine outcomes can occur from any circumstance or action. I will leave that subject alone now, but you should also study the manuscripts describing the beings known as lesser angels and their actions."

"OK, you are not seriously suggesting I am something angelic, right? I don't think that has any validity, based on what I have done or how I feel." Despite my words, I made a mental note of looking up and reading about lesser angels.

"I merely suggest that you are perhaps not what you've always thought you were," he continued. "But then, most of us aren't. And it takes effort to see that."

"I can give that some thought," I said.

"You should. My role for a very long time has been as a protector within the Church, including the office of the Pope. I see and deal with risks mostly, but I also see and deal with other things you may not believe exist. In your case, I know something unusual is at work. You may not be a member of the Church, but you are someone that we will look after as best we can without interfering with you."

"Thanks for that, I think."

"One other thing I need to tell you," Michael said.

"I get free bus tickets to Rome and a harem allowance?"

"Not exactly. I need you to know something regarding the virus suspected of creating vampires and other creatures, even though it is a closely guarded secret. I'm divulging this because I want you to take some time to mull this over, including the ramifications, and perhaps help give us an explanation if there is one. We need a fresh perspective."

"This should be good. Hit me."

"Our best virologists believe that the virus is not natural. Someone created it artificially, or they engineered an existing one, to produce specific effects on the host."

"Holy shit," I exclaimed. "Pardon the expression, of course. But who the hell could do that more than a thousand years ago?"

"Pardon granted. And that is a very valid question. Based on some very good viral detective work, with random mutations and lots of genetic procedures I do not understand fully, we believe this virus is much older than a thousand years."

"I'll need to consider that for a while. Do you have any technical background files you can release to me that won't get me shot for a low security clearance? I can try to put some thoughts together."

"I'll get you a file. You don't have the clearance, but in this case, we are at a dead end and need some outside help. It will be here this afternoon."

"Huh. Oh, what about animals? Could that virus or a similar one affect animals and turn them into monsters?"

"I really do not know, but that could add more researchers to the Center. That's a new team for every hour of conversation on average with you. Without a doubt, the most expensive day I have had."

"Happy to boost your budget."

"This virus may be bad news for you. From our studies of existing documents, fragments of stories, and some accounts of witnesses that were recorded, there seem to be three outcomes for those exposed to the virus. Most, perhaps ninety percent, simply sicken and die quickly."

I thought about that for a second. "With that high of a lethality rate then the survivors must be super spreaders," I said.

"Exactly. The second group, most of the remaining ten percent, gets sick but recovers enough to turn into ravenous and murderous creatures that range widely and kill just about anything they come across."

"Ah, the lower vamps, werewolves, and zombies. And that group can spread the virus easily."

"Yes. But because of their obvious behavior, they are easy to spot and easily killed once the authorities concentrate on them."

"The 'townspeople with pitchforks' welcome committee' or the machine gunners in more recent times, I presume."

He nodded yes, then continued, "The third group, and there are very few of them, master the infection and actually benefit from it physically."

It took me a second to do the math. Oh crap, this was not good. "OK. From my calculations, for the Ninth Legion's under-strength quota of five thousand men, there would be approximately four and a half thousand to die quickly, another five hundred raving lunatics impersonating zombies or werewolves, and a couple dozen that master the infection, which would be like the senior vampires that Hollywood portrays on television today."

"Yes," Michael said.

"You think the assassin trying to kill me is likely a master vampire?" I asked.

"Yes."

"Crap."

"You needed to know that, so you don't underestimate the danger. I will leave tonight or tomorrow to continue assembling the Center facility and personnel. Jo will go with me. That should give her some time to consider your situation and develop her perspective. Meanwhile, if there are any further developments on the jinn investigation, or thoughts on the origin of the virus, please call me."

"Will do."

"With the Center taking priority, I am afraid your training scheduled for next week is postponed again."

"That won't be a problem. I have some thinking to do, anyway."

"I'll leave you now. If you will wait a moment, I will have the virus file delivered to you." He left through the back door of the study. Five minutes later, one of Michael's people came in with a tiny envelope. He handed it to me and left. It felt like a USB drive. I took that as my cue and left.

I headed back to my house, then spent the day and the weekend inside and never ventured out. I had a couple of large whiteboards in my study and I filled them up and erased them a few times. It was a good way to organize thoughts and make flexible plans. I was going through my past seventy-five years and sifting through memories, following random patterns, and looking for a killer on one board. The other board contained relevant Ninth Legion memories. Somewhere there had to be a connection between them. Something that would lead me to the someone I needed to find. That link randomly appeared while I was in the shower, thinking about nothing. I dried off, sat down and began remembering a very ancient former colleague I unfortunately knew for a few years, and a German officer I had met only briefly. Now I finally had a place to start.

Caius Domitius was one of the Ninth Legion's lower tribunes and known as a political animal. He gained the appointment because of his family's ties to one of those creatures ascending to power. He was the third son of a senator from one of the lower houses in Rome. His two older brothers had already achieved a measure of success. I assumed he competed with them, but while I heard they were competent, he was not. He did not have any friends, but he had followers. Smarmy to those above him, petty to those around him, and horrible to those below him. He was cunning at all times.

The cohort they assigned him to, the second, had occasional disappearances, attributed to desertion. Duty on the Limes meant lax discipline, and that things happened differently than in other Legions, but his cohort's desertion rate was higher than even our normal range. There were also disappearances from the local villages, more so than most places along the Limes.

I rarely interacted with him and he had no use for me as I could provide no rung upon which he could climb. I was in the tenth cohort, which also minimized any contact. There was no official Legion interaction during the day. However, over a few years, I saw him at the drinking establishments when off duty. I did not like him and avoided him. On one occasion, his men started a loud argument with mine, but I quieted them back down before actual fighting began. I saw him smirking from where he was sitting. He had actually instigated the argument, then went and sat down before punches were thrown. I thought the actions fit him well from everything I had observed about him.

I then thought about my time during the Great War, Part Two. I heard there was a Nazi colonel or Oberfuhrer visiting Amsterdam in 1944, possibly in anticipation of a Hitler visit. Nobody thought the visit would happen since they had sent such a small contingent—just the colonel and three of his staff. Nor did anyone expect Hitler to be leaving Berlin when the war was going so poorly for his forces.

The colonel was Karl Dietrich and had been one of those in charge of the Nazi school near Eifel, the Ordensburg Vogelsang. One of Hitler's grand plans, sending little boys off to his school, make them good Nazis and talented athletes to compete in the Olympics, and then go shoot innocent people in the head. Quite a curriculum.

Karl was not on my target list as he was not assigned to the Netherlands, nor to my knowledge had he spent any time doing evil things. The Dutch Underground had asked me to monitor him while in town. They suspected he was into more than just investigating the area for a Fuhrer visit and possibly was spying for someone in Berlin.

Something else made me wary of him. There had been disappearances of boys at the school during Karl's assignment. The only reason I knew about it was because both Belgian and German authorities would conduct an occasional search for the missing boys, since the school was near the border. No boys, nor any bodies, were ever found. Most thought that the boys drowned in the turbulent river near the school. I thought it seemed more like the work of a predator.

I monitored Karl while he was in Amsterdam. I followed them when he and his staff went to a restaurant and I went in and sat at the bar. He looked familiar, but I just thought that I must have seen him elsewhere prior to the restaurant. The odd thing was that among the more than a dozen other customers, plus the colonel and his three staff, I could sense everyone around me but the colonel. I could see and hear him just fine, but he did not register on my special radar screen at all. Very unusual.

They left the restaurant that evening with nothing unusual occurring and left Amsterdam the following morning. I did not see him or hear anything about him after that.

Could the two men be the same? Karl was larger than what I could remember of Caius, but then I was larger than I was when in the Legion, as well. Both men had been in places with strings of unexplained disappearances. If Karl was a master vampire, then that explained the disappearances at the school. But was Caius a vampire back in Roman days? Or just a serial killer?

Then I realized something that was so minor but so important. Caius hated the camp smell as he was too good for the camp life. He always burned herbs in his tent. And I had picked up a similar faint smell in that Amsterdam restaurant. Damn, my past kept coming back at me. And that smell was like what I had encountered three times recently.

It was time to get some help and contact Monk. Hopefully, he could determine who Karl was. Then search each century backwards to find who he might have been, as far as possible. Even more carefully, Monk could work it forward to see who Karl had become after the war, and possibly determine where he was now. I doubted it would be that easy, but I needed to start somewhere.

Chapter Fifteen

I got the call at midnight. No rest for the weary, as sometimes Americans forgot about time zones existing outside their continent. It was from a number that could not be ignored. And I instinctively knew that all my current plans were about to be postponed. I answered and said hello in English.

There was a pause and then a female voice spoke up and said the words I did not want to hear. "We need you. Some of ours have gone missing and I think it's bad."

"Nan. What is happening and where?"

"Four teenage girls were headed to Fort Smith for a college visit. Their car was found outside Fort Smith a day later, but not the girls. Two of them are our own, Melissa and Stacey."

"Where was the car found?" I already had a bad feeling creeping up my neck.

"Moffett. Just across the bridge from Fort Smith."

Shit, I thought. Then I thought a second shit. This was going to get bad.

"I will be there tomorrow night. Can you meet me at either the Fort Smith or Northwest Arkansas airports? And do you have backup resources I can access, both hardware and people?"

"Let's meet at the Northwest Arkansas airport. I can get you what you need easier up there than in Fort Smith."

"Got it. I will text my flight information to your number and plan to see you tomorrow night. Anything else?"

"No, just thank you for coming. I don't think we have any other good options."

"We will see. Hope for the best. Meanwhile, I will prepare for the worst. I'll also text you the list of some needed items. Bye until tomorrow."

"Goodbye." She ended the call.

Shit. This blew my chances of quickly finding the shooter, master vampire, or jinn. Maybe this was a temporary delay and I could get back on it in a week. I just hated losing the time. But some things were more important.

On the positive side, I would not have any free time to think about Jo. On the downside, this would be something I would keep from Michael, which also prevented me from asking for backup from his people. I had a bad feeling I was going to need it. If it was dangerous enough to quarantine the area for his people, then I could use some background. But I did not need Michael to know about it, since if it went bad, they might come looking for my last whereabouts and possibly find my family, which I didn't want to happen. If it went well, there could still be questions about how something big and dangerous got taken out mysteriously; he was smart enough to put that together with me traveling to the States to reach the right conclusion. But I had no choice. Better to ask forgiveness than permission, and those guys were supposed to be big on forgiveness.

I was back at Schiphol the next morning on an expensive flight to Atlanta. I called Thomas from the airport to let him know I would be out of town. It was unexpected, but I should be back in a week. Then ten hours of plane fun, an Atlanta layover, then on to Arkansas. Living the dream life of an air traveler. I spent a lot of stupid time going over possibilities with no information and no answers. The only conclusion I kept coming up with was no matter what I did, those girls were already dead. Nan and the elders probably realized it, too, but they were desperately hoping they were alive, so that was the only reason they called me. Even though I did not know the girls, it still hurt knowing they were family. Something or somebody was going to get killed very dead before this was over.

One distraction I used was the thumb drive Michael had given me to review. Holy crap. I was already juggling enough crazy stuff. Karma was kicking me in the nuts for all those slow years, apparently. The information was explosive and, so far, unexplainable. I parked it in the back of my mind for the next few days. I might percolate something in my subconscious or die in Moffett. Either outcome would solve the problem from my perspective.

The Northwest Arkansas International Airport was a nice newer airport in the middle of nowhere, but on the edge of Walmartville, as the locals called the area. A few massive corporations and their influence had changed a formerly sleepy corner of Arkansas into a sprawling mess of suburbs and decentralized retail outlets. I picked up my rental, a Toyota 4Runner, and headed to meet Nan at a restaurant in Siloam Springs. She had driven over from Tahlequah, and we had decided by text to meet somewhere in between. We could talk at the restaurant, and then drive down to Fort Smith to start a war.

I pulled into a Mexican restaurant and parked. I did not see her outside, so I went in and found her at the bar. A gorgeous Cherokee woman, just like her great-grandmother. She was getting some glances. Bet they would not guess she was at least ninety years old, especially since she didn't look a day over twenty-five. I had only made it a few steps into the place when she turned around, stood up and walked to me in one fluid motion. She had sensed me from a distance; it was the hawk in her. We hugged briefly.

"Nan," I said, using her nickname, "it is good to see you despite the reason."

"Elder kingfisher," she said, invoking an old family joke. "It is great to see you again after so long."

We just smiled at each other and wandered over to an empty table. Some women were looking at her to judge the competition, since some guys had stupidly watched her. We sat and once the chips and salsa arrived, we ordered drinks. There was something reassuring about going to any Mexican restaurant and having the same service everywhere. We did not need any small talk to get started.

"What information do you need?" she asked.

"I will need everything you know since I am coming into this cold," I said. "A summary first. Then we can go over the details. I assume you have a copy of the police report, description of the girls, and all the rest. How special were the two that were our own?"

Nan immediately reacted to my past tense referral of the girls. She said her next sentences with emphasis and flashing eyes. "They are both special. I think they may both be shifters, although it is still too early to know for sure."

"Damn," was all I said. Shifters usually developed their unique talent closer to twenty. The girls were probably too young to shift and escape danger. Losing two of them in one generation was a severe blow to our family and to the people. The drinks came, and I had more time to think.

"Any chance this event could have forced an early change with either?" I asked.

"I don't know. But I think I know what you are asking. If trauma prompted an early change, that could be an advantage for their survival. It could, however, have other repercussions long-term."

"Yes, I hope they have had some advantage, since it has already been forty-eight hours and with no trace so far. That might be their only chance."

"We should talk no more of this here." I protested, but she waved me quiet. "I am riding with you tonight so we can talk on the way down and at the hotel in Fort Smith. Meanwhile, let's enjoy our meal and talk about other things."

I nodded agreement and had more chips. Nan asked me about my life over the past few years. I told her about me, mostly living in the Netherlands with visits to Asheville and work travel to lots of places. I asked her about relatives I knew existed, but many of whom I had not met. When the tribe split and went west, including many who were forced to do so, I was out of the US and had missed the entire era. Actually, I'd missed most of the century other than a trip out west. Two offspring had eventually gone to Oklahoma as the people there needed their talents to build everything new while keeping their culture. Because my later visits were in the east, mostly North Carolina, I did not know many of the later generations that lived in Oklahoma.

We caught up with major events and finished our meal relatively quickly. She had gone into little detail about relatives, as she knew I would not get much from it due to lack of context. We finished, and I paid, and then we left in our cars. I followed her to a gas station. She knew the owner so would leave her car there to be picked up the next day by an acquaintance.

I helped her grab a couple of bags from her trunk to throw in my SUV. It really wasn't necessary, as she was as strong as I was, but it was a habit for me. We got in my car and began the trip south.

"What can you tell me about Melissa and Stacey?" I asked Nan.

"Both are good girls, excellent students, and both play sports in high school, volleyball and softball," Nan answered. "They were also active in the community, dated some of the local boys, and stayed out of trouble. We kept an eye on them just in case anything might start early, but as you know, that is very rare. Of course, they could compete in sports, as their talents had not manifested yet since they were not twenty. They and two of their friends went to visit other friends at college in Fort Smith, and they also wanted to visit the campus. We don't know why they might have stopped at Moffett, or if they disappeared elsewhere and the car was left there."

"I have a strong feeling they disappeared there, probably where the car was found."

"There just isn't anything there for them. No reason to be there. The town itself, as you know, has nothing but a junkyard on one side of the main highway and the stockyards on the other side. Nobody they know lived there."

"What was the weather like at the time?"

"Typical heat and humidity for late May and early June. Lots of storms, so the fields are muddy with fog at night coming off the river."

"Do you know any of the history of the disappearance of the large village down on the Poteau River, the Spiro Mounds site?"

"Just what the history books and Google have to say. None of the original people from there apparently left any descendants to carry the stories. Newer people that came afterward have lots of strange stories, as do the first US soldiers that settled Fort Smith. And you know about the more recent bizarre disappearances and deaths in Moffett itself."

"Yes, it seems like an unfortunate place." I changed subjects. "Which hotel are we going to?"

"The historical society was having a special deal, so I got us two rooms in old Hanging Judge Parker's prison overlooking the gallows."

I gave her the fisheye stare, and she laughed. She knew I did not like the old Fort Smith Historic Site, since to me there was still an air of violence, death and suffering that suffused the place. One of the easiest places to sense ghosts other than Edinburgh. She could pick up the same vibes.

"The rooms are at the Courtyard just down the street. Just in case we need to walk the bridge over to Moffett. Although, with all the items you requested, I'm sure we will drive over."

"I will be, at least." I noticed her unhappiness at that statement. "You will be back up and won't be setting foot in Moffett unless things go completely sideways."

"Hell no, I am going in with you."

"We will discuss further in the morning, but you know as well as I do just how few of the special remain. If the two girls are really gone and then you are lost, that leaves what, one of Hia's direct descendants, left for the whole West?"

She did not reply, but I knew the conversation was not even close to being over.

"I need your help and advice on this, so what do you sense so far about this situation?" I asked. "Does it feel more like it is something in the supernatural realm, or more human in nature, or is it something nonhuman but a natural presence?"

She thought for a moment. "Can you be more specific about what you mean?"

"For example, is it supernatural, like ghosts or demons? Or more of a human issue like a badass motorcycle gang or a serial killer? Or something nonhuman but natural, like the Loch Ness monster, since, if real, it could be a remnant dinosaur?"

She was thoughtful for another moment. "OK, I think I get it. Let me think about that for a while and let it settle in my mind. We rode a few minutes in the quiet. "What I sense is that it is more like the last one," she said. "I get nothing like ghosts or Uya shifters. I also am not detecting that psychic darkness that indicates evil humans and their actions. Definitely closer to the last case you mentioned, but I can't get a handle on it. I don't sense it is like anything I have encountered before. Maybe something unusual or multiple things involved. I also do not get any sense of just a normal accident or anything weird like alien abduction, although I don't believe in that, anyway. Aliens, I can believe. I just don't get the random abduction part."

I was listening and thinking about her words. "This may be terrible, then," I said. "Something like that has probably been around a very long time. It has escaped detection even these days because it has killed anything that has ever come into contact with it, or it has some sort of abnormally superior camouflage capabilities, or both. And it likely is smart. Or it is so different we just don't even detect it. Those stories go back long enough to worry me and that tells me it is great at survival, even over centuries."

"Is that not like looking in a mirror?"

"Yeah, I guess so. One or more critters like me could be bad, but I don't think so in this case. I might as well let you know about something I have been working on in the Netherlands as it could affect you here."

She was looking sideways at me. She knew I would not bring it up unless it was important.

"I have been working as a contractor with the Church the past few weeks." I could tell Nan was not happy with that revelation. "It happened after I was chasing something that they were also after, and during the chase, I bailed out their guy. From him, I found out they were already tracking me, which led to further conversations and a job offer. From everything I know, they only tracked me in Europe, but I am letting you know so you can take steps to keep off their radar. Because of our work relationship, during a conversation I found out they knew about Moffett being dangerous. Nothing specific was divulged, but I found out that they have quarantined the area for their people for some years in the future. Whatever they know, it must be bad. They also told me it would be dangerous for me to come back here. They don't know I am here, and I have no intention of telling them. But I can't get any backup from them, so that's why I asked you to call in some extra manpower on top of the equipment list."

"Are you sure they don't know about your American life and that you are here now?"

"As sure as I can be," I answered. "I have been tracking their tracking and nothing has shown up. Right now, they are too busy working on something else to keep up with me. But if I don't get this taken care of in a week, then they might get suspicious. They think I'm working off grid on another deep case."

"I don't know the details, but they lost a priest here some years ago, along with a few other people. The law from both Arkansas and Oklahoma was involved, but nothing was found or resolved. That probably led to more scrutiny we didn't hear about."

"They probably sent in a team similar to what I have heard about in Europe. If that team was lost, you wouldn't have heard about it, but it probably would have triggered the quarantine."

Our conversation tailed off as we arrived in town. I had not been in Fort Smith for some years, so it looked different. Some new hotels and businesses, or at least new to me. I guess tornadoes and floods are good for occasional renewal, but this also looked like there was new money in town. I pulled into the hotel and we went inside.

Chapter Sixteen

Ten minutes later, we had our bags in the rooms and we met back downstairs to make plans. I was tired but could go another two days without sleep if I had to, and Nan could also miss sleep for a few days. Despite this, I was determined to get a few hours of sleep, or at least have time for some quiet thinking. We sat in the lounge area and sipped some iced tea. I looked at her and admired her for the person she was. As one of my and Hia's direct descendants, Nan was a full Nunehi shapeshifter. She worked in healthcare and also ran a food cooperative, doing what she could to help the people as per her nature and calling. She had flirted with getting into the tribal government but had wisely left that course alone. Melissa and Stacey were her great nieces. This was hard for her, but I had to protect her at all costs.

"Who do you have lined up to come in tomorrow?" I asked.

"Henry, you'll remember him from twenty years ago, is the eldest, plus four others that are younger that you have not met," Nan responded. "Henry is the rock, and two of his guys are solid. But the two youngest are still hot-headed enough to need direction, or a boot in the ass."

"Easy enough to correct. I would still like one more person, if possible, trained and tough," I said. "I am assigning two of them to you, even though you won't be in the action directly. That leaves me three if we don't get another."

"I can't get anyone good that quickly. And why do you insist on protecting me?"

"I'm being cautious because this is going to go bad. I feel it strongly in my gut. I've learned to trust that feeling as my source of prescience. Regardless, we have little time and we will go with what we have."

She nodded. "I get it, but don't like it."

"I'll take Henry since he is good, and the two young hotheads as cannon fodder. You get the other two. Are they bringing down the hardware?"

"Yes," she answered. "I also have them bringing the more standard items you asked for. Really, you think motorcycle leathers are appropriate?"

"They will do OK for protection once I put in the Kevlar armor, and won't be nearly as noticeable as other alternatives. The dry suit will give me a different kind of protection. And I do expect to get wet at some point. There is just too much of a coincidence of water around these events. But I will look a little odd, even for Oklahoma."

"It is late, and I'd like to prepare my mind for tomorrow. Meet you for breakfast at seven?"

"Yes, let's do that. I am going for a quick walk across the bridge to get another impression of the place."

"Goodnight and try to be careful." She left for the elevator.

I walked outside and turned left down the sidewalk on Rogers Avenue. I could be in Moffett in about twenty minutes at a fast pace. Just not too fast since the police might notice at this time of night. It was probably unnecessary, but I wanted to get another feel for the place and the danger and see if I could make any sense of it. Plus, it would provide an opportunity for thinking and planning the next few days' activities. I decided I also needed some sleep afterward as I figured the next thirty-six hours straight, I would be awake and active. As I got to the bridge and began crossing the long expanse, the occasional car passing was loud enough to cover any sound.

There was some distant lightning coming across from deeper in Oklahoma, but it was too far away to hear any thunder. Off to the right of the bridge, I could glimpse the cattle stockyards, but the breeze was blowing away so I couldn't smell them. At the end of the bridge, I continued straight a little further and then left again onto the inappropriately named Grand Avenue.

When I got to the first dirt road past the junkyard, I went left again to get to the boat ramp on the river. It was a warm and humid night, with an occasional mosquito buzzing past. The area was swampy the closer I got to the river, and a large drainage ditch followed the dirt path. I got down to the boat ramp where a couple of old pickups were parked with empty boat trailers. I hoped they were not out in the river at night.

I stood for a while but did not get the same intense feeling I had gotten years before. It was still there, but I thought not as intense. I stood in the dark but had no thoughts or premonitions. I sent out, in my mind at least, a notice to whatever was out there that I was coming for it. After a few minutes, I headed back to the bridge and continued on to the hotel.

Nan and I met at seven in the hotel lobby and then walked down the street for breakfast. The sun was already building up for a sweltering day, and I hoped no thunderstorms were on the way. Back east, either Asheville or the Netherlands, thunderstorms were common enough but usually mild. The bastard storms out here in Oklahoma would come across the plains with a vengeance, with wind, hail, and what I called photo lightning, where it flashed so often that even at night it wasn't dark between the flashes, and the thunder was continuous. Which was bad because it masked the sound of the F4 tornado embedded in the same cloud. They had hit Fort Smith more than once, and any storm out here could turn ugly in minutes.

After we ate, we walked and sweated our way back to the hotel to get my car. We drove back over the bridge to the town of Muldrow to meet Henry and his guys. We parked at the casino to wait for them. Then we would head for more rural ground away from prying eyes.

"How do you feel this morning about all this?" Nan asked.

"About the same as yesterday. I honestly do not know what this is going to turn into, but I think it's going to be bad. The crazy thing is, I'm not as worried about the girls as I should be. I just don't get the sense that they are dead."

"I know. I have the same feeling about them, which is good since I usually can tell when family has passed."

"So, let's keep on hoping for the best. And after last night, I think we also need to get at least one small boat or a couple of kayaks. Whatever this is, I believe we are going into the water."

Nan nodded. "Henry is bringing down a boat today, anyway. After we meet up, I will go with him to get a couple of kayaks at that place that rents them downriver. Two-day rental enough?"

"Should be good. One way or another, it will be over by then. I wouldn't put a lot down on the deposit; I'm not sure they will ever get those boats back." Nan just laughed.

A large navy four-door pickup with a camper top and towing a small jon boat pulled into the lot. Nan stuck her arm out the window and waved. The truck came in our direction, then I started the car and pulled back out onto the highway as they followed. I went back toward Fort Smith and turned left at the second massive cornfield. Casinos are good places to meet since everyone knows where they are or can find them. But since there are lots of cameras even in the parking lot, we were going somewhere more private.

From the highway I turned onto a dirt road, and after about half a mile, I pulled to the side at an oil well and pump. They scattered these pumps all over the river valley in the fields. They probably only pulled up a few dozen gallons of oil a day, but if you owned a few thousand acres and two dozen wells, it added up. Even multimillionaires liked to count their pennies.

I parked and got out, as did Nan. The truck parked behind us and a large, older, in-shape Native American man got out of the driver's door. I walked up and shook his hand. Four other men got out of the truck as well.

"Henry, good to see you again."

He nodded and said, "Same to you. But let's not do this too often."

"Agreed." Nan came over, and Henry bowed his head.

"Blessings upon you, Henry," Nan said. That seemed to make him happy. Then she stepped closer and hugged the big man. He looked a lot less happy.

"Thank you, first woman." His reply was a formal address. "And these two are John and Samuel," as he pointed out the two men that looked about my age. "These two are Jimmy and Ned," as he introduced the two younger men, just out of their teens I thought.

Nan and I nodded at each of the four as Henry introduced them.

"I have some things in back you need to see," Henry said to me.

He and I and Nan walked to the rear of the truck. Henry opened it and pulled three locked cases, among the half-dozen in the truck, onto the tailgate. He used a key to unlock all three. The first contained several firearms I had requested. They all looked good. I looked in the second box and checked the bladed weapons and ammunition for the guns. Once again, everything was in order. As I looked in the last case, Henry said, "This was the difficult stuff to get. Some had to come out of the National Guard Armory."

"I hope that wasn't too much of a problem."

"Nah, just once won't get us into trouble. But we won't be able to get another haul like this for a few years."

I pillaged through the case of grenades, flash bangs, incendiaries and other fun fireworks. Fourth of July was about to come early, possibly even tonight.

"Thank you. Everything is here as expected. And you have plenty of goodies for the rest of your guys to prepare for the festivities?"

"Those other boxes are for us. We all got our favorites. No grenades for the young ones though, as I didn't want to have any unfortunate accidents."

"Wise," I said, thinking of the two youngest men. Youth does not always lead to stupidity, but I rarely betted against it.

Nan and I walked back around to the front of the truck where the other four men were talking as Henry locked everything back up and pushed the cases back in the pickup bed. Jimmy and Ned were not shy about checking Nan out. Well, I just won that bet on stupidity. They either didn't know who she was or were playing some dumb game with themselves. She noticed but just flashed me an evil smile. She was going to hurt them, but probably only a little. Then they made another mistake when they started whispering among themselves. Both Nan and I had much better-than-average hearing. They were trash talking like dumb teenagers.

"This guy doesn't look like much. What's an old man and a girl doing here?" I believe he was Jimmy.

"No idea. Maybe she can cook for us. Not too bad looking if you like older chicks." That would be Ned.

I was not sure which one she was considering breaking first. I gave Nan an evil grin. "Do you want me to take this, or are you doing the honors?"

"Age before beauty, usually. But I'll take it from here. They don't know as much as they should yet. I'll try not to break them too much in case you need them later."

The other two older guys, John and Samuel, backed up and looked interested. They had never met me but knew the stories, and I was pretty sure they knew all about Nan. They were old enough to know some stories have a factual basis. Henry had come from behind the truck and caught the end of the exchange. He kept walking past us and over to John and Samuel. He was muttering "dumbasses" toward the boys as he walked.

"Hey Nan, after you teach them some manners, can we get an early lunch? I hear the barbeque place has good banana pudding."

"Sure thing. This won't take long." With a big smile, she walked over to the two boys.

"You boys ever wonder what happens if you piss off the alpha?" I asked Tweedle Dum and Dee.

"Alpha? Nah dude, she's just a girl," Ned said. He mistakenly followed that up with a leer toward Nan.

Nan jumped between them faster than they could even follow and smacked both of them on the ass, hard, as she passed, then spun around toward them. They both yelped in pain and surprise. They could not decide whether to be confused or pissed. Boys. Dumb. Yep. They weren't learning their lesson yet.

"Miss Nan, why'd you smack us for? We were just being friendly," Jimmy said.

"Yeah, we were just kidding around," Ned said.

She stepped between them again incredibly quickly and grabbed them each by the ear. Not gently either. It looked painful.

She led them over to the truck and the other older guys. "I think these two aren't ripe yet. Might want to let them mature in the field a little longer," she said. She let them go, and they were standing awkwardly and rubbing their ears.

"I never saw nobody move that fast before," Ned said.

I heard Henry again say "dumbasses". The boys looked a little confused and embarrassed.

"Fun is over," I said. "You both should apologize to Nan. She's at least four times older than you, so show some respect. Meanwhile, I plan to work you to death for the next two days, and if you survive that, then maybe I'll get you killed on our hunt. We have family to find, so serious time starts now."

They both said "sorry" to Nan and tried to walk to the truck without favoring their bruised buttocks. They also looked like they were trying to do the math in their head and coming up short.

I moved back to the truck and went through all the boxes again, planning out what I would carry tonight and what I would give out to my backup. It was all a guess, since I did not know what we were facing. But since I was going to put myself as bait, I went heavy. With the heat and humidity, unpleasantness was a given. Yet better safe and heavy and hot than dead and light and comfortable. I took the boxes out of the truck and put them in my cargo area once I dropped the back seats down. Henry took the rest of the gang in the truck to get some kayaks and food.

I had printed some maps, Henry had brought USGS maps of the area, and Nan had left me her computer so I could pull up online maps. The east bank of the river was fairly populated with residences and businesses of Fort Smith. Further downriver was Van Buren, and more people. Fewer odd events had occurred recently in the more populated areas. When Fort Smith was a much smaller town 150 years ago there were more incidents. But upriver and on the west bank there was little population. The majority of the disappearances and unlikely events were centered near the tiny town of Moffett, on the west bank, over the past few decades.

I thought that this must be an ambush predator that was shy around crowded areas. Therefore, it made sense that it was probably upriver, using the river to come down and do whatever it was doing. Feeding? Protecting territory? Or both? Tonight, we would hunt upriver.

Around two hours later, the truck pulled back up with two kayaks strapped in the jon boat. They had stopped for barbeque and brought my lunch back. It was getting hot, so we drove back over to Moffett proper and down to the sandy boat ramp on the river. The willows would at least give some shade. We gathered at the back of the truck, and I showed them the maps and told them what I thought while we ate. Everyone agreed, and Nan added some information about a public use area just south and upriver that nobody ever used anymore. Henry added in his hunting experience from the general area and pointed out a couple of likely places a predator could easily hide. He said if he were a bear, then those places would be appealing. Unfortunately, those places included the most difficult and forbidding terrain in the area. Slightly high spots surrounded by swamp, vines and river debris; one was on an island off an old slough and the other was just on the side of the riverbank. Both were close to each other.

"Henry, are there bears in the area and how well can they swim?"

"There used to be some along the river wilds, but I have not heard of any lately. I don't know if many would roam down from the Ouchita Mountains, but they could if they were hungry. As for swimming, they are better than I am. Even if the river was flooding, they could stay with the current and be fine."

"Nan, any idea if there are any Uya here, and if any of them could be bears?"

"We have not had a problem with Uya here for a long time. Most left even before I was born. I have heard that some could turn into bears."

I thought for a moment. "OK, let's just make up a wild hypothesis that we are after Uya in bear form in one of these two places. Right now, I can't think of anything worse, so going with that should prepare us for the worst-case scenario."

"So how do we hunt it or them?"

"That is what we are going to decide for the next couple of hours. That will give us time to set up down there before dark and get the bait in place."

"What is the bait?" Henry asked, smiling.

"Why, that would be me and the dumbasses." The dumbasses were not smiling.

Chapter Seventeen

We stayed at the boat ramp for another couple of hours and talked over all kinds of hunting methods, and which of the two places to stalk first, knowing all the time that our plans were just theoretical until we got on site. But it was the best we could do with what we had. I motioned to Nan, and we walked away from the others.

"Nan, do you have any feeling at all about these locations? I know you can sometimes feel Uya from a distance. Or do you need to take a solo flight out there to get closer? I don't think there are any gun freaks around that might take a shot at you."

"I don't get any sense around here of what I have been told the Uya feels like. I may take a quick look at those two spots. That should give me something if there are Uya around."

"Maybe we should drive down closer, so you won't be in hawk form too long."

"Probably a good idea."

We went back to the guys and explained we were going closer to look over the area, even though it was early. Everyone loaded up, Henry and the guys in his truck, and Nan with me. We headed south and west, which was upriver along this stretch of the Arkansas River.

We drove down a series of muddy, yet sandy roads as the river meandered sometimes close and sometimes far away across extensive fields. The first spot we were looking for was where a creek came into the river, forming a large swamp with some cleared area in the middle. Sand had built up a few feet in the clearing from flooding. Then there was an old river slough forming a rough island that also had a sandy center. The satellite map showed a rough road going to the first location, but the bridge over the creek was missing—that was why we had a boat and two kayaks.

As we got to the first spot, we had a bit of luck. There was a nearly new bridge across the creek, but it did not look sturdy. We both stopped and everyone got out to look over the scene. The road we were on was packed sand and sat a few feet higher than the land across the way. There were also some sight lines across to the slough island.

"Henry, how partial are you to the camper top?" I asked.

"Could be that I get rid of it. This looks like an excellent spotter location for both grounds out there. And we put the jon boat in the creek if we need river access."

"Exactly what I was thinking. Since mine is a rental, I'll chance the bridge and park where you can set up as my cover. Me and the boys will take the kayaks down to the slough in case we need to get across to the island."

"What about us?" Nan asked, standing with Sam and John.

"Nan, you are the spotter and will stay here since you have the best eyesight. And you two," I said, pointing at Sam and John, "will be here loaded for bear and protect her with your lives."

The three of them didn't look happy, but Henry was nodding approval. Henry and Nan started getting the camper top off the truck while John and Sam were muscling the jon boat down to the creek. I got the Tweedle brothers and put the kayaks on top of the 4Runner and drove across the bridge and to the far side of the clearing. We put the kayaks on the side of the swamp, directly across from the island. I then staked out a place with a folding camp chair where I would wait this evening, then put two more chairs a few feet behind me and further from the water for the dumbasses. I needed to quit thinking of them like that; ever since Nan had grabbed their ears, they had been very respectful.

I then placed most of the weapons and goodies around my chair. I also had some three-gallon buckets, and I loaded each up with a gun and ammo. Each I placed around the clearing. I wanted access to more firepower when things went sideways. And things always went sideways. I gave each of the boys a short barrel rifle with multiple magazines. My only advice to them was to shoot whatever showed up, but not me in the back. I then drove back toward the bridge and parked with plenty of clearing on all sides and on a slight rise. Henry would set up here as my main backup. The rest of the goodies in the boxes were his to use as he saw fit. It seemed to be all coming together. I just did not know if any of it would work.

Henry came across the bridge to my car. "Good spot," was all he said. He then rummaged through the boxes and pulled out a 6.5 Creedmoor semi-auto rifle with scope, plus a shotgun and a pistol. "This should do for now."

I agreed and walked across the bridge and up the rise to the truck. Nan and her guards were sitting in the bed on camp chairs. I handed John and Sam each a set of night vision goggles.

"You guys can come down to my car and get whatever weapons you need. Everyone else is set up. Nan doesn't need these goggles, but you guys can try them out. You also need to take turns keeping an eye back down the road in case something tries to flank us."

They both nodded and climbed down to head to my car.

"You still thinking about taking a flight around the area?" I asked Nan.

"No, not now. I feel like whatever we are after is here or nearby."

"I agree. I noticed that although there is a bridge now, there are no tire tracks. Nowhere in the sand are any deer tracks or other animal sign. I think everything and everyone are afraid to come here."

"Yes, it feels like whatever took the girls is here," she said. "I just hope we are in time to get them back."

"I think so, but I bet we will soon find out," I answered.

I walked back across the bridge and to my car. The last thing I needed to do was the last thing I wanted to do. Henry just smirked when I opened the boxes. I stripped down and tried pulling on the dry suit. Since I was already hot and sweaty, it was not cooperating. I finally got it on and walked back and dove into the creek. I swam down the creek and swampy area to the river, then headed against the current back up to where the kayaks were. I wanted to get a feel for the water and currents, as I assumed that I would spend some time there soon.

The entire area had bad currents with unpredictable swirls, with lots of strainers - the jumble of limbs and debris under the water that would trap and drown anyone caught against the mass. With all the strainers and the currents, I decided nobody should be in the boats or in the water unless absolutely necessary. I climbed out of the water at the kayaks and walked back to my car.

Henry greeted me with, "It seems unnaturally quiet out here. No tick deer or waterfowl or anything moving."

I nodded. "Not even tracks on the sand or even the banks I just covered. There is nothing here."

"Oh, something is here alright. I got a feeling we will see it, too."

"Hope so," I answered, as enthusiastically as I could. The water had cooled me off some, but my torso was cooking up a sweat. Then I pulled on the motorcycle leathers after adding the Kevlar inserts. Let the sauna begin.

"You really are expecting trouble," Henry said soberly.

"Yep, I have been doing this a long time, and I get a gut feeling this one is going to be bad."

He went back to the box and got two more grenades. My sentiment exactly.

I walked back past the boys and sat in my chair. They were looking at me like I was crazy. I picked up my guns and checked through everything again before dark. We still had half an hour of light when we all met back at the 4Runner for a bag of junk food and soft drinks. Nobody really said much, and as it got dark, I took the opportunity to talk to them.

"We have done everything we can to set this up right. I intend to get this over with, get the girls, and get out of here. Good luck everyone." Lots of 'yeps' and 'same to you's'. I walked back to my chair to enjoy the wait and the bugs in my face, all the while sweating like a pig.

As the evening cooled, a slight fog came in from the river. Some bugs were making noise, but it was still quiet for this time of year. An hour after dark, even those bugs went quiet. Good news was, maybe now I could shoot something and strip out of my personal sauna. Bad news was, maybe I was going to get eaten. There was no moon and no storms tonight, so it was completely black.

I sensed more than saw or heard something to my right. It was still partially in the water but so big that it was also close to me. I silently clicked off the safety, ready to start the party. I also clicked my radio I was wearing to give Henry a heads up. I slowly stood with the gun. I popped a couple of glow sticks in my pocket, closed my eyes for a second and threw them out to the left of the black blob, between it and the water.

Holy crap, that thing was big. And not at all what I was expecting. Matte black dimpled skin, shiny in some spots; a thick, snakelike body from a fantasy book. At least thirty feet of it, from what I could see out of the water. Not including the tail. The head, though, was not shaped right for a snake and had some sort of bony or cartilaginous growths coming out on each side of the top of its head. The glow sticks had not startled it. I imagine nothing had startled it in a long time. I could hear the boys behind me scrambling out of their chairs and heard safeties clicking off.

"Don't shoot yet," I yelled. I had meant to say it quietly, but that big thing was scary.

That got its attention. It made a strange noise; the body quivered sickeningly. Then it opened its mouth and spit or coughed a slug of gunk toward us. It was breaking apart as it hurtled toward me and I half-turned away. A smaller glob of phlegm hit me on the back and right side. The boys took a more direct hit. They both immediately dropped, with one acting like a dying cockroach on the ground and screaming about spiders. The other one, Jimmy, was curled in a fetal position and moaning about tornadoes. What. The. Hell? My mind was racing overtime. Damn. It was amphibious. Which meant toxic. Which meant...

Salamanders, why did it have to be salamanders? Not that this giant was not incredibly dangerous, but who would ever brag about kicking a salamander's ass? I would guess there just was not much credibility in the monster hunter community for slaying a giant gummy lizard. I decided to just go with what the people who knew it best, the Native Americans, had called it over the centuries—Great Serpent, or Great Horned Serpent. Of course, it wasn't actually that great and definitely not a serpent, but this seemed like a good time to be a traditionalist. Looked better on the resume.

While I was ruminating on that crucial matter, the gummy lizard was getting prepped to eat me. It was giving me the threat display, puffing itself up, getting ready to spit another couple of gallons of nerve gas snot in my direction. I had already been loogied once, and since I did not feel like another, I emptied the gun clip into its head, followed by a grenade into the mouth while it was still open and protesting about the bullets. The explosion was intense and splattered everything within twenty yards with gummy gore, mostly red, that used to be its head. I had used a strong concussion grenade rather than a fragment grenade, so at least there was little metal shrapnel in the gore. I started thinking I had seen nothing that disgusting since I was perusing street food in Shanghai; flavor of the day was ick on a stick, a red monstrosity that looked like a cross between octopus and hermit crab. That image still shook me. And just what sauce goes with tentacles?

Anyway, I realized I had been sniffing a little more of the toxin than I had realized, because that was twice that I had almost drifted off from the subject at hand. If the gummy lizard had been faster, I might have been in real trouble. But I doubt it had run into anything as resistant to its charms as I had been. Still, there was something off, something important that I was missing. Maybe I would remember after I had a nap. The noise on the edge of my mind finally broke through. It was Nan's voice, screaming something at me. It's always something, I thought. I had probably gotten gore on her new shoes. Wait, no, it was something important, sounded like 'behind you'. I remembered something vague about salamanders sometimes hunt together. But that would mean—holy crap! While my mind was wandering around like a lost puppy, the gummy lizard number two was sneaking up behind me.

I spun around to see Gummy Deuce moving my way. It was amazing how something so large, with such little legs, could move so fast. I was thinking about what color nail polish would look good on those claws when my hind brain kicked into survival mode and my left hand pulled out the nine-mil pistol and started blasting away. It did not seem to hurt it too badly, but it noticed enough to stop and snap its eyes closed. I was wondering if I was violating any Oklahoma hunting regs on giant gummy lizards when I also tossed an incendiary grenade on the ground in front of it. It went off in a great kaleidoscope of fire and the critter turned around and hauled ass back to the river. Do gummies have an ass? I pondered that existential question. Right until Nan poured a cooler of ice-cold water over me. I finally had a moment of clarity.

"Ma'am don't touch me or get any closer. This toxic gunk is messing with my mind."

"You don't say. Do you realize you just called me ma'am?"

"I'm not realizing a lot right now, except that me and the boys need detox and quick. But save a gallon of gunk because I'm going to need it for a potion."

"OK, and way ahead of you on the detox." She hit me with a powder I later realized was baking soda and then a gallon of milk. It was a crude way of carrying around a buffer for chemical poisons, but it was relatively effective. She and her two helpers did the same for the two boys. They had put on Tyvek suits and gloves from the truck before coming across the bridge. I must have been out for a while.

The three of them then cut the clothes off the two boys and hit them again with the soda and milk. They were still completely out of it but were no longer screaming about tornadoes and spiders. I pulled off the motorcycle leathers but left on the dry suit. I figured that was what had saved me. Nan poured more baking soda and milk over my head and hands since that was what had been exposed. I didn't mind since I was on a tropical island in the Arctic Ocean; Jo was wearing a thong bikini, and I was in a Santa suit, riding a white horse like Sinterklaas. Zwarte Piet was playing disco music so loud I could not hear what the horse was saying. My mixed metaphor brain would keep a psychologist in e-book authorships for years if I didn't get this stuff out of my system.

I woke up lying on the sand exactly where I had fallen again. My colleagues had brought the truck over and loaded up the two boys in the back. They were heading in my direction, so I knew I was next. Nan was telling me we had to leave, since the gunshots and grenades would draw attention. I was not too worried since this was rural Oklahoma. The two guys, John and Sam, picked me up, and I realized I was headed for the bed of the truck, where the two boys were curled up. We passed Henry, and I saw him smile down at me. I think there was a 'dumbass' in there somewhere.

"Nan, I am having a powerful vision, probably from the lizard spit. I can clearly see in my mind that the girls are over on that island across the slough. Look up in the oak tree on the south side. They aren't in great shape, so you and Henry need to take the boat and get them."

I saw Nan's face peering down at me. "How do you know that? Can you see them?"

"I am seeing lots of things right now, but yeah, I see them, and they are there. You're also looking very hawkish, I must say. And one of those guys over there looks like a menagerie of different things, but I can't tell which guy it is."

Henry just nodded, but John and Sam looked perplexed.

"We will get them, don't you worry. John will drive you back to the hotel and get you guys in the showers while Henry and Sam go with me."

"That's good, meanwhile I'll be on Christmas Island, but don't come knocking until after I open my present."

She just shook her head. That's all I remember; except I think on the ride over the bridge, I had my head hanging from the side of the truck with my tongue out. Because I thought I was a dog.

Chapter Eighteen

I woke up in the morning feeling like I had a hangover. Or from what I remember, a hangover might have felt like, since I had not had one in many centuries. I was in bed in my hotel room. Slightly damp but clean. The door to the room next door was partially open. Oddly, I didn't remember that, and Nan was a couple of rooms down the hall. I rolled to my feet quickly but quietly and went to the door. The other side was quiet, but I heard Henry ask, "Are you awake, Tinkerbell? Or should I say Lassie?"

"Yeah, hilarious. I hear the casino is looking for stand up talent."

"Tried it once. The crowd did not appreciate me," he responded. "You get dressed and we will head down and meet Ms. Nancy. Still a few things to take care of now that you are back on our astral plane."

Maybe he had given up on comedy routines a little too soon, but I kept quiet and got dressed. We went to the lobby, met Nan, who was already there with Sam. John was still at the site from the previous evening. We walked down to the brewpub. Once there, we sat down and started discussing what the hell had happened. I really wanted to know from their perspective as well as what transpired toward the end once my brain went soft. There was not really anything new to add, though. One thing I did not know was that while I was shooting at the second one with my pistol, Henry had also been peppering it. I imagine that did a lot more than my pistol to persuade it to take off. I thanked Henry, and he responded, "Always happy to help out a dumbass." Based on that, I guess I was now the Great Dumbass Fisher, which I said out loud. Nan laughed, at least.

"You said last night something about the salamanders being the Great Serpents," Nan said. "Do you really think that?"

"Makes sense to me," I responded. "Great big black things that look like snakes, especially if they are in mud or water with their legs hidden. And those bony ridges on their head are like some drawings I've seen. They den up in the riverbanks most likely and drag their prey there, which is like the old story descriptions of going to the underworld. And as we now know personally, they pack enough hallucinogens to make anything think they are gods."

"That stuff was affecting me from fifty yards away," Henry said. "Think it was coming in with the fog."

"Makes sense. They are so potent, I bet when they excrete the stuff through their skin it rides on the fog, wind, or water. Stuns anything near them and makes for easy meals. And lots of strange events that spark stories. Not to mention disappearances all around this area."

Everyone else had come to the same conclusion. A lot of things were clearer now about the area's history.

"Nan, do you remember from your mother how to make the Uya shifter binder and cleanser potions?" I asked.

"Yes, but we have not made those in many years. The Uya had left North Carolina before the people came west, and they have not been a problem here in Oklahoma for a century."

"Can you make it from the gunk of that big fellow? I imagine that the mountain salamander we used centuries ago is likely extinct."

"I think so. The properties may be slightly different, but from what I saw of you and Jimmy and Ned, the hallucinogenic portion of it works well. When we get a first batch made, do you want to try it on yourself?"

"Uh, probably not. I'm still having disturbing flashbacks of an imaginary island. But if it works, I need a gallon of the stuff for a project back in Europe. That is assuming I can get it back there without exposing people and turning the airport into a bunch of slobbering idiots. And keep a batch handy here, too. I hear there have been some problems in Mexico with Uya shifters working with the cartels. That is just the other side of Texas from here. They could be here in a day if they moved north."

"We have heard about the problems down there," Henry said. "We were not sure it was the Uya, but it sounded like them."

"Sure, I will get some help and we will have a batch made in less than a week," Nan said.

"Is the carcass of that thing still where it was?" I asked.

"Yes, John is there to keep an eye on it and keep anyone from stumbling across it. Why?"

"We need to incinerate it. Will have to do it when the wind is not blowing since I would guess the smoke is as toxic as the rest of it. Still have any incendiary grenades?"

Henry nodded a yes. "Sam let's go take care of it now, before the afternoon wind stirs," he said.

"Thanks guys," I said as they were leaving. "Oh, could you grab a chunk of that thing and freeze it? Then send it Fed Ex to my address in Amsterdam."

"You keeping a tissue culture library of new beasties?" Henry asked.

Once again, he had surprised me. I wished I could get him to Europe on some hunts.

"Something like that," I responded.

He nodded, and they left.

"OK, Nan, tell me the rest, including anything I should already know, just in case my brain is not working yet," I said.

Nan summarized that the two girls, Stacey and Melissa, were in a tree on the brushy island in the river, just the other side of an old slough that had filled in with mud and vines. My premonition had been accurate. They were filthy, hungry, and completely disoriented. From what Nan could get out of them when they were found was that they remembered little of the real-time events as the hallucinogen was actively working on them. After they were attacked and spit on, apparently the salamanders had dragged them back to the island judging by the large bruise impressions on their skin from the salamander's mouths. Then their flight or fight systems kicked in and activated their shifter stage early. As hawks, they got to the tree, but no farther, then returned to human form. Based on my experience with the hallucinogen, they were lucky to have gotten away. They would spend some weeks or months with Nan as she helped them recover and coached them on their new abilities. They should be OK but would need time and care to heal. Their family, my family many generations down the line, had already come and picked them up to take them back home. Over the next weeks Nan would let me know if they remembered any more of their experience.

The other two girls were not found, but we all knew they were likely eaten by the giant salamanders, or Great Serpents. I also told Nan to keep all of our people informed of what had happened so they could avoid the place. I knew that eventually Michael would find out and I'd have to brief him on certain parts of the operation. It was important that he knew to keep the curfew on for his people. I knew this whole thing was not over, and not just because one salamander had escaped. I was betting the girls had been dragged to the island as food for what would be new hatchlings from a nest. It only made sense and although these things were dangerous, I felt certain it was not my call to cause another extinction event. They had been here a lot longer than humans had.

That afternoon, I checked out of the Fort Smith hotel and drove north to another hotel near Fayetteville to be closer to Nan and the airport. I would have made calls, especially back to Thomas, but I didn't want there to be records of my location. I drove over to visit Nan and the two girls. Both were teen beauties, but the ordeal had left them solemn and still shaken. Nan introduced me as the family patriarch, the Great Fisher, she said again teasingly, from centuries past. I am not sure they believed it, but now maybe there was a better chance that they would understand that the world they thought they knew as teenagers was a very different and dangerous place. And that they were special in this new world and would live much longer lives than other humans.

I sat down with them over iced tea and told them about their ancestors. How I had come to America and met my wife, a shifter, just as they were, and what happened afterward. That they were stewards and shepherds of the people now and would live long and prosperous lives. But that also brought obligations to use that gift for the people and not themselves. They seemed OK with that, and I'm sure Nan had already told them. Nan wasn't happy about it, but I also told them about their shifter cousins in North Carolina and how they operated there and why. And I invited them to come to Europe and learn new things once they were well and had adapted to their new lives. They seemed appreciative and thanked me for the information.

Afterward, Nan asked me about why I told them about the North Carolina group and invited them to Europe. I told her they needed to know, and we were too small a group as it was, and there needed to be more interaction between the east and the west groups in the US. As for Europe, the more education and experience the girls got then the more prepared they would be, and hopefully safer and more adaptable. Somewhere recently in my mind, I decided to be more active with my extended family and try to ensure their survival. I would have to be careful though to keep the Church out of my business. And killer Roman Nazi vampires that might be following me.

I spent two more days there as I had decided to skip the planned stop in Asheville on my return to Europe. Instead of spending the few days back east, I felt I needed to head back to Amsterdam. It was time to continue with my projects there. I had not contacted Monk at all over the past week to keep any chances of communication from being intercepted, and I really needed to know what was happening there. Monk had mentioned that the Americans were good at intercepting communications and were even better with international calls and texts. Better safe than sorry.

I did spend part of that last day with Nan. We ended up having lunch and then sitting outside in the Arkansas heat on the Fayetteville town square. I had hoped to spend a day fishing the White River, but it would have to wait. I could tell Nan wanted to talk. And I needed to tell her more about my recent work and the risks to her that came with it. As we sat down, Nan first told me that an odd thing was happening with Stacey and Melissa; as Nan coached them into changing, they would manifest as hawks, but sometimes for a split second during the transition there was a flash of something that looked like a salamander. Nan was perplexed, but I told her that possibly they had picked up some salamander DNA. Maybe, but I just did not know. Evolution works in mysterious ways.

Then it was time for a new conversation.

"You are not stopping in Asheville," she said. "I guess that means you won't be contacting the eastern people this trip?"

"No, I have already spent too much time away. I also want to minimize the risk by association with all our people."

"Are you that afraid of the Church finding out about us?"

"Not that much. But there are other players you need to know about and be able to protect yourselves from. I also have recently found that I am not as unique as I thought. There are probably other colleagues of mine from the Roman Legions, and possibly even older beings out there. They are what you might think of as master vampires from the movies and TV that you know. Unfortunately, I don't know what powers they truly have compared to mine. But one of them is hunting me as I hunt him in return. The only thing I know is that I can see and hear them, just like any other person, but I can't sense them."

Nan looked thoughtful. "You mean you can't sense them as prey?"

"That is a good way of putting it. If you run across anyone like that, then you should probably slowly move away, then watch them from a distance. And there may be other creatures that can mimic that trait as well but are not vampires. I simply don't have enough information or experience to know yet."

"That is good to know, and also good that you are cautious of them."

"I plan to be very cautious indeed," I said. "In fact, that will be a new use for the Uya binder. I don't know yet, but I believe that will work on a vampire, as well as the cleanser, if it gets that far. Use the potions if you find yourself attacked by something similar to what I have described."

"We will prepare our people for that," she said. "I also must ask if you are planning to become more active with our people here and back east?"

"Yes. My involvement will bring risks, but I think the world is dangerous enough now to warrant that risk. That is also why the west and east peoples need to be closer and work together."

"You foresee an unknown risk to us?"

"Yes, there are simply too many enemies and odd occurrences to all be coincidences. The world is moving to a new and dangerous place, and our small group needs to be better prepared in order to survive. My few hundred years of observation and experience tell me that not only are threats to certain of us worse than before, the risks are accelerating."

"We welcome your return to us." Her voice was formal and somewhat sad. I looked at her, a little surprised. She noticed and continued, "Our mothers have told us of your departure and rare returns over the years. We assumed it was because you were unhappy with us."

I was floored. It took me a moment to come up with a reply. "Nan, my leaving had nothing to do with you or any of the people. It was my way of leaving behind my grief at losing Hia, my only true mate over the centuries. I am just now getting over that loss. I am sorry that I caused you any pain in that way and I will try to remedy the wound that I have caused and come back to aid the people."

"If you survive your other troubles."

"True, but there have always been other troubles, and I have survived all of them. So, I will be more active with the people. Please let all of them know that by the late fall moon we need to meet as a people and prepare for the future."

She nodded and looked grateful. "This week I have seen that the stories about you are true. I am happy that you are coming back to us."

I hugged her there on that bench in the square. It seemed benches were becoming my new style of communicating for important conversations. I might have even shed a tear, but that was likely just sweat from the Arkansas humidity. Over the past two centuries, I realized what an ass I had been to my family. I didn't know how to undo all those years of hard feelings, but I would start this year to atone for my neglect.

We left the square and went to her car where she gave me two jars of devil's brew, labeled A and B. Nan, with help, had been brewing up both the binder and cleanser potions. I was getting a quart of each. I was hoping to never use that much of either, but the past couple of months had alerted me to the reality that I may not be as unique as I had thought. And there were things as dangerous as I was out there, and soon I'd be hunting them both for myself and for the Church. Better to have an unknown advantage in my pocket when I ran across something big and scary. That just might keep me from getting eaten someday. I also had some other ideas on how to use the binder potion to my advantage; one idea being what I had told Nan about immobilizing vampires.

We said our goodbyes at her car, and I told her how to contact me through Monk as a last resort, for any major emergencies. I was sad to see her go. Back at my hotel I poured the two potions into oversize bourbon bottles, shrink-wrapped them, put them in heavy duty sealed plastic bags, wrapped them in bubble wrap, then put them in my checked baggage, which was a newly purchased hard side roller bag. I hoped it was enough protection. Otherwise, neither the plane nor I would make it to Amsterdam, but probably nobody on the plane would know or care afterward if that stuff leaked. I thought it was worth the risk, considering what I was planning. I was sure neither the government nor Michael would look too kindly on me using chemical weapons, but I felt it was needed.

The long flight to Amsterdam was not as restful as normal, knowing what was in the cargo hold. The squirrel cage spinning in my brain was squeaky. Spurred by the last talk with Nan, I spent time thinking about another episode in my past. I had approached George Vanderbilt in 1903 with a plan to conserve enough land in the Southern Appalachians to protect the Nunehi and other things in that expanse. He thought I was crazy at first, so it took some convincing. But since he was conservation-minded anyway, we came to an agreement.

The project ended up protecting large pieces of the forests and mountains in the southern Appalachians. The rest of the plan was more variable regarding success. As I look back over the last hundred years, I can definitely say it was a success; I can also say it was a failure. We never got close to the million acres total I felt was needed. Certainly not any contiguous acreage that was even a portion of that size. But we got much of the George Vanderbilt acreage, which became the basis for Pisgah National Forest after he died unexpectedly young. We also were instrumental in forming the Nantahala National Forest and the Joyce Kilmer Forest. Eventually, through Teddy Roosevelt and other conservationists, we got the Smoky Mountain National Park. Those tracts, plus the Qualla Boundary area, made a difference, ensuring the survival of the environment and our people in it. Part of the failure in the project was not getting some areas in time before they were clear cut or mined, and never getting the contiguous acreage needed to preserve the area completely. But it was enough to save some things.

Reliving all that history sparked a vague plan in my brain, something to both protect my descendants and bring the two clans from the East and West together. That plan might also give me some purpose beyond just existing for another few hundred years. By the end of the flight, I had a good idea of what I needed to do.

What I never expected from that effort is how it would affect my family and me, and how it would lead us into saving humanity much later. I didn't know it, but it was a turning point, a big step back toward humanity. Even more unexpectedly, that it would catapult me into an entirely new world of time travel and teleportation. Events that would soon teach me that doing good things resulted in unexpected returns.

Chapter Nineteen

I was relieved when I found my bag intact at the luggage claim. Thankfully, nobody in the building was acting weird. Or at least any weirder than normal for Schiphol, which was still one of the best places in the world for people watching, even at seven in the morning. I took a taxi to prevent any unfortunate collateral events should the train have an accident. When I got home, I noticed a message on my phone. The screen showed an unfamiliar number with an area code from Oklahoma. I got an uneasy feeling. I clicked on the number to play the voicemail and I heard Henry's voice say, "call me" and nothing else.

Well, it was early in the morning for me, so it would be nearly the middle of the night for him. It must be important. I did not even know Henry had a cell phone. I dialed him and he answered on the first ring.

"Morning Henry," I said.

"Evening," he replied.

"I thought you might be asleep, considering the time on your end."

"But you called anyway," he said in a neutral tone.

"Thought it might be important."

"Could be. That is why I was up waiting for your call."

"I am not getting a good feeling about this."

"You should not. When we went back out to get your pound of flesh and burn that thing, I took a good look around. Felt funny, like something was watching me. Found some prints in the mud. Human-like. But webbed toes."

"Damn."

"After taking care of that thing, I went back upstate and called in some hunting buddies. We geared up, just in case, and went back all careful like. Spent nearly two days looking around."

"You thinking these new guys are associated with our newly departed leather bag of LSD spit?"

"Could be," he answered. "Or could be they were hunting it, too. Just don't know and saw no further signs of anything there."

"Still no sign of the other two girls?" I was thinking of some ugly thoughts about where they might be.

"Nothing. My gut says they are gone. Not sure if they were eaten or taken, but they are not there anymore, either way."

"Ever run across prints like that before or hear about anything like that?" I asked.

"Nope, but I will ask some of the elders in case there is something in the old stories," he said.

"Thanks for all that. You need me back over?"

"Nope."

"Call me if you do, and I know she will kill me for it, but try to keep Nan out of it if possible."

"Other than you keeping her in the truck the other night, I've seen nobody get Nan to do anything other than what she wanted. I guess that was a fluke."

"Yep, probably was, and I won't expect it again this century. Let me know if anything comes up."

"Will do," he said, and ended the call.

Damn. Now I would have to get Michael involved. Damn. A taxi took me back to the Amsterdam house. It was less risky than riding the train. I eased my two special packages out of the luggage, put them in my cold room, then put on plenty of personal protection and opened each box, splitting half of each container into one of two new, smaller glass jars. I wanted to hide a batch of each here in Amsterdam and keep the other batch in my apartment in Woerden, carefully locked up in the vaults at each place. When I drove to Woerden with the half batch, I would be driving carefully.

After that, I felt I needed a walk outside after the plane ride. It was bordering on too warm, and I hoped another heat wave was not coming in for the week. A country with so much water and so little air conditioning could get miserable on some summer days. I had broken down and installed mini-split units to provide me with cool air at both the house and the apartment. I had decided I was old enough to enjoy some comforts.

When I returned, I decided to call Michael. Not sure where he was or what he was doing, but it would be good to know if anything was happening with any movement of master vampires, if they could actually track any. Or if there was anything new with the jinn trail.

"Hi Michael," I said.

"Salute, the wandering Roman has returned," he said.

"Not much of a Roman these days."

"None of us are. That is not such a bad thing."

"Hey, don't go cracking on us. We invented concrete, after all."

"Look what that did for Soviet era architecture."

"Yeah, well, can't help that once again humankind misapplied perfectly good technology. How were things in my absence, or how are they now?"

"Quite busy with all the recent developments you provided. The Center is already twice the size and staff that we had originally envisioned."

"OK, so then you can thank me for helping you to build an empire?"

"Or hate you for causing me four times the trouble."

"That's right, because problems caused by people increase geometrically."

"Very much so. Enough that I have considered shanghaiing you and forcing you to be a department head. I gather however, you would be much more valuable in the field, especially the closer we get to having the Center operational."

"Because of having more information about who and where to hunt?" I asked.

"Partially. But it is also because the more we do, and the more people we position, the more that leaks out. We have increased our monitoring efforts outside the Center through the traditional network and have already heard chatter in a couple of different arenas. Eventually, that will have to be addressed. I'm concerned that threats will result from information leaking out."

"I'm sure you can form a new department to handle everything."

"Bureaucracy will be the death of all of us."

"What doesn't kill us just annoys us endlessly?"

"I assume you are calling to tell me you were back in the country."

"Yes, just back in a few hours ago."

"Perhaps I should be offended you didn't ring me immediately."

"Nope, actually you are my last call, so that gives you the place of honor if this were a published scientific paper in some countries."

"I'm sure that bit of trivia will go far in saving your life, and in wasting mine."

"Yeah," was my snappy reply. "Anything relevant to my hunt in particular, or things that I need to know about?"

"Nothing particular about your master vampire, and nothing new on the jinn, either. I would be interested in getting you back in the cottage for strategy and tactics training with some of my staff over the next few weeks. We never got to that, and it will be helpful to complete that step. I really think it will be necessary to contract you for some work as soon as I can get free from the Center startup."

"Anything specific in mind?"

"Yes. Do you have any issue working in Alaska, Italy, or Russia?"

"Nope, been to all three, although Russia is a very volatile place right now. Anything particularly nasty happening in those countries?"

"Threats surfacing in all three. I expect to tell you more in a few weeks."

"What about the trouble brewing in Mexico you mentioned a while back?" I asked.

"It is still an issue, but we are employing an alternative approach. If that does not work, that might be another possibility, but it is hot there this time of year."

"Definitely is. I always prefer comfort when I hunt."

"Your comfort is paramount to us. Changing subjects, we should soon complete the Center startup. Are you going anywhere for the summer holidays?"

"No, I'm staying in the country through the summer. I'm planning to keep myself busy."

"I never know if that is a good thing or not with you."

"Neither do I most days. The only thing I have going for me is a few centuries of never getting caught."

"Now that is a bullet point to put on the resume."

"Better on there than another bullet through me."

"Last question, and it pertains to this topic of you staying busy: did anything happen in America that I or the Center should be concerned with?"

"Hmm, a definite yes. I'm not ready to divulge anything, as I have not worked through it all myself yet. A definite curve ball got thrown my way just recently that has me rethinking everything that happened, and I will probably need some of Jo's time to do research on what, for me, at least, may be a completely new critter."

"Well, well, for a moment there, I thought you might try to be mysterious or ominous. Any intention of elaborating?"

"I will give you the story soon, and there is not any imminent threat I'm aware of."

"OK, and it's not like I have any time or resources to deal with anything new, anyway. Just give it to me when you are ready. Since you mentioned Jo, she will be back at the cottage for a few days this week to both give her a break and give you more time to finish up any background sessions."

"Thanks. Is it safe for me to show up and meet her?"

"You mean to ask, 'is she still mad at me' or similar? We have had time to talk, and she has studied your background paper. I think you are safe. It would be best for you to rethink before you kill again and have to explain that to her, however."

"OK, I have received the message loud and clear. No more murders."

"That's the spirit. Do yoga, not murder."

"Will do. I might have to put that on a self-help book cover, though. Take care down there. Keep yourself and everyone safe."

"We shall. Ah, I just got a text back from my trainer. Can you be at the cottage starting next week for further training with him?"

"Yes, I can do that."

"Good, talk to you soon."

I spent another day running errands and talking on the phone to accountants. The weather was still very warm, so I kept on my bicycle. The canals were full of kids in the water and on boats. Summer in the Netherlands was idyllic, except for those occasional heat waves. The following day, I drove over to the cottage as it was time to see Jo.

I arrived early and wandered out to the garden as the birds were in full raucous mode. All the young ones were hatched and in training. They seemed to spend much of their effort convincing their parents to feed them. There was a family of robins in one corner, and an entire clan of swallows along the edge of the gardens. Sitting in the sun with the birds singing was quite relaxing. It was a good way to prepare for meeting Jo for the first time since our last unfortunate conversation. She opened the door and walked into the garden to greet me.

"Hey, Jo."

"Hi, how are you?"

"I have been neither shot nor eaten by a monster lately, so I'm good."

"I never know when you are serious or kidding."

"Does that make me mysterious?"

"I think that annoying is the most appropriate term."

"I can do annoying very well. How are you doing?"

"Good, but busy," Jo said. "There is a lot of work, so the schedule is five to six days at twelve hours a day, then home every other weekend. Being here for a very few days is actually a break."

"I am glad you could get a break here, as I'd like to talk about our last conversation. You have my apology for springing that on you so poorly. And for the incident itself, as I should have held him for the police. I can only promise you I'm not a bloodthirsty murderer."

"Well, it shocked me, after spending time with you on the job and getting to know you, then realizing you had a habit of killing people. I have never been in that situation as I consider myself a nonviolent person and assume that others are the same."

"So how do we get past this, or is this something that prevents us from working together?"

"I am prepared to continue as we have been. Michael explained your background to help me understand some of your actions. I also read and reread your background paper. I don't think that excuses your actions, but I can better understand the context. However, I still can't condone it. If you continue those actions, then I will refuse to work with you."

"Understood, and I plan to make better decisions. Michael has made me realize those actions damage my soul and have a lasting impact. But because of upcoming Church work, I may have to resort to lethal action for evil non-human creatures."

"I don't like that either, but I can accept it."

"To be honest, I have never enjoyed killing either, even if in past centuries I felt it was necessary. Now I have multiple good reasons not to do it again."

"Good. I think that is settled. Now, how do you want to spend the next two days?"

"I need a crash course in North American mythology to start. I also want to take you somewhere tomorrow that is completely unrelated to work."

"North American myths and monsters are not my specialty, but I can tell you what I know from other studies and from some peripheral Church documents I have read. If you want to take me somewhere tomorrow that is relaxing and fun, then I accept. If it is boring or taxing, then I'll decline."

"I can promise you tomorrow will be fun and relaxing. Now about those monsters..." We spent the rest of the morning having an informal discussion about North American creatures. Most of the information was from the Southwest US and Mexico. I wondered about that for a bit but then realized it made sense as that is where the Church was in residence the longest. We took a break for lunch, then went back to our earlier discussions.

We finished early. Jo asked me about the following day so she would know what to wear.

"We will spend the day doing something completely Dutch that everyone must do in Amsterdam at least once."

"What is that, before I agree?"

"We will bicycle the loop around Vondel Park, watch people, and then you get to buy me an ice cream," I said.

She thought for a minute, then finally smiled. "OK."

I picked her up the next morning, and we went to my Amsterdam house.

"Nice," she said, standing on the terrace over the canal.

"It'll do," I said. "Now let's get to the park since it looks like a nice day and no rain."

We went back downstairs, and I got the two bikes out of my storage unit in the garage. We took the streets for a short distance and dodged the stoned tourists, wandering aimlessly off the sidewalks. Many young Brits, and those from other nations, were still taking cheap flights or the ferry over, heading to the coffee shops and getting stoned out of their minds. They quickly became traffic obstacles and occasional speed bumps.

A few blocks away, we got on the bike path and had an easy ride to the Vondel. It is basically a promenade and park for all of Amsterdam's finest, whether families, stoners, executives, or the occasional tourist. Fields, ponds, and mini forests gave everyone the opportunity for some outdoor recreation. Dogs, frisbees, and bikes were in abundance, and nobody was having a bad time. We rode the paved loop around a few times, then stopped for ice cream and sat on a bench.

"This is great," Jo said.

"Yes, like I imagine a tame Woodstock or Piccadilly Circus would be, but practical since it's Dutch. You can see just about everyone here, from the prime minister on his bike to the actual families that live here. What you don't see are people misbehaving or much police activity."

"Thanks for bringing me. It's a pleasant diversion in this storm of work."

"No problem. And now you are officially Dutch. Just remember when on your bike to avoid anything large and hit nothing square."

"Pardon?"

"If you have to run into something large or dangerous, go at an angle so it's a glancing blow. Hurts less that way."

"If you say so; it must be all that time you spent in America that addled your language."

"Of course. I also blame everything on the Americans. Now, as we sit here, you will notice the next best thing about the park is the people watching."

"Yes, I can see just about everything and everyone here. Other than the one couple having a spat, everyone here is happy. Even the dogs play well together."

"Yep, we as a race could probably learn something from them. Ready to proceed?"

"Just ten more minutes," she answered. "I need to soak in all this positive karma."

We pedaled back to my place and parked the bikes. We had stopped on the way to get a few items at the market so I could put together something simple and fresh for us. I finished my task, poured a nice but light wine, and we ate on the balcony. I had sliced some fresh bread thinly and toasted it, spread a thin layer of mashed avocado, then layered on mozzarella, tomato, and avocado steeped in olive oil, basil, and a little balsamic vinegar.

"Wow," Jo said. "Simple and tasty. I like it. Why the avocado paste on the bread, though?"

"It holds the salt on the toast, but also keeps the juice from the topping from making the toast soggy," I answered.

We finished with a little more conversation, enjoying the wine, food, and the view. It was more pleasant sharing with her than being alone. Afterward,

I took the plates in, then started tea and made us both a cup. She smelled it, then took a sip.

"This is... interesting," she said.

I laughed. "Yes, the first time I tried it, I could not decide if I loved it or hated it. I had gotten it by mistake thinking it was a breakfast tea. But it has grown on me and now become a staple."

"What is it?"

"A Harney and Sons Paris tea. Extra fruity. So, the Center is running, or can you even talk about it without having to kill me afterwards?"

"Of course, I can't divulge much, but nothing really secret is going on yet. Just lots of bringing people in, finding them office space and furniture, getting bids on equipment, and lots of meetings to discuss what we will be doing. Which means tons of bureaucracy building."

"OK, so now you've told me, please kill me and put me out of my misery. Just listening to that has taken away my will to live."

"Yes, it sucks the joy out of life. And what have you been working on?" she asked.

"Oh, not much. Had to run over to America for a personal reason, which ended up being work, which is why I asked about North American myths. I'll probably tell you about it eventually, but honestly, I'm not ready to get into it. The search for my personal shooter seems to be at mostly a standstill. Nothing further on the jinn search. Have you heard or seen anything about that?"

"No, nothing new that is jinn-related."

We finished up our day with small talk, and then I drove her back to the cottage. We were both quiet on the drive while listening to music. But it was a comfortable quiet, and I was encouraged that we were back to nearly normal.

"Thank you for a very pleasant day," she said.

"My pleasure."

I took a card from my wallet and handed it to her. On one side was the printed name "Ceryl" and nothing else. On the back was a cell phone number, mine, and below that a set of twenty numbers; five blocks of four numbers each.

"Ceryl? Funny, you don't look waxy."

"It's a name I use, and has become a version of my real name, and only a few of the people closest to me know it. And no, not the waxy definition. It's the other definition from North America."

She looked at me questioningly.

"Google it later," I said. "It will make more sense to you then."

She turned the card over. "Your cell, I presume, but what are the other numbers?"

"Your way to contact me anywhere in the world. Put those numbers in a cell phone and I will get pinged to contact you with whatever message you can squeeze into ten seconds. Don't use your regular cell though, because whatever phone you used to type in those numbers in will erase itself and become inoperable. So, your message may need to provide contact info if you are forced to use your own cell."

"I have never heard of that technology before."

"Nobody has, or likely will, for some time. Please use that number discreetly and only when you must reach me."

"Thank you, I think."

"You are welcome. I have to go, but thanks again for spending the day with me. See you when you get back up here."

"Bye, Sen, and thanks again."

I exited through the front door and walked to the car.

My phone buzzed with a text from Jo.

"Kingfisher? I think I understand. Must be a story there. Take care, Jo." I thought about a response. Something funny but epic, sweet but sane, and not too romantic. I came up with nothing. Instead, I sent her the passcode to my house along with the address. My text also included, "Use it whenever you might need it. Should be paid up for the next decade." I might literally be sending the wrong message, but I wanted her to use it if she needed it. I would have to add her to my list of approved guests, of which she was the only one at the moment, or the booby traps would make it a short but loud stay.

I was starting the car when my phone rang and I answered, "Hi Michael."

"Hello. I have news on your jinn. Can you meet Jo at the cottage so we can discuss?" Michael was all business, so it must be important.

"Actually, I'm at the cottage and was just leaving. I can go back in and we can call you from there."

"Good. Ring me on the video in the study, as I need to show you some pictures."

"Sure, talk to you in a few minutes."

I went back in and texted Jo, as I didn't see her. She came in from the back with a questioning look.

"Michael has news for us on the jinn front and wants to videoconference about it."

We went through the tedious process of turning the equipment on, logging in, and finally connected. Would humans ever develop simple technology?

Michael was in a suit on the other end. Very unusual.

"Hello. We have found the jinn in a canal in Venice. Despite standard surveillance and video cameras in the area, he simply appeared there. We also are reviewing all surveillance records, but there is no record of him arriving there."

"You said he was in the canal, so I presume he was drowned?" I asked.

"Not exactly. The body was in a boat filled with dirt and some mud. The body was under the dirt and nailed to the wooden boat."

Jo looked surprised. She and Michael continued the conversation while I tuned out for a moment. I was stunned to hear Michael's words, and they prompted me to relive old, and not so good, memories, until I realized the conversation had stopped. Jo was looking at me, as was Michael, through the screen. I began speaking.

"The body was nailed face down in the boat, with the arms at right angles to the torso, like a crucifix. There was just enough dirt to cover the body but not sink the boat. Either they poured water or wine near the head to create mud. You will find death occurred either from asphyxiation or drowning, or both, from the mud around the head."

Now Michael was looking surprised. Jo was unhappy. I suspect she may have thought I was involved with the murder.

"Yes," Michael said. "You say that with some conviction, as if you are familiar with the method."

"Unfortunately, yes, I am. Caius, my old friend from the Ninth, or one of his just sent a message."

"I think you need to explain," Jo said. "This sounds like a ritual killing, but one I am unfamiliar with."

"It's a derivation of a rite practiced by some Legions in the far north. The crucifix position, the dirt, and the muddy water all have Roman origins of ritual killing."

"Yes, the Romans had many ways of killing people, including crucifixion," Jo said. "The ritual killings and sacrifice, while rare, included live entombment or drowning."

"The reason they did it in a boat, or sometimes, on an island, is because of the Druidic influence of the north. Someone with magic, or protected by magic from others, had to be killed while surrounded by water to 'ground out' the magic."

"That sounds familiar, as I have seen similar rites described in manuscripts."

"In this case, someone familiar with the northern Legion's manner of executing a witch or warlock used both entombment and drowning. The dirt signifies live burial, and the liquid poured near the head guaranteed drowning even if it was in mud. It was done in the basement of one the flooded houses, or in a boathouse, probably to keep the jinn from escaping. I guess the jinn either outlived his usefulness or betrayed Caius."

"We need to decide what we should we do next." Michael said. "Based on the question of - does this murder signify the end of a program or the beginning of something new? Jo, what do you think?"

"I'm not sure, but as Sen said, this is a message. But I think one that only a very few could read. It seems logical that they meant it for Sen."

"I agree," Michael said. "But it was also done in Italy, so it could also be meant for us as well. I believe our threat level just rose a notch."

After more discussion and a view of the morbid pictures, none of us had any further answers. I left Jo at the cottage as she was packing to leave for some days back at the Center. I spent the rest of the evening mulling over the jinn's demise, as I was still missing something, but it was not coming to me.

Chapter Twenty

I called Thomas at work the next day. I knew his time was limited, but he would give me a few minutes. "Thomas, how are you this fine morning?"

"My life is great, and improving just from hearing your voice," he said, with just the right touch of sarcasm. "And how is the traveler from America?"

"I am well, except for the lower IQ resulting from American television. But I'll recover quickly."

"Ah, I keep expecting it to get better over there. Perhaps someday."

This was our typical exchange when I came back from America. I saw the country as a once great nation that was now gorging itself on obvious stupidity and moving down the escalator to second-world status. It saddened me because I was really more American than Dutch, based on the time I spent there in the past century. Thomas knew the American persona via movies and television. He once had that unique European perspective that America was always a place to strive for, whether for vacation travel or perhaps even to emigrate to as past generations had. But recently, many in the EU had finally seen the America I had observed the past twenty years, and the shine was gone.

"Now that I'm back, how about that guy's night out?"

"We can do that. For Jan's birthday bash, we were planning to take him to a bar to celebrate. How does that sound?"

"That sounds fine," I said. "Text me the address and I'll be there."

"I'll do it later today. Just not sure which place yet."

"How are Kate and Anna?" I asked.

"They are wonderful, as always," he responded. "They asked about you and are planning another dinner. Speaking of that, how is Jo?"

"She is fine, and we are still platonic colleagues, before you ask."

"Very boring. You will be required to provide the evening's entertainment, so make something happen or make something up."

"Uh, OK, I'll come up with some nonsense."

"I'm giving you a hard time, of course. It's just that we like her and you two seemed good together. When she comes back in country, we need another party."

"Sure, we will do that," I said. "She seemed to very much like you guys. Makes me question her judgment somewhat, but otherwise she is alright. You still must tell me about your recent love interest."

"Yes, yes, now I have to go do some work and make the planes fly on time. See you Tuesday?"

"Yes, I'll be there, ready for the inquisition. Assume the same place and time?"

"Yes, and goodbye for now. Bring us a good story."

We ended the call. There really wasn't much I could tell them, but I had a feeling it was going to be simultaneously fun and embarrassing for me. I was looking forward to it. I would also get a few shots in on Thomas and his new relationship. That was my hope, at least.

I sat out on the balcony over the canal with my melancholy thoughts. I had time to ponder my life, which was not always a good thing. If I admitted to the truth, it was that I had become a coward. I had tired of seeing my family and friends grow old and die in my past lives. Sometimes I could sense the accusation they logically carried. Why were they dying when I was young and defying age and death? It was easier for me to be a nomad and leave before time progressed to that point for my loved ones. I doubt it was easier for them, but since I was not there, I could rationalize that it was better. I had sold myself on the excuse that I left to keep people from becoming suspicious and possibly harming me. In reality, my departure was always because I was afraid to watch those that I loved grow old, sicken, and die. Survivor's guilt built up over several centuries. I had honestly grown tired of my life. I guess my midlife crisis took a while longer to arrive than with most men, or perhaps I had been in the middle of it for a few centuries and had not realized it.

That, plus my overall boredom with life in the past century, had left me emotionally distant from humans until recently. It was time to change my life and be present where I was, and with whom I chose, even to their end. I must admit I had been having more fun the past month than most of the past century. Except for the getting shot part. Even that was exciting, in a way. Thinking along those lines brought up just what I felt for Jo. Was it really her I was attracted to, or was she just a part of the whole new exciting situation I had found myself in? It is sometimes difficult to know your own motivations. I could read other people better than myself.

I had expected to have a few weeks relatively free this summer. But between picking up the hunt for my favorite Roman Nazi vampire and going back to the cottage for some training sessions, I really foresaw little free time. On the positive side, there was not much time to brood.

My thoughts circled back to my vampire problem. I had made a connection between the original being and then what or who he had become during the war a few days before. Based on the newer identity, I could come up with some theories on both who he was and how he might shadow me. As I sat on the balcony, I opened my computer and worked, my primary method of getting through a funk. That or a week in Portugal.

My IT specialist, probably the guy that did networking for God himself, had come up with a few nuggets. I was having him shadow everything online that I took part in, from surfing the internet to banking and restaurant reservations, since I had been shot. I also had him shadowing my accountant's and lawyer's web presence. All highly illegal, of course, and also expensive. He was stalking behind me to trace anyone shadowing me. I assumed my suspect was also savvy in the same regard, but I expected my guy was better than his guy. As it so happened, I was right. The nuggets were that someone, very good with computers, was shadowing me. Monk could follow them without detection and could soon backtrack them. Or perhaps his guy was better, and they were setting up their own trap for me, in which case I was doomed. I sent a series of further notes and queries to him regarding my suspicions of Caius' activities.

My calling him Monk was for no particular reason other than to give him a name. I initially had imagined a solitary figure never talking, just hunched over a computer in some cellar somewhere. The one time I had met him, it was an entirely different reality.

My initial introduction to Monk was by computer via a series of rather unsavory characters that had used him to purify their identities. I sent him several easy projects to see how good he was. He taunted me by doing everything quickly, then stating he could better spend his time doing actual work. He also had a reputation as impossible to find. It took me a week. But I cheated since I needed little sleep and used other means than most people.

I watched him one afternoon as he walked home. He turned down his canal toward an upscale house in Gouda. Gouda, really? A world class computer expert and hacker living in an expensive house in cheese central? I sprinted to the back of his house, to where I had already opened the back door in his courtyard. I moved into the foyer and jumped up into the ceiling, splaying my arms and legs to hang there like a spider. The fancy keypad activated, and the lock opened. He came in and took off his coat and scarf. A taller, thin blond guy in his mid-twenties, looking like one of thousands on any train in the Netherlands.

After he had hung up his jacket and scarf, I reached down with one hand and grabbed his collar and lifted his head toward my face. To say I surprised him was an understatement. I have heard quieter screams from pigs during slaughter and Viking shieldmaidens on raids. He was bouncing around so hard he was about to hurt himself. Without letting him go, I lowered him until his feet touched the floor, then I dropped down in front of him.

"Hello, if you calm down and promise to behave yourself, I will let you go."

After a few 'hhhuuhhsss' noises, he finally got out a coherent sentence. "Who, who are you, and what do you want?"

"I am the guy you thought was too easy to work for, so I made your life more interesting."

"Oh, oh shit."

"OK, first, I needed to make a memorable entrance to get your attention. Do you understand?"

He nodded.

"Second, I have no intention of hurting you. Can I let you go now?"

He nodded again. I dropped my hand from his neck.

"In fact, I have a lot of work for you, which will earn you a lot of money. In return, I just need you to keep me anonymous and hidden from everyone you know or ever will know. I will ask for actions that most governments consider illegal, many of which you have already conducted. But I won't ask you to do anything major that is unethical or immoral."

The color was returning to his face, so I hoped his brain was now functional. "How did you stay in the ceiling and pick me up like that?"

"Before I answer that, and I will, have you followed me so far?" He nodded again. "Good. I needed to get your attention. As we progress into our professional relationship, you will get curious about me. I understand that. You will search for me and eventually find anomalies that will lead you down some paths in my past. I don't care about that and would expect it. But once you do that, you need to bury or delete anything you find and never share it. If you don't, then I will come back, and as Governor Tryon in London found out, being smothered by your intestines is not a noble end. Got that?"

He lost a little color again but nodded.

"Exactly what I am is not important. Just know I have been alive for a long time, have lots of experience, and am stronger and faster than any human."

Then I moved behind him faster than he could follow. As he turned, I moved just as fast back to my original position. Even as he spun back again as fast as he could, he was much too slow to follow me.

"OK, I have made my point, I think. After tonight, I doubt we will ever meet again. Are you ready to make some serious money without getting into too much trouble?"

"Yes, I am. What did you have in mind?"

"Well, first I need hardware; I am thinking a paired device that only we can access, that can evade all detection and would destruct with any tampering effort. Then I need a number code that can be sent from any cell phone that would allow a message to go to you and then me no matter where I am in the world; and then that cell phone disabled once that code has been sent from it. And I have several other devices and data uses in mind, plus there will be lots of illegal searches for people. Is gold an acceptable payment?"

I continued with a list of goodies, and he looked dazed for the next ten minutes. But once he realized he was in no danger from me and how much I would pay him, he got down to business and really appreciated the types of things I was asking him to develop. I petted his cat while we chatted, and he opened a bottle of wine. Not a monk at all.

Tonight, I was giving Monk a new target to search for, along with strong warnings. My instructions were to use all available resources in his search without regard for cost; timeline was two weeks, so he would know it was not an immediate need; the target was extremely well protected and efforts to find him would likely result in countermeasures and backtracking, with possibly lethal consequences. And that the simple, easy and safe stuff could be given to others to spread the risk and work more efficiently. I wanted Monk to get the search right, but also to impress upon him the risk, so he would protect himself.

My plan was shaping up. As it got dark, I poured a glass of wine from the bottle opened the night before. I hoped to get Caius tracked in a week. Then I could begin plans to end what was becoming a serious threat rather than an annoyance. Regardless of whether Caius alone or with accomplices was messing with me, it was time to stop this business before someone got hurt. Well, someone other than Caius.

An odd text showed up in the morning, alerting me it was Monk. I called a number that had too many digits to be real. Monk answered immediately.

"The text I just sent you, click on the link in it and wait five seconds, then restart your phone. I will call you in two minutes," he said and then hung up.

I knew better than to be offended about what he was doing, and I would not understand beyond a basic level. I restarted my phone, then a moment later it rang, and I answered.

"What was that about?" I asked.

"I am protected on my end for this conversation, and now your phone is protected and untraceable, at least for fifteen minutes. I thought a conversation in this case would be better than emails or in person. Besides, this is a beta test."

"Good with me. What you got?"

"Multiple hits from cameras showing someone is physically surveilling your house, your apartment, and your car. Looks like a small white van is involved in most of those photos. I ran an analysis to piece together the partial plates in the system. No match, so they are using false plates."

"Or worse, they have access to the system."

"Good point. I can also check that. Maybe that will lead somewhere if someone was not careful."

"No people identified?"

"Nothing, they are very good. Even with the photos I got, I couldn't determine if the person was male or female. I put in a different algorithm and the gait analysis comes out male. Same person at two different locations, actually. Just don't know who it is yet. Unless they make a mistake, it is unlikely I'll find out anything else. I do not foresee that as a likelihood."

"Any chance of getting satellite images?"

"I could, but right now that is a sort of last resort, never to be repeated, type of action. There will be some future opportunity though as I have it on good authority that some of the new internet satellites being launched are also carrying cameras. All that is off-the-record stuff. I just have to find a way in."

"Good, that could help in future cases, even if it doesn't for this one. Any more on that target I sent you to search?"

"Not really, but I did not start searching until last night. It has been an interesting chase, and right now I'm down the rabbit hole, following some crazy leads."

"With this guy, I have to stress that the crazier it is, the more likely it is true. He is also as dangerous as anybody you have ever searched for, so be careful."

"Got it, and I've never been more careful. But wow, if crazier equals truer, I should have a good story for you soon."

"Good. I'm sure it will be interesting. Cover your tracks like you're in a litter box."

"OK, I am uncertain if I like that phrase, but I will do it. One thing about your guy, is it possible he's a part of some family, like he's doing the same thing as his grandfather?"

"Not likely at all. You must assume it's the same person. Yes, before you ask, he's been alive longer than almost anyone else you know."

"Almost anyone else I know, huh?"

"Yes, and just know it's the same guy."

"Got it. We need to end this call. The time block is almost up."

"Thanks. Contact me when you get closer to them."

We both hung up. I was expecting my phone to melt or flash and disappear, but it did nothing. Then it was time to get back on the bike for a two-hundred-kilometer ride to pass the time.

I drove over to the cottage the following morning. I parked and went into the familiar front room. A man came in from the back. He looked vaguely like a commando but was wearing glasses and carrying a book. My kind of guy.

"Hello," I said.

"Good morning, I am Simon."

"I am your student for the next two weeks, apparently."

"Ah yes, I was expecting you. Michael wanted me to bore you to death with arcane Church procedures. I was thinking more about weapons training first thing each morning, then current strategies, operations, and logistics in the afternoon. Save the junk for the last two days. We might even forget about it by then."

Yes, definitely my kind of guy. "Sounds good to me. Bullets or blades?" I asked.

"Both. You ever use a sword?"

I just grinned.

"I'll take that as a yes. You would be surprised how many don't have that talent. It comes in really useful with some of our jobs. How about hand to hand?"

"I've done black belts for three of the Eastern styles, Greco-Roman wrestling, some Brazilian jiujitsu, and a year of Krav Maga in France with an Israeli."

"Good. What would you say your style is?"

"Win at all costs, so I don't get my ass beat."

"Yes, I can work with that. I'll have the gym prepared. This is going to be a lot more enjoyable than I was expecting."

I just smiled again. But he was correct. It was an enjoyable week, then got even more intense the second week. I had to dial back, but he was an excellent adaptive fighter and we learned from each other. I don't know what style we ended up with after those two weeks, but I hoped they had been taping it, as it would make an excellent training session. If I ever needed a fight trainer, I was definitely stealing this guy from Michael.

On another bike ride, I got a ping from Monk, and then we went through our elaborate pre-game warmup. When he called five minutes later, he gave me a brief on his latest findings.

"I traced your guy as a Nazi colonel attached to a couple of different generals in Berlin, before that to a Nazi school in Eifel, then he was in England in World War I, then briefly appeared in Czarist Russia, and I have a hit in Prussia some years before that. Around 1850, I may have had a hit in Frankfurt. I have another dozen fragments but nothing verified. Does any of that information confirm any of your observations?"

"He was a Nazi colonel and at the Eifel school. I don't know about the rest. My next point of verification may be a stretch for your resources."

"I doubt it. Give it to me. Double or nothing; I bet I get it within forty-eight hours."

"I'll take that bet. Ninth Roman Legion, near Utrecht, 300 AD."

"Schijt! You must be joking."

"Nope, it's your bet, and it is the truth. Although if you can pull it off, I'd be happy to pay."

"Not likely, but I will try. I will have to check a unique set of sources. On the positive side, my efforts will be untraceable; on the downside, it will be tedious."

"I'll leave it to you. Any hits on anything else?"

"Nothing anywhere. Were you expecting recent activity?"

"I was not sure. But this guy comes around for a while, then disappears for years. That is one reason I need more information, so I can track him and force him to come back out of hiding. Damn, I just thought of something obvious."

"What?"

"Can you access traffic cameras around Woerden?"

"Of course."

"On the date I'll give you in a moment, check the cameras for anything moving out of the city center heading west, late evening." I gave him the date of the night I was shot. "If that white van shows up, then maybe we will be a little closer. Regardless, there should be a vehicle leaving at a high rate of speed that is involved in this."

"I'll get on it. Double or nothing on that?"

"I'm paying you regardless, so betting is useless. How about this - I dare you to find the info, or you have to swim naked down the Gouda canal."

He laughed. "I would draw too large a crowd of young women and be cited by the police for an unlicensed parade."

"Yeah, yeah. Just find my guy, and we are good. On a related matter, I'm sending you a photo of some graffiti in Utrecht for language analysis. Probably nothing but take a look when you get a chance."

"Very good. We will speak later."

It was not much, but every little piece could help. Maybe the Woerden escape vehicle could be a lead. Every time they stuck their head out of a hole, it increased the chance they would make a mistake.

Chapter Twenty-One

My friends and I met at the restaurant as planned. I was expecting some teasing, but I knew it was all in fun and love. We hugged and kissed air three times on the cheek per Dutch custom. We went to the bar first to wait on the table since we were a few minutes early. As soon as we ordered drinks, the running of the gauntlet commenced.

"How are you doing? And how is our new and even smarter friend Jo?" Kate asked in the opening salvo.

"I am well, thanks. I believe she is fine, and, of course, still very smart."

"Good, and we look forward to seeing her again," Thomas said.

They all smiled at each other conspiratorially.

"We will see her again, won't we?" Anna asked.

"I believe so. Hey guys, thanks for caring, but Jo and I are not and won't be an item. Besides, I have a lot of work to do instead."

"Isn't she somehow tied in with where you work?" Anna asked.

I had to grin at that. That is what I liked about them. They were good folks, gentle but firm and direct. The best of the Dutch. Humor, but no bullshit. I was not born in the Netherlands but was glad I settled here and did not think I would ever permanently leave, not with people like this. Living here for a few hundred years might make me part Dutch, but I still wasn't, not really, but I adored the people here.

"Yes, we work together, but now she is at another location. Besides, workplace romantic relationships are frowned upon, aren't they?"

The other three burst into laughter.

"Where do you think people meet other people these days?" asked Kate. "It's either meet at work or chat someone up online. So, you are just part of a trend."

"Great. I'm part of a trend. I should start saying 'perfect' in all my conversations, maybe get a Twitter account."

"No changing the topic yet," Anna said. She guided us back to my paltry dating life. "By the way, what does your online profile say?"

"What? I don't do that stuff online." They all laughed again.

"It is no wonder that you are floundering in the dating sea," Thomas said. "There's nothing left for you but church."

I must have had a funny look on my face.

"Oh my, so you know her from church, too. How quaint," Kate said.

"Um, well, not exactly," I said.

They were looking confused and very amused at me.

"How do you both know her and not know her at church?" Kate asked.

"Well, the Church funds her research. I do some part-time work in that area as well. So, the workplace we share is Church-related."

They thought that was hilarious, and it got the biggest laugh of the night.

"Oh, well, I think we can finally change the subject," Thomas said. "Unless we turn this into a prayer meeting."

"Yes, we can all feel safer now that we know Sen can administer last rites," Kate said.

That finally ended my questioning. We went to the table and settled in there.

"Thomas, now that I have had my interrogation, what about your new thing?"

"Thing? He is definitely not a thing. And you will get to meet him later tonight at Jan's birthday party if you decide to come with me."

"Have either of you met him yet?" I asked.

Both Kate and Anna shook their heads no. "Not yet, so this must be serious," Anna said.

"But he will be with us at the next dinner, right?" Kate asked, pointedly, at Thomas.

"Oh yes, that would be a good time for introductions. He would have joined us tonight except he had a corporate dinner."

The evening continued pleasantly. I had stopped thinking about all the other things spinning around in my universe and enjoyed the moment. After dinner, we said our goodbyes, and I walked with Thomas to the party. It had cooled off as we walked along the canals. It was very peaceful. That was the pleasant thing about Amsterdam at night—once a block or two away from the tourist areas, it was very residential and quiet. We chatted and walked several blocks to another concentration of restaurants and bars.

Thomas's friends were a riot as usual. Some could drink heavily, but they didn't need to do that to have a good time. Laughter and camaraderie really are contagious. Their motto was "The night is still young, so plenty of time to recover from mistakes." I watched it unfold as a few of our group peeled off from time to time to chat up others in the bar. It was a lively crowd because most people would soon be leaving for extended vacations, so this was the feeding frenzy before the lull. Although it was Jan's birthday, any such occasion was useful for throwing a crazy wild party. Drinking and socializing were art forms perfected by the Dutch.

I was subdued and quiet, but Thomas and his new beau Willem were doing their best to keep me company. I was enjoying the evening except for the blaring eurotrash music that most bars employed to entice their patrons to shout conversations and buy more drinks. Thomas and Willem were well matched, physically and intellectually. Willem was an international food buyer for a massive company, so we had in common a few topics of conversation. I kept a close business eye on a few things, like food oils and cocoa, because of my investments.

The mood had dimmed a little around the table. From the snippets of conversation, my overtaxed ears picked up that there were a couple of people missing tonight from the larger crowd. Not unusual, except another couple of guys had also gone missing in the spring. People orbited in and out through this social solar system, but everyone would show back up in a few weeks with a good story. These guys kept up with each other pretty well, so if they were worried, there was probably something real behind the vague unease. My predatory instincts had clicked on alert for a threat to the herd. Perhaps someone was taking men at a slow but steady rate. Too early to tell for sure, but I decided I needed to take the rumors seriously and start investigating. Somebody might be due for a late-night canal swim.

"Hey, are you going to brood all evening and keep scaring the good-looking ones away?" Thomas asked.

I looked up at the lively, ever-changing crowd all around us. "I don't see that I'm having any repulsive effect, but I will try to buck up and shed my grumpies."

"Good. Come back to the living. Just because you aren't having sex doesn't mean you can't celebrate with those of us who are."

"Oh, you ass." I lightly punched him in the arm.

"No, he's my ass," Willem said. They both howled in laughter.

I had another drink, joined in the banter, and left rather early. Early with these guys was relative, as often they would stay until the place closed at three am, then have more conversation outside in the courtyard. Then, somehow, they would go to their high-level executive jobs and plow through the day.

Before I left, I talked to Thomas. "I overheard talk that some of your crowd had moved on without keeping contact."

"Yes, I'm not sure if it is anything or not, but about four or five guys have dropped out the past few months. Too early for vacation. Usually by now someone has heard from them or they have shown back up."

"Has anyone mentioned that to the police?"

"Oh no, I don't think anyone has gone to that length yet. But if it keeps happening, I think we might."

"OK, just curious. Let me know if anything changes."

"Right, because as the part-time Church deacon, you will wreak righteous vengeance."

"Maybe." I laughed off the comment.

I left and walked toward home. I used the time to make plans for a new hunt. This crowd I knew well enough to plot out the nights they partied, the bars they traveled between, and I had a decent idea of who the couple of hundred were that made up the extended group. Or I knew enough to know if anyone unusual, or new, was in the group.

I needed to get started, as probably half the group would soon disappear for several weeks. That was life in most of Europe, where summer holidays were a real thing. For most, it was mandatory to leave work for a paid vacation. Four weeks was not an uncommon length of time. That, plus the other holidays during the year, and the shortened work week for most, contributed to a happier, healthier, and more productive citizenry than almost anywhere else.

So, although vacation was a good thing, it was speeding up my plans. I would start this new project the following week. It might be even easier once the crowd thinned to pick out a new face. If there even was a killer, but something seemed off, my gut told me. My instincts told me a predator was encroaching on my territory.

A few days later, I spent some time each night in or near the usual hang-outs. I saw a lot of familiar faces and was getting some curious looks since I was hanging around more than usual. Everyone knew I was straight, and even those that didn't know me at all could figure it out in less than three seconds. I did not know how that worked, but I knew it was a real thing.

I was in a bar eating some terrible versions of borrels when Thomas and Willem came in one night. I nearly bolted out but had nowhere to go, since they were between me and both the entrance and the toilet. Thomas picked me out a few seconds later and came over to the bar.

"OK, now you have my attention," he said. "Either you have transcended to a higher plane of being and are now attracted to men, or something strange is going on."

I laughed at the phrase, but I knew he had caught me. "I guess that the line of 'I was just in the neighborhood' would not explain myself?"

"Not even a little. Now tell me what is going on."

"Well, the entire story would take a few days and a lot of drinks to convince you. But at the risk of being more odd than usual, I will try a bit of truth. I am keeping an eye out for anything or anyone unusual that might be a threat."

"OK, and what would you do if you found that?"

"Depends. If it was not an imminent threat, I will send a dossier to the police to give them an opportunity to take action."

"I think, my friend, that we should have that long talk soon," Thomas said. "I always knew there was a lot more about you than what shows on the surface, but I wasn't expecting you to be this serious."

"I am exactly who you know me as; I have never kept that hidden from you. What you don't know is that my part-time Church work is to observe, investigate, and detain those that mean harm." I was taking a chance, but I thought Thomas could handle it. After all, running one of the world's biggest airports must require balls the size of watermelons. He did not disappoint.

"You really need to explain that further."

"I can do that. All I do is keep an eye on things and protect those around me, and others that need it. I am also not the only one in this line of work. What I can tell you right now is that if someone is harming this crowd, then there will probably be news headlines that someone has been apprehended for the disappearances. Regardless, though, the disappearances will stop."

"That is reassuring, but I didn't realize you worked in that field."

"It is mostly a new thing with the Church, although I've had experience in the past. You can now go back and tell Willem—your guy over there who is really wondering what we are talking about for so long—that you both have a guardian angel watching your backs. Or that I am still desolate over lost love. Either should work, and both have some truth in them."

He smiled, and then we hugged. It was good to have friends. He went back to Willem to order dinner and then I left, chatting with them briefly on the way out. Thomas gave me a knowing look, telling me he was going to get a better explanation out of me. After I left, I sent him a text that I would give him the truth once my assignment was complete. If it was not before the summer holidays, then we would meet as soon as possible when he got back.

I spent my days at the cottage with Simon, learning more about operations and how they interacted with other groups. How to travel, access funds, weapons caches, contacts in different locations. We talked about espionage, threat assessments, and sabotage. I cut him off when he started talking about expense forms. I told him there would be no expense forms or other paperwork from me. He looked doubtful, so I told him to check with Michael, as I was on a contract basis only, and they would only get a final invoice from me after the job, if completed.

It kept me sensitized to another issue. Michael had kept me apprised about unusual chatter around the Center operations, which to me meant the possibility of threats. I don't think he would have mentioned it unless he thought it was valid, and he was keeping me close to the cottage for training. I think he wanted me to stay because the threats were valid. The most concrete example for me was the dead jinn. I was now regretting having Jo with me during that brief investigation.

Those thoughts led me to make a brief call to Michael one afternoon after leaving Simon. I had considered some options that might get me in real trouble. In the past, I had noticed how sometimes something minor could go very wrong. This might be one of those times. He answered the phone immediately.

"Good afternoon," I said.

"Good day to you. How can I be of assistance?"

"You know, I prefer to ask for forgiveness rather than permission. I figure that is a safe bet, anyway, considering who you represent. But today I'm here for permission."

"It depends on what you are about to ask—I can go Old Testament wrath, or New Testament forgiveness."

"It is good that your faith provides options. That way, you can cover all your bases."

"Yes, we are always right, no matter the situation. Makes the work so much easier. Now, what are you plotting?"

"Theoretically, if someone were to put a tracker on a vehicle, it would be good if that action were not seen as a threat. And if–"

"Stop there." He thought for a moment and then continued, "Theoretically, her black sedan has been assigned and is parked out front of where she was staying before and will stay again on her next visit. Theoretically, again, a tracker would not interfere with our current operations nor be seen as a threat and removed. I believe that gives me a tiny shred of plausible deniability. You, however, may unleash holy hell on yourself if she discovers your actions. But

I sense you would do it anyhow, and ultimately I would have to agree that it is not a terrible idea."

"Thanks, theoretically."

We ended the call. I guess that went well. Well enough that I drove over to Den Haag that evening and planted the tracker. When Jo was in the Netherlands, I would know where she was traveling in the car. It was likely overkill considering how safe this country was. I doubted she would get into trouble.

I kept up my nightly surveillance at the usual bars and dance venues for another week. My ears might never be the same. But I now had an even better idea of who belonged in the crowd and who did not. As I was prowling once again in a bar in Amsterdam, I saw an unfamiliar young man working through the crowd. He seemed friendly enough and confident enough to keep approaching groups of guys, but most everyone quickly shied away from him after only a moment. My predator senses picked up.

I watched him eventually approach someone I knew named Edwin. I could hear them, and the young man's English was accented, probably German or Austrian. Edwin was as straight as I was, so why was he trying to pick him up? Something was odd.

After the younger man left, I went over to Edwin. I asked him about his encounter.

"Oh, that is Kim. He's a little creepy."

"Why creepy?" I asked.

"He is always hanging around the bars, chatting people up, but seems fake somehow," he said.

"Maybe he is trying too hard?"

"Maybe. He also seems confused, like he is new to the lifestyle and does not know the rules," Edwin said.

"How long has he been around?" I asked.

"A few months now."

This was someone I needed to investigate. I found an empty seat at the bar where I could obliquely keep watch on Kim. He didn't look like a Kim, and his accent did not fit a Kim. I arbitrarily decided it was a fake name. That is why I was a good detective—in the absence of facts, I made shit up.

More guys drifted in, some singly and others in small groups. Kim targeted each one that had arrived solo. The first he approached only gave him five seconds, but another guy seemed more interested. They had drinks and stood on the edge of the crowd that was dancing to more of that horrible sound they called dance music. After about fifteen minutes, Kim and his new friend wandered toward the exit. I followed at a distance. Not that they would have noticed me with all the people around, both inside and outside. Neither could they have possibly heard me walking behind with their auditory function impaired.

They walked down a block and turned left. Then another block and into an alley. I was getting uneasy, because I was going to walk into an abduction or disturb two guys making out. It turned out to be the former.

I heard a familiar sound as I turned into the alley. A sedan was sitting in the alley with the rear door open. Kim had his arms around the other guy and had a taser in one hand he had obviously just used. The other guy was unconscious, and Kim was trying to maneuver him into the backseat. I moved at full speed and easily plucked the taser from his hand and applied it to the back of Kim's neck. He went out like he had just been tased I thought with amusement. I grabbed the other guy as I let Kim fall. I put that guy on the car hood and then roughly tossed Kim in the backseat.

I carried the other guy out of the alley and back toward the bar. Before I got to the last turn, I set him down and propped him on the stoop of a row house in a well-lit area. He should be safe for a moment. I walked back to the bar and saw one of the bar workers that I vaguely knew standing outside with a small group. I told him that, as I was leaving, I saw someone that had just left the bar go around the corner, stumble and pass out. He walked with me to the corner, saw him, and told me he would get another guy to help and go pick him up. Most of these folks were protective of each other, so I felt OK leaving things as they were. I trotted off and went back to the car.

Kim was still out in the back. I put on my gloves. I opened the door and went through his pockets and got his car keys and wallet. An obvious fake ID with the name of Kim on it. An Austrian driver's license with the name of Walter on it. That seemed more realistic. I got in the driver's seat and started the car. I scrolled through the GPS unit until I saw a home listing, then I punched it I took Sleeping Beauty toward what his car claimed was his place.

I drove out of Amsterdam, heading northwest. I entered the concrete dominion of the newer area of Sloterdijk. Lots of soulless buildings, some nice and some transient. The best part of this area was the train station, because that is how you could leave. I found a lower rent concrete block building that the GPS showed was his home base. On arrival, I thought the address had looked familiar. I suppose I should not have been surprised that the building was the same as the one Jo and I had visited while backtracking the jinn.

I parked illegally. Might as well give old Walter another headache, regardless of how the rest of the evening progressed. I threw him over my shoulder and walked to the entrance, then I placed Walter at my side so it would look like I was assisting a drunk friend. No keypad, but the door had a key lock on it. The second key I tried on the key set opened it. This time of night, there was no attendant in the hideous orange lobby. I did not know which apartment was his, so I needed to go through his stuff. I found his residency card in the wallet with the number. Up we went.

The place was just as attractive inside as it was outside. A one bedroom, one bath flat with a small second room too small for a bedroom, and a kitchenette.

I dropped Walter on the sofa. I checked throughout the apartment. In the second small room, a door closed off a utility area. Nothing there, but a light smell, similar to the jinn's or Caius' scent. This was my third time smelling it. I was now sure that it was close to Caius' odor. This was an obscure clue which I still couldn't read.

I went through the refrigerator but there was not much there. In the freezer were a couple of frozen dinners. One of them was open. Who opens and cooks a frozen dinner, then puts it back in the freezer? Who even eats those anymore? I pulled it out and opened it to find four driver's licenses. All were males, three from the Netherlands and one from Belgium. One guy looked somewhat familiar. So, there was more evidence here somewhere. I just needed to find it.

I went back through the apartment. All concrete walls and ceiling, so few hiding places. Unless he had rented a jackhammer. Across the back of the bedroom closet was a cheap wooden wall, about three feet tall and a foot deep. It definitely had been added, as it was not concrete - a sure sign my deductive reasoning was working overtime. I pulled on it and it came free from the wall. The space behind contained two small duffel bags. The back of the wooden partition had some hooks in place, and hanging from it were several items, including a crucifix and rosary beads, and a few other religious items I didn't recognize.

I emptied the bags on the bed to find one that was full of handcuffs, zip-ties, another taser, duct tape, and two knives. The other bag was full of religious material, including a Bible, several small books in German, and a pamphlet that had both Christian and vaguely Nazi symbology on the cover. I was pretty sure I had found a nut job killer, fueled by some kind of perverted religious belief. That would make my next decision a lot easier.

I dumped a glass of water on Walter's face. His eyes opened, and he tried to move. He didn't get far as I had used his handcuffs on him, and duct taped his mouth. He squirmed and tried to scream as he fully realized his situation. I let him simmer in that position as I played with one of his knives.

"If I take the tape off your mouth, will you behave and not scream?"

He nodded his head.

I ripped off the tape as hard as I could. His eyes teared up. Poor guy.

"Who are you?" he asked.

"I'm the guy putting you out of business, but I'm interested in what you have been doing." I held up the four licenses.

He spouted some gibberish about good and evil, and then he started yelling. A taser to the chest silenced the ranting as I did not need to hear anymore. I thought about what to do and who to call but decided it could wait a day while Walter enjoyed lying on the sofa by himself. No reason to kill him. There was overwhelming evidence so the legal system could deal with him. Then I had a powerful urge to kill him. I paused, thought about it, then rejected it. I realized that Michael was right, and there was no good reason for this murder. But I was going to need to think about where that urge came from.

I didn't think he could get out of his handcuffs unless he had a key stashed somewhere, but I needed to keep him immobilized, so I went the old school route. I took off Walter's shoes and socks and, using my penknife, I jabbed it through the back of each of his ankles, just under the Achilles tendon. One zip-tie went through both wounds and then I fastened it to where his ankles were only a couple of inches apart. Now he was literally hobbled. The last time I had seen this procedure, it was done with freshly boiled rawhide. It was sterile, so less chance of a local infection, and once you tied the knot, it was impossible to untie, so it had to be cut with a knife. It was very effective to keep captives from running off in 1750s America. I then zip-tied the ankle zip to the sofa arm. I zip-tied his wrists together, besides the handcuffs, and then zip-tied that to the other sofa arm. That should immobilize him once he woke up. I put the duct tape back across his mouth with some small holes in it, as I didn't want to restrict his breathing. I wondered if my decision to hobble him came from the previous urge to kill him, then turned into something merely vicious rather than murderous. Another avenue of my psyche I would need to explore.

I put the four licenses on the bed with all the rest of the crap. I walked out of the apartment, closed the door, left the building, and took my gloves off. It was easy to walk the few blocks to the train station and ride back to my stop. I walked home and sat on my balcony in the warm evening. I thought I was probably a lot more comfortable than Walter would be when he woke up. But someone would come to pick him up whenever I called. I thought about not calling, but I did not want that on my conscience. Better he should spend most of the rest of his life in a cell.

It didn't have to be that way, but you had to live with your decisions. I'm sure he was thinking he was doing the right thing and that he would never get caught. But he was doing it on my territory. That made him fair game, but lucky for him, I was trying to be a better person.

Chapter Twenty-Two

As I ate breakfast, I thought about whom to call to pick up Walter. I knew some of the Amsterdam police force, but then I decided it may be better to call in an anonymous tip. Considering how I had left him I might get charged with animal cruelty. The police would probably decide that one of his potential victims had turned the tables and disabled him. I needed to go get one of my throwaway phones so the police could not trace it. Then I thought about the four he had killed. Just in spite, I would let him sit for another day. The Netherlands prisons were nice, so he was due for a day of suffering. An extra day was not long enough to die of thirst or infection from his ankle wounds. With that last thought, I forgot about him.

I got a text that Jo was back in the country and we would meet in a couple of days. I pulled out the device that received the tracker signal and checked it as I had not used one before. Monk had approved of it, so I felt confident it would work. According to the device history, the car had been driven to the airport. Probably one of Michael's people had driven it to pick her up. Other than that, it had been in Den Haag or at the cottage. The detection range was impressive since I was over thirty kilometers, or twenty miles away from the car most of the time.

I thought about seeing her again and how it might go. The safe bet was to continue to be nice and professional, keep rebuilding trust. I also needed to think about how my relationship with the Church should proceed. The upcoming projects sounded interesting, so I should choose one and see how it went. This time of year, either Alaska or Italy would have the best weather. Mexico could wait for cooler weather. Russia could wait for years until things went back to normal, or what passed for it there.

I had left the tracker monitor on, so I was aware when Jo's car deviated from what I considered as normal routine and drove out of Den Haag, east and north, toward no obvious destination. Because that behavior seemed odd, I was going to investigate and follow the car. But I would not interfere with whatever she was doing. Probably not my business, plus I didn't want to give away that I had her tagged. We were due to meet at the cottage the following day, and I had no intention of antagonizing her beforehand.

There was nothing in that direction but tulip fields, either barren or planted with cover crops this time of year. Definitely not a reason to drive out there other than to waste some time. And I didn't think that she was a time waster. The other potential destination in the area was a golf course, but I knew she didn't play golf.

Since I was in Woerden, I got on the A-12 and headed west at a fast clip. Once you knew where the speed detection cameras were located, you could speed between them. I exited and turned north and continued past several places where I had spent a few lifetimes digging ditches in my early career. Some might have been ones I dug, but there were a few thousand ditches scattered over a hundred thousand hectares.

My tracker screen showed she was just ahead, but no longer moving. I slowed, not sure whether to pull into the dirt lane leading into the edge of the field where she was. Then, when I saw what was happening, I accelerated into the field and toward the back of Jo's car. A dark SUV was hauling ass in the opposite direction, down the lane on the far side of the field. There was a swath of fresh dirt spun up in tire tracks where it had turned around at high speed. Jo's car door was open on the driver's side, and there was a body on the ground beside the car. I sped up before slamming on the brakes and skidding in the dirt, stopping near her car. I was already out before my car stopped moving.

When I reached Jo, she was unconscious, and blood covered her right side. I saw two entry wounds, one just above her right breast and the other just above and to the right side of her navel. I checked her back and there were no exit wounds although her right shoulder blade felt off, possibly fractured. Based on the size of the holes and lack of exit wounds, the weapon must have fired a small caliber round at subsonic speed and was probably suppressed. In a few seconds, I went over all options I could think of to treat and save her. If the bullets did not fragment, then she was in grave condition; if either or both had fragmented, she was almost certainly going to die. Ambulances were too far away to arrive on time. My first aid skills would not keep her alive long enough for the medics to get there, so I'd watch her die.

The only option to keep her alive would require the hardest decision so far in my long life. Despite all the uncertainties, I had little choice - I would have to turn her into a version of me. Time slowed as the potential futures screeched through my mind if I turned her. The treatment could go poorly, and she might go into a zombie state. But she might be fine and live a good long life. Then would I subconsciously think that I did this to provide company for me, or even a companion? If she survived, she'd hate me as all her loved ones died around her in a few years. Regardless, I was altering her life in an unforgivable manner, without her permission. Saving her life could easily ruin her life, but she would be alive. I would live with that.

I sprinted to my car and popped open yet another secret compartment in the right rear above the wheel well. I pulled out the small cold box kept there at frigid temperatures by a small compressor powered by the battery, backed up with the solar panel built into the roof rack. Inside the box was a black bag.

I also grabbed the sizable first aid kit and ran back to Jo and shut off my mind to all the massive misgivings that almost paralyzed me. I condensed down all thoughts to just those necessary to treat her.

I ripped her shirt buttons free and used my knife to cut it free from her arms and neck, then slit her bra as well and pulled both garments free, but kept her shirt close by to use as a compression bandage as she would likely bleed though all the bandages in my kit. I then noticed that the top wound was showing signs her lung was hit. Fate just kept throwing grenades in my face. I pulled out a tube of wound superglue, opened it, and doused both holes. The top hole also got a piece of tape to close it completely against the suction from the lung. Her breathing was shallow and irregular, and her pulse felt weak. Shock was already in progress. I picked her up as carefully as possible along with my kit and the black bag and got her back to my car instead of treating her in the field. I knew that moving her was risky, but I needed a better place to work on her. At the back of my car, I opened the emergency foil blanket, wrapped her in it, and placed her on her left side.

The right lung was hit by the upper bullet, and no way of knowing what the lower bullet had hit. Worst case was colon and intestine perforations, which would eventually kill her from sepsis. The other worst case was the bullet had gone on into the kidney, which would kill her more quickly from internal bleeding. I had only been there for two minutes, working feverishly on her, but it seemed like an hour. Just like I had thought seconds ago, I realized that I no longer had a choice. I opened the black bag.

I removed a small syringe full of clear liquid, a much large syringe full of what looked like dark spinach puree, and a small scalpel. Damn. The thought flashed through my mind that this was about to be rough. I pushed the small syringe into the vein at her left elbow and emptied it. A second later, I slit her pants from the waist down the right leg with my knife, and then also cut through her panties. Without thinking, I pushed the large syringe, pre-coated with silicon, into her rectum and pushed the plunger fully down, then removed it. If she survived this, I hoped to never have to tell her about that part. I rolled her onto her back, then pushed myself up and over her, then slit open the inside of my bottom lip with the scalpel. I kissed her for several seconds with my mouth open on hers. Her breathing had almost stopped. I was getting prepared to do CPR, even though I knew how slim the odds were of keeping her alive with that procedure.

She suddenly convulsed. Shit, she was dying right there under me. I pulled up from her, and she convulsed again. Her eyes were open and wild. I did not know whether to hold her down and restrain her or let her struggle freely since I did not know which might injure her more. She then did something completely surprising by closing her eyes, lying still, and breathing shallowly but rapidly. My first aid skills were about exhausted, but I slid up front and started the car and turned on the heat. I went out the door, then back around to the rear of the car. I pulled out an epinephrine pen from the first aid kit and stuck it into her thigh.

All the damage I could do to her had been done. Concentrated viral particles harvested from my blood went into her arm; a fecal implant harvested from my well, inner workings into her, well, inner workings; and my blood and saliva poured directly into her mouth. It was all I could do, and since I had never done it before, I wasn't sure how it would turn out. I kept telling myself it was to save her. She would either survive and turn into something like me, or survive and turn into a raving mad zombie, or she could die without recovering at all. But it was now out of my control.

I needed to make two calls. The first was to 112, the Dutch version of 911, to get an ambulance on the way. I told them a female had been shot twice, and I was giving first aid, but she wasn't doing well. I gave them the basic address for the field, plus the GPS location on my phone. They told me to stay on the line, but I hung up. They were Dutch, they would understand.

I finished removing what was left of her pants, then re-wrapped the blanket around her before I jogged over and gathered up her bloody clothes from the field and put them into a pile in the back of my car. I climbed back in and held her through the blanket while pulling out my phone again.

The second call was to Michael.

"Hello."

"Michael. I'm with Jo and she has taken two bullets to the right torso. I have done what I can but not sure it's enough. We are out in a tulip field outside Hogeveen and in my car. An ambulance is on the way. We should be going to the hospital in Den Haag. Because of the shooting and my unorthodox treatment of her wounds, I think you better get involved as quickly as possible before this goes even further to hell."

He listened without wasting words on asking questions.

"I will have the hospital prepared before you arrive. I'm also sending a team to your current location to clean things up. Is there any imminent danger?"

"Thanks. No imminent danger, but I will be with her and kill the hell out of any threats that show up. See you at the hospital." I ended the call and kept a hold of Jo. Her breathing was better, but she still looked like hell. Naked, bloody, with two holes in her. And maybe a zombie, one I might have to kill.

Twelve minutes later, I could hear the ambulance on the main road, slowing to search for us. It finally found the lane and sped up. From the time I had first arrived to find her until the ambulance got there, it had been twenty-five minutes total. I had taken three extra minutes to treat her before calling the ambulance, but I didn't think those few minutes mattered, considering her wounds. I don't know if she would have lived those next twenty minutes without my intervention. That, at least, was my rationalization.

Two guys piled out of the ambulance and warily looked at me while walking up with two large bags. I then heard another siren, which must be the police. They visibly relaxed. They don't get many gunshot wounds in the country and I'm sure they were worried about me, all bloody sitting in the hatch of a car with a naked body wrapped in a foil blanket. I realized this was going to get messy quick unless Michael could work his magic.

I slid out of the car, showing them my hands, and pointed to Jo. I unnecessarily told them someone had shot her. They moved to her and opened the blanket carefully. They did not like what they were looking at. One dug in the bag and pulled out an IV. The other was talking rapidly into his radio while opening the other bag to remove a set of sensors to put on her chest. As soon as the IV was set, the first one looked at me.

"Did you treat her? Put on the glue and use the blanket?"

"Yes, I found her over there by her car, shot, and brought her here to start first aid. I didn't know if I should move her, but I had to get aid started. I also gave her an epinephrine shot."

"Probably should not have moved her, but everything else you did was excellent work." He turned away from me and went back to help his partner remove the stretcher as the police car pulled up.

Two tall young men got out and walked up to me. I could tell they were sizing me up. Was I the good Samaritan or the jealous boyfriend shooter? Either way, their day had just gotten extremely complicated.

"Meneer? You were the one to phone?" The police officer was asking questions in Dutch.

I answered in English, hoping that would get me some allowances during the questions. "Yes. As I drove up, I found her here by that car while a dark SUV spun around and went that way." I pointed toward the other end of the field. "I started first aid as best I could and then called to request an ambulance."

They both looked at the obvious tire ruts, looked at her car and my car. So far, everything looked legitimate. I just needed to keep them trusting me long enough to get to the hospital without being detained.

"Do you know this woman?"

"Yes, we are colleagues on a research project. We were to meet in Den Haag today when she called and said she was visiting the tulip fields. She said we could meet here first since it was on the way from Woerden for me." The whole thing sounded lame, even to me. But it was the only partial lie I could come up with.

"What is your name, and could we also see some identification?"

"Yes, my name is Ceryl Vogel, and here is my license and passport." I handed them my two documents. I was not too worried about what I told them, as the name and documents I just handed them would be deleted by tomorrow and replaced with new ones. During the exchange, the medics had hooked another sensor on to Jo, and now they were grabbing the blanket to slide her on the stretcher. The policeman glanced at my documents. One of them took a photo with his phone.

"Do you have any idea who might be in the other vehicle, or did you see them or a license plate?"

"No. While I was still driving up, the car was already halfway down the lane. They turned left, but I saw no person or a plate at that distance." I wasn't even looking at them while I was speaking, as I was distracted by what was going on with Jo. The medics were moving the stretcher toward the ambulance. "Look, I know you have many questions, but can we continue this in the ambulance? I really need to be with her until she gets to the hospital safely." Probably not the best thing to have said as they both tensed back up.

"Why would you say that? Do you expect her to be in further danger?"

"Possibly, but I doubt it with all the attention here now. There will be guards at the hospital waiting for her." They perked up. I wasn't helping any by making them more suspicious about who she was or who might have shot her. The EMTs had her in the ambulance and one was checking her monitors while the other was talking into his radio. Obviously, they would leave any second. "Why don't one of you go with me in the ambulance, while the other drives your car, plus call in another car for backup on the way to the hospital?"

"No, we need you to stay with us. We have more questions and need to secure the scene until our team arrives."

"Not going to happen. I will be in that ambulance until the guards receive her at the hospital." Perhaps that came out a bit forcefully or threateningly, as both stepped back while one began speaking into his radio. I began walking to the ambulance as one stepped back to his car and grabbed something, while the other kept two steps behind me and to the side. Guess he didn't want to be in the line of fire. I had no desire to do it, but if they were going to be obstinate, I would have to take them both out before they could shoot me. The EMT in the back with Jo looked up and began shrinking back toward the cab as he sensed what was about to happen. He thought I was quickly going to join Jo in the ambulance on the other stretcher, with holes in me as well. He was about to be enlightened, with a front-row seat of me taking down two police officers in two seconds.

Both were behind me and closing in. Excellent, as I needed to let them both get in range. Then a sound saved them both from a terrible day. A helicopter came over us fast and dropped immediately into the field beside us. I had not seen flying like that since a drunk mercenary pilot in Thailand dropped off a released kidnappee on a river barge. The EMT in the back of the ambulance jumped out and released the brake on the stretcher while the driver got out and came around to help remove it from the ambulance. As soon as the helicopter touched the ground, both back doors opened and Michael and two military commandos, armed to the teeth, ran to us. The commandos followed Jo's stretcher and helped load it onto the helicopter, but only one jumped in. Michael stood in front of me for half a second, then I smiled and shook his hand. He winked and ran back to the helicopter. As soon as he was in, it lifted off and zoomed toward Den Haag. It was a large medical copter, so

I guessed there were multiple commandos on board without even crowding the space. The other commando on the ground jogged back towards us and then stood by my vehicle. The police officers looked a bit shocked.

"Well, I guess now I can ride with you to the hospital."

I had to wait a few minutes before two additional police cars arrived. Three officers and a supervisor. I suppose my actions before the helicopter arrived might have triggered some overreaction. The ambulance had departed, so I sat down on the edge of the field. The commando had said nothing or moved from beside my car. Once the supervisor got out of his car, he talked to his two officers for a minute, then came over to me. I was trying to look relaxed and inoffensive as possible.

"Hello, would you be willing to ride with me to the hospital so I can ask some necessary questions?" he asked.

"Absolutely. I need a ride since I have no intention of annoying that well-armed gentleman by my car. And I'll answer what I can."

The supervisor just gave a half-smile and nodded.

Chapter Twenty-Three

The trip to the hospital was only twenty minutes by car. There were two police officers in the front, with the supervisor and I in the back. I gave the same story, all true, as I had given the first two police officers. I got mostly polite nods and very brief questions.

Toward the end he asked, "You said that she and you were colleagues; who do you work for?"

"That is a question best left to the people you are about to meet at the hospital." I don't think he expected that kind of answer to such a normal question. "I am not intentionally being difficult, but I am being vague because my employer requires it."

"You realize that puts this entire matter into a different light."

"It probably should, because I have a suspicion this was an assassination attempt. And this is probably about to float way up past everyone's jurisdiction."

He didn't look happy, but I was trying to prepare him for the shitshow that was brewing at the hospital. I think he suspected as much after the reports of the helicopter appearance and the stoic commando at my vehicle.

"What is your role in this matter?" he asked.

"Until today, I was researching information about some interesting but mostly harmless topics. Dr. York, the victim, was helping me with that research."

He looked confused for a second. I doubt that in his line of work he saw researchers get shot. We arrived at the hospital, and all four of us got out. Waiting nearby were two men in suits I assumed were Michael's men, as well as a commando. The police supervisor did not look too surprised.

The supervisor said, "The two patrolmen at the scene did not think you were lying, but they reported you as dangerous. I have been doing this for thirty years and I think they are right. But if I can assist you, please let me know." He handed me his card.

"Thank you, and I will behave while in your city," I said. "On a totally different matter, I was going to alert the Amsterdam authorities, but today went a little differently than planned. There is a serial killer handcuffed in his apartment near Amsterdam, in Sloterdijk, along with all the evidence of his crimes. Would you like the address?"

"Uh, sure. Would you care to enlighten me on how you came to know about this individual or how he found himself handcuffed?"

"I really have nothing further to add. I will be around for more questions after you pick him up. Everything you find will be self-explanatory."

I could not tell if he was happy hearing that or not. Either he was about to get a nice coup for an arrest and a lot of notoriety, or he would find out I was wasting his time and was probably insane. I told him the address. Then he nodded and we shook hands. I trotted off to find the ICU ward. He walked over to Michael's men.

I arrived on the third floor of the massive building. My dirty and bloody appearance had kept people from speaking to me. Maybe I should wear this outfit more often. I came around the last corner and ran into Michael, another younger version of Michael that I assumed was Brother Somebody or other, and three more of his commando friends. Between me and the commandos, the few people in the waiting area all decided they had somewhere else to be.

Michael said to his men, "Secure the downstairs, answer any further questions from the police inspector, and guard the room."

Brother Somebody and one commando went for the elevator, the other two commandos went through the ICU doors that were supposedly off limits and down the hallway. They all knew what to do without being specifically told.

"How is she?" was all I could ask.

"Remarkably well, considering she should have died an hour ago," he said, while looking at me speculatively. "Serious trauma involving several organs, blood loss, and shock. She will be in surgery a while longer to remove the bullets and repair the damage. But overall, the doctors seemed shocked by her resilience."

I decided to keep quiet for the moment. "Thank God."

"Indeed," Michael responded.

"I have a feeling the master vampire I am chasing did this, and I feel terrible. I will continue feeling bad right up to the time I skin him, de-vein him, and puree him piece by piece in a woodchipper."

"That was our initial assessment as well," Michael said. "But that changed a half-hour ago. Our lead resource scientist at the Center, Jo's counterpart, was found in a car that was smashed at the bottom of a ravine in the Dolomite Mountains. He had three bullet holes in him. Obviously not a random crash."

"Damn, I guess that explains the extra security, then. This is a hit on the Center?"

"Apparently," he answered.

"So, where is your security?" I prodded him.

"As I suspect you have guessed, I normally don't need any security," he said.

We both sat down in the empty waiting room.

"I guess this is where I fess up and tell you how she survived."

"I can logically determine the general how. At some point, we probably need to discuss the details of that in regard to her further care and recovery."

"Yes," I said, "if she survives as herself and I don't have to kill her if she turns zombie." It felt worse saying that out loud than it did thinking it. I had to stop and compose myself. "And if she is herself, and then I become responsible for her burden of outliving everyone she has ever known."

Michael put his hand on my arm. "I know you did what you thought best," he said. "If you do a good thing for the right reasons, eventually the universe will accept it and smile upon the act. Jo will follow suit."

"Eventually; hah, that could be a long time in our case."

"I did not say it would be easy, or even soon. Especially when you tell her the full story."

"Damn, you mean I have to tell her? Isn't that incumbent upon you as her employer or healthcare provider or something?"

"No, only you can provide that truth to her. She was lucid for a moment in the helicopter, and all I told her was that it was you that saved her. She may not remember that after surgery, but me saying that calmed her, and she went back to sleep. I feel that you two have a bond that is about to become even stronger, but I warn you that the future will not be easy."

"I think the same thing and am afraid of how long she will hate me," I said.

"No good deed goes unpunished, per the cliché," he said.

A doctor came down the hallway and looked at us, or really just looked at Michael and ignored me. "Do you have any news yet?" he asked her. She said nothing but looked pointedly at me. It was obvious she would say nothing in front of me, as I looked like a homeless person a ketchup bottle had exploded upon. "It is OK. He is family and the one that treated her first."

"Oh, good to meet you then," she said to me and finally relaxed. I just nodded and waited. "She is stable, but still in a serious condition. We removed the unfragmented bullets without complications. It was odd, though; it was like the bullets did not cause any collateral damage to the surrounding tissue and organs. Maybe it's a new type of firearm or round, I wouldn't know. I feel like we did more damage retrieving the bullets than they had done on their own." Neither Michael nor I said anything; the truth wouldn't do in this case.

"With the existing trauma and blood loss, I would say she will be here at least a week, possibly two, as we continue monitoring her progress and ward off infections," she continued.

Michael said, "I believe she will be up and around well before that. We will also transfer her to another facility tomorrow." I suppose he was prepping the doctor on what to expect. She looked incredulous and a little miffed.

"I'm the doctor here and there is no way she will be ready to transfer, much less leave ICU by then."

"I know you are the doctor, but there are extenuating circumstances involved in this case," Michael answered. "I'm not trying to argue with you, but we have seen this before. Patients like Jo have healed much quicker than expected." He was looking at me as he said that last sentence.

"Well, I suppose we will see. I would welcome such a quick recovery. I just don't imagine that it could happen based on my experience."

Michael just gave her a fatherly smile and bowed his head.

"Can I see her?" I asked.

"She is waking, so maybe you can for just a couple of minutes."

I gave her a grateful look and followed her down the hall while Michael stayed in the waiting area and watched us leave. We entered the open room—it was the only one with two commandos outside it—to see a bed with a small Jo in it hooked up to at least four monitors, IVs, and other colorful beeping things. I should have been a medical doctor.

I walked over to her and grabbed the hand that had the least number of things attached to it. She opened her eyes halfway and gave a slight smile.

"How are you doing, sunshine?"

"Oh, cut the crap," she said in a low voice. "I feel like a bloody lorry has hit me." I had to smile at that.

"Do you remember anything at all today?"

"I was driving out of Den Haag when I got a text that I thought was from you, asking to meet in a tulip field for a picnic. I pulled in toward a car I thought was yours, but just as I got out, I realized it was black instead of grey, and it was definitely a Range Rover. Then something hit me hard. I was in a helicopter, I think. And Michael said you had saved me."

"That's good that you remember," I said, as I was getting dirty looks from the doctor. My time was up. "You sleep now, and I will stay with you either here or in the waiting room." She gave another half-smile and closed her eyes.

I turned around while the doctor scanned the machines, then followed me out into the hall.

"She is already doing better than expected," the doctor said. "I'm not sure why, but maybe she will heal quickly."

"I am sure of it. Do you know who Michael is, or rather who he is with?"

She shook her head no.

"He is with the Church, so he's counting on a miracle, and he's usually right."

She looked at me skeptically. I would not say anymore, but I would rather have Jo's recovery thought of as a miracle than any in-depth tests conducted to determine how she beat those bullet wounds in two days. We walked back to the waiting area, and the doctor left. I walked with Michael to the opposite side of the room.

"She said the car was a Range Rover, and I guess she should know," I said to Michael. "She had gotten a text she thought was from me asking her to meet at the tulip field, so maybe you can trace something from her phone."

"We already have the phone," he said, "but no leads on the message."

"Some things make little sense, though. Two bullets fired, but not particularly well placed, and out in a field with no cover or control of the situation for witnesses. It sounds sloppy."

"We think it was a last-minute contract job," Michael said. "Probably not the 'A' team, which, of course, was good for Jo. The area in the field is now secure. Is it OK if one of mine drives your car here as the keys were in it? I assume your surprises and traps are inactive."

"Yes, I had time to turn everything off and secure all my goodies before the police arrived," I said. "Would have been imprudent of me if one of them had died after turning the radio on."

"Always thinking of the uninformed, I like that," he said.

"Other than the vague threats you mentioned before, anything else odd happening lately?"

"Possibly some intel that either your master vampire or another has been in the country. But quiet, other than the Center chatter. Have you heard anything else about your master vampire?" he asked.

"No, completely quiet the past few weeks."

"I suppose that is a positive with everything else going on."

"I will stay here with Jo," I said. "I know you have two guys here, but I can be backup if anything else shows up here, especially if a master is lurking. I also will need the time to think about how to tell her about her recovery and her added centuries."

"I am sure you will give her the truth compassionately," Michael said. "I will leave you here, as I need to attend to several other things and make sure everyone is safe."

"Are any of Jo's family traveling here to visit her in the hospital?" I asked.

"No, too much of a security risk," he said. "When I realized what was happening, I informed them but also downplayed her injuries as I did not think awkward questions after her miraculous recovery would be welcome."

I nodded. "Goodbye then, and thanks for your help today."

"It is what I do for our flock, especially the wounded ones." He left, and I sat down to ponder my next and perhaps last conversation with Jo.

I alternated between thinking and drowsing the afternoon and evening in a most uncomfortable chair. One of Michael's men had dropped off a change of clothes, towel, and soap. I could at least look presentable after some time in the bathroom.

Something was bothering me about the entire episode. I contacted Monk and asked him to research the recent local shooting incident and the accident in northern Italy. I gave him a few other details, and then also asked him to cross reference both incidents with the individual I already had him searching for but doing so as carefully as possible. He said he'd be right on it or would be as soon as the soccer game ended. It's always funny when computer geeks talk smack.

I saw the doctor in the hall a few minutes later and walked down. I asked her about staying in the room with Jo, but she was adamant I could not, so I went back to the waiting room. Then sometime past midnight, the doctor came in to see me. She must have been working one of those wonderful twelve-hour shifts.

"She is awake and insists on seeing you," the doctor said. "I don't know how, since she should be completely out of it, yet her condition has improved drastically. Your friend must have been right." She looked confused, with a little touch of wonder. Good things to see on a trauma surgeon's face.

I trotted down the hall. I noticed they had replaced the commandos with new, almost identical guys. As I walked into her room, I realized it was time to fess up.

Jo was sitting up and looking good, considering all that had happened to her.

"Hey, did you bring me something to eat?" she asked.

"I think the doc would frown on that, since you are not supposed to even be awake for a few more days," I answered.

"Well, all I know is that I am starving and bored sitting here," she said.

"I don't think I can bring you any food, but I would be happy to keep you company," I said.

"I'd like that," she replied. "And I'm sure I can talk you into smuggling me something. But I wanted to ask you about what happened today since I remember almost nothing after getting out of the car."

"I drove in behind you, probably just a minute after they shot you. A dark SUV had already spun around and was heading the opposite way out of the field. I found you and started first aid, then called the ambulance and Michael." I left out some of the more unsavory parts on purpose.

"How did you appear there so quickly?"

Damn, she had me there. But this was no time to lie. Conceal maybe, but no lies.

"I was tracking your car since you came back into the country," I said. I continued on quickly as I saw the look on her face. "Michael had mentioned threats involving the Center, and I thought the jinn's body was a clear threat message. Mostly to me, but you were with me long enough to be seen when we investigated his trail. I put a tracker in your car and left you alone. I acted when I saw you do something unusual and leave Den Haag for the countryside, when tulips aren't blooming. My gut told me to see where you were going."

"Thanks, but that still makes me uncomfortable."

"Welcome to the world of international espionage and assassinations. Yay, now you get to have bodyguards and everything."

She didn't look happy.

"But now that I have made you unhappy, I might as well tell you something."

"Well, that's a great lead in for telling me something terrible. So much for bedside manners."

I reached over and grabbed her hand. Now she looked scared. I was direct. "About twelve hours ago, you were shot and left for dead in a field with two very serious wounds, from which you should not have recovered."

"Yes, but you were there quickly and able to save my life."

"And now you are sitting up having a conversation and begging for food, which are actions that most patients would exhibit only after two weeks of recovery."

She looked confused, more than scared. "What are you trying to tell me?"

"There was only one way to save you. It's a decision I made without your consent, and possibly the wrong one. But do you remember some time back at the cottage in Meije, when we were first discussing all my special characteristics and how the Center should start its studies?"

"Yes," she said tentatively.

"Part of the discussion was how the condition might be transferred to others."

"Yes."

"Well congratulations, you are the newest, and so far, only guinea pig to get that opportunity."

She looked at me as the comprehension came over her face. Her eyes teared up, and she looked away while squeezing my hand tightly. She finally looked back at me. "I'm not sure whether to thank you or curse you. But you saved me. What does this mean?"

"I expect you to do both—profusely thank me and scream obscenities at me. I will give you time to do both. And I don't know what it means yet. I hope it means you will be healthy and live a long life."

She just looked at me and sighed. She was obviously thinking about all the positives and negatives I had just saddled her with. I sat with her, holding her hand, despite the protests from the nurses coming in to check on her. Once they saw how well she was doing, they left us alone. This was going to be a lengthy journey for both of us.

After they left, she looked up at me. Her eyes were still shiny, but she was refusing to cry. "Right now, I think I want to be alone for a while. I have to get my thoughts in order and I'd rather not talk to you about this. I'll let the nurses or Michael know if I need to see to you."

I nodded and left. My dismissal told me she was going to need time to adjust to her new situation. Her decision did not surprise me, but it saddened me she did not want me around.

Chapter Twenty-Four

As I left Jo's room, I saw Michael near the elevator. "Is she doing better, as expected?" he asked.

"Yes, she is. I've also been blacklisted for some time. She said she would let you or the staff know if she wanted to see me again. Not unexpected, but it still stings."

"Of course, it does. But she will need you to navigate this new life. We will transfer her to our facility in town today as our doctors have flown in. It's here in Den Haag, so I will text you the address."

"Thanks. I'm going to Woerden to get cleaned up. Let me know if anything changes and I can be back in less than an hour." I drove back to my apartment and spent the rest of the day and the next, riding a bike and thinking too much. I also had a brief conversation with a particular police supervisor about a sloppy serial killer found in Sloterdijk. Once he realized I would not give him any further information, he thanked me and ended the call. I threw the burner phone away after talking to him.

Michael called and asked me to come to the Church clinic the next morning. "Did Jo ask to see me?" I asked.

"No, she didn't. But we have to discuss how to make this work and get back to business. And since this is business and not personal, I'm deciding to have the meeting."

"OK, I'll be there. But she needs to know that is your call, so you can take the blame."

"Not a problem for me. I normally make people mad or uncomfortable. In her case, however, I can easily deflect her ire toward you."

"Thanks for that. See you in the morning."

After a healthy dose of caffeine, I drove to the private hospital. A very nice building set into a more residential area of Den Haag, near the Peace Palace.

Michael and I walked into Jo's room. She acknowledged Michael but ignored me.

"You seem to be doing very well this morning," said Captain Obvious. "Your treatment appears to agree with you."

She glared at him. No reason to poke the bear this early, but he seemed to enjoy my squirming. About then I noticed there were no commandos nearby. There would be no one to restrain her when she got out of bed and kicked Michael's ass. He definitely would not get any help from me, as I would be busy recording the event on my cell phone.

"I know that you two have talked and will need more time to address the obvious issue resulting from this unfortunate event. I must apologize to you, Jo, for our lapse in operational security. That won't happen again. And you," he said, looking at me, "are to be commended for doing what we could not do, however unorthodox your actions were."

I appreciated Michael's efforts, but I doubted that would get me back into Jo's good graces anytime soon.

"What happens now?" Jo asked.

"So far you have recovered nicely, but we are keeping you here at our hospital in case of any side effects for two more days. For the next couple of weeks, I encourage you to take time off and be with your family. I hope that afterward you will come back to the Center and continue your work. But you don't have to make those decisions right now."

"Thanks. I will need time to think about what I'm going to do. When I decide to come back to the Center, I want to take a more active role rather than just research. I also need a crash course in weapons and self-defense."

"Understandable, and after that training I would expect that you tell me what you want to do; other than my current role, any position will be open to you," Michael said. He looked at me but did not speak. Then he went and closed the door. Not a good sign. "We have had multiple operational failures resulting in a heightened threat level the past forty-eight hours."

"You must do something right to get all that attention," I said. "But you need to up your game before they beat the hell out of you and yours."

"Quite right, and already in progress. I would also ask that you join us full time to help us cope with the multiple additional threats."

I really considered it. Not for him, but for her. When I looked over at Jo, she looked uncertain. That decided for me. "Thanks for the offer, again, but I am still not ready for that. Although we are still after some of the same folks, I need some independence for a few other things."

"I suppose that would include ridding North America of some previously unknown and quite nasty creatures?"

Damn, he had already gotten wind of that. His sources were excellent. Jo was now looking very attentive. "That is certainly part of it. Surprised you heard so quickly. At some point, I'll fill you in on the newest member of the menagerie. And I have some meat in my freezer for the lab folks."

"I look forward to it, as I'm sure Doctor York will," he said, looking at Jo, then turned back to me. "I am surprised you survived, but I'm glad you did, so you could help here this week."

Jo was pissed. I don't know if it was from doing something stupid as Michael was implying, or if it was from me not telling her the whole story. Either way, it was not going well for me. Time to change the subject and get everything stirred up. I hoped that work talk would get Jo's mind off of hating me.

"I have had further time to think about the jinn investigation. Ultimately, the situation makes little sense, and I think our premise is wrong. Michael, is it likely that the jinn was making himself and his trail very visible, because he was trailing and marking a master vampire, to give us clues to follow and a warning? Isn't that more likely than the jinn himself caused the evil along that trail? The jinn could have killed James in that alley, but he did not. When cornered in Utrecht, he disappeared. Perhaps Brother James and I mistook the situation and acted with violence, when we should have had a conversation with the jinn instead."

"Because the typical behavior of a jinn is not to randomly harm or kill humans, that argument does make sense. But the jinn would need to be directed to follow that course. The question becomes, who would direct those actions? That would show an unknown but beneficent party," Michael said.

"What other evidence makes you think the jinn was acting as a marker for us to get involved and follow the master vampire?" Jo asked. She was finally getting into the conversation.

"Caius had a very distinct smell. The jinn was putting out a similar smell, but different. And jinns rarely have a smell like that. Almost as if he was leading me. I also caught a serial killer earlier this week in Sloterdijk in that same building we visited. Same thing there with the smell. There are too many coincidences to be chance."

Michael and Jo looked surprised at the mention of a new serial killer. I summarized events of my investigation and capture of the culprit.

"Is he still alive?" asked Jo.

"Yes, I tied him up and let the police know, and made sure all the evidence was available so there would be no question of his guilt. I had a momentary urge to end him, but recent conversations have convinced me to ignore those impulses."

Both of them looked relieved. Wow, everyone assumed I killed rather than captured. I needed to work on my people skills.

"If the jinn was trying to help us, then we must assume Caius or something similar was up to something major. But it seemed random and rather mundane, getting people to kill or harm other people. I don't see a strategy there," Jo said.

"I don't either," I said. "But it could have been a diversion away from something bigger. Perhaps Caius spreads chaos while something else is happening and we are looking at the diversion. Michael, can you get your network to check for other occurrences like this around Europe and other continents?"

"Yes, I will. It smells like a ruse. Caius could distract us while a vanguard of the enemy is approaching elsewhere. That makes the jinn a harbinger, alerting us to the danger so we can follow the trail and eliminate those threats quickly. Clear those distractions so we can see the real threat. Jo, what do you think?"

"That is a more logical conclusion than a random jinn showing up to cause problems. The graffiti on the building in Utrecht was a warning to us, seen from that context. How imminent is the threat if this was a diversion?"

"Possibly a few months away, as the unrest in Utrecht, the drug dealer in Amsterdam, and the serial killer in Sloterdijk would have all developed into major problems by then," Michael said. "If the pattern shows up in other countries, then I believe we will have the answer as to the time frame. Leaving us to determine what the real threat is, and secondarily who our unknown benefactor is."

The conversation stopped for a minute as we contemplated all the new twists in our reality.

"I need to change the subject and add to the Center's to-do list," I said.

"Oh good, this should cost me another few million euros," Michael said.

"Since we are changing subjects, my aside is that I expect a full briefing on your North American jaunt," Jo said to me. "I am bored sitting here and that should make an interesting story, especially if you have a new species to add."

I nodded a yes to her. It seemed like a good omen that she still wanted me to keep her company.

"I take it that Jo is now at the highest security clearance?" I asked Michael.

"She is now. I was just joking about you costing me an extra few million, but I think you are serious."

"I am," I said, "and this ought to keep you both entertained a while. And reasons to increase security even more."

I had their attention, so time to plow on.

"Michael, I have had some time to think about your viral origin problem."

He looked slightly unhappy and glanced at Jo. I barged on instead.

"I have narrowed it down to two possibilities, however unlikely they are. First, it is plausible that there are aliens from outside our world involved, either hanging around nearby or even living on Earth undetected."

"Oh, my god," Jo said.

"May not be his jurisdiction in this case."

"The second hypothesis, and the one I think more likely, is the virus was introduced from time travelers."

"Interesting. Please proceed," Michael said.

"They will develop the virus in the future with advanced technology, then bring it backward into our past for unknown reasons. The precise technology for time travel is unknown, and I don't believe it has been invented here yet. The viral technology also has not been invented. I think they did the travel mechanism and the viral manipulations in the future."

"That seems unlikely, as both the travel mechanism and all the scenarios getting someone to a particular time and place in the past would be problematic."

"The first part I cannot answer, and not sure anyone today could. The second part is simple, though."

"Then how?"

"Quantum entanglement. If you have particles of an object, you can link them across any length of space and with no time constraints. If you had the right technology linked to the particles, then you could travel to when and where you needed to."

"I don't see how the traveler would have the objects in the first place to get the correct particles, though. If they are in the future, they can't easily get those objects from the past. That seems like a paradox."

"Oh, I don't know," I said with a grin. "Who do you think has the world's largest collection of ancient artifacts that one could use for linkage to times past?"

"Damnation. Relics?"

"Relics indeed."

I watched as his mind raced through the possibilities. "This is a serious problem. That indicates we have further traitors in the Church."

"It's possible, though, to track the relics to get an idea of who might take them or sample them," Jo said.

"Exactly," I said. "I have the guy that can do it, but you will have to provide the computing power, which will be substantial."

"And add a new section to the Center at substantial cost," he said.

"Of course," I said.

"Jo, can it be done, or do we need more resources?" Michael asked.

She thought for a moment. "Yes, we can start that process. But those records need to be digitized I think, to be useful for computer input to look for patterns. We probably don't have enough people for that, as it will be an extensive database."

"Is that where you were going with this?" Michael asked me.

"Absolutely. She took the words right out of my mind. I would suggest you also begin digitally recording images in Church possession, whether illustrations, paintings, sculpture, or manuscripts. That could be of even more benefit than the relic tracing."

"I am not sure I follow that logic," Michael said.

Jo chimed right in, "I think it's about facial recognition, looking for patterns of any faces that show up more than once in different time frames. That would help pinpoint any travelers."

"Bingo. And you are on fire today."

"Perhaps I should get shot more often," she said.

"Really poor joke," I said. She just looked at me with a half-smile.

"I see you two have discussed this before," Michael said.

"Well, actually no," I said. "Everything today is pure real-time synthesis. Maybe you need to get shot to get smarter and keep up."

"I've done that before. But all that it taught me was to try harder to stay out of the path of future bullets."

"A worthy endeavor. Regardless, I think with my guy and your hardware we can find enough patterns in the different databases to track these guys. I also think the jinn could have been using time travel or teleportation. That explains his propensity for disappearing and appearing."

"But that means that the third-party director was using time travel or teleportation. Does that show they are also from the future?" Jo asked.

"That is a good point. And one to add to the list of mysteries."

"We can evaluate that possibility," Michael said. He seemed too unsurprised by much of the discussion, which told me he knew much more than he was letting on.

"The other topic to cover is security of this operation," I said. "Similar to the other Center projects, they will probably target this one for acquisition or destruction. I can think of multiple governments and private entities that would like to have this system once operational. And, of course, the travelers themselves, once they learn of it, will start terminating your staff."

"They may already know about it since they are in the future and the Center might have interacted with or had an influence on them," Jo said.

"Yes, if it works like that. That's for the physics crowd and paradox paranoiacs to discuss and advise the Center management."

"Regardless, the Center security has been upgraded the past forty-eight hours, and I see now it will have to be both strengthened and hidden much better than we had planned. I think the traveler project should even be as separate as possible from all other projects to minimize collateral damage should the worst case occur."

That brought the conversation to a halt, as we all considered collateral damage. A threat from a group in the future that possibly already knew what we were planning. Nothing like having formidable enemies to keep your wits sharpened.

Finally, after a few minutes, Jo said, "Time for you two to leave. I really have to go to the toilet, and I would prefer not trekking across the room in this joke of a hospital gown with witnesses present."

"Oh, that is not a problem for this one here. I believe he is already a witness to all possibilities partially covered by any hospital gown," Michael said.

Son of a bitch. He was lobbing a dirty nuke right at me.

Jo was looking at me furiously. "What the hell is he talking about?" she basically yelled in a low voice. Such a thing should have been impossible, but I had just heard it.

"The applications of the required treatments in the field were unusual," Michael continued, emptying the gasoline onto me. "It requires, I am told, certain liberties with the patient. Of course, the saving of a life was worth the indiscretions."

Son of a bitch, son of a bitch. I could feel my face getting red, a sure and flashing sign of guilt. Jo did not miss that either.

"What did you do?" she asked in a voice that was even lower than before. Reminded me of a lion growling before charging.

I decided the truth was better than fiction, or concealment. Not that either was possible with Michael in the room. I glanced over, and he winked at me. Son of a bitch, I thought thrice. He was still standing in the room and enjoying this immensely, despite my fervent wish that he had been transported to Mongolia. I would proceed carefully and employ the most clinical language possible.

"Well, I had thought a lot over the years about a situation arising that would require saving a human life as a last resort, which you already know about. After much study and some guesswork, I came up with a three-part solution that I decided would give the best outcome."

Jo was not looking any happier. I decided it was probably all the urine backing up. "The first was harvesting viral particles from my blood and plasma, concentrating and stabilizing it, and putting it in a syringe for veinous injection. That was what I injected into your arm. The second part was harvesting and stabilizing a culture for a fecal implant."

"You didn't." It came out as a hiss.

"I did."

"Oh my God," she muttered.

"He was not there, so I inserted it myself," I said. Her nonverbal response suggested that she did not find that funny. Michael threw a little more gasoline by letting go with a little chuckle.

"You said three parts. What other kind of hell did you subject me to?" Jo asked.

"For the third treatment, I cut open my lip and pressed it against your open mouth for a minute. I had to make sure my fresh blood and saliva got into your system as quickly as possible."

"Oh." Somehow, she seemed less offended than I expected. Not exactly the response I would have given if somebody had told me they leaked their body fluids down my throat while I was passed out. "Thanks for saving me. We will talk more about this later. Now both of you get out before I burst my bladder and have to stay here another day."

Chapter Twenty-Five

Caius

My servant brought me a glass of wine. I thought again about purchasing a vineyard to make my vintage. A bottle of Caius Estate Reserve sounded nice. Or Domitius Vineyards? I might have to work on the name and ensure it met all the marketing buzzwords. Those thoughts of wine somehow sent me to the weirdness of the sacrament. I might be a vampire, which could disqualify me, but I truly drank blood and ingested bodies regularly. Maybe I should be a saint. Did that come with health benefits? Not that I needed them, as I stayed in perfect health. Nor did I think the Church would offer me any employment opportunities. That would be something, a vampire suing the Church for species discrimination.

My thoughts turned serious as I moved on to a recent problem. An ancient comrade, one who should not exist, had come to my attention during the Great Extermination some seventy years ago. Back then, I was experiencing strange sensations while visiting a restaurant in Amsterdam. It was odd enough that I followed up as best I could during the post-War period in Europe. Amazingly, I determined he was from my distant past and I could finally place him as my old Legionnaire colleague. A vague memory of an officer of the Legion, really just an asshole, with a stick inserted. He made a habit of doing the right thing and taking care of his men. I was very young and did not have my powers yet, so I never killed him. But I should have had my loyal men kill him at the Camp since we regularly killed others.

Once I realized who he was, I had a few other opportunities, but whether due to luck or some interference, the job was never finished. Or rather, those I hired had not finished their jobs. I killed them instead, but I did not eat them afterward as they were too old and gristly. The one group I hired botched the train accident, which they paid for with their lives. Another time, a single assassin had tampered with the brakes on Senecus' car. The idiot had picked the wrong car, as the headlines the next day revealed the tragic auto accident that killed four people. For that mistake, I ripped his throat out. The recent shooter in the tower had been close to killing him but had left too soon to get a final shot. The damned jinn had shown up and spooked the shooter. It was always something, and perhaps I should see to it myself. I just needed to get those future humans interested in killing Senecus. Then they could pay me to do what I was already going to do. Another win-win for me.

But before I could follow up on Senecus, I had gotten a demand from those pathetic futurions. They might be a few hundred years ahead of us, with advanced technology, but often I wondered about their intelligence. I nominally worked for them through others, but they did not impress me. They had detected some chance that a low-ranking researcher could pose a threat to their interests. But those morons could not even determine exactly which person was the threat, so they sanctioned two people. Both were in some new, secret department that Michael was overseeing. The only direction they sent was that both would need to be killed to end the threat. Not exactly efficient, but I suppose it was effective.

They gave me thirty hours to arrange the deaths of both people. Through our Church contacts, I could find both of them, as they were based in Italy. But the Church contact, Paolo, got mouthy with me as I explained the information I required. But I finally got what I needed on the targets, as well as the contact for the two gentlemen that were professionals and could kill both targets easily. My interest was piqued when Paolo mentioned that one target had worked both with Michael and the even older, personal enemy from the Legion. It was all a win-win for me. I would get a hefty payday, would be owed a favor from those idiot Sky Lords, and put a damper on both Michael's and Senecus' day. All for just a phone call. I could even text the one target while posing as Senecus to draw them to the hit team. What an ironic and delicious turn of events. This was just too good. I called the hit team and set it up.

But then, of course, my evening plans went to hell. In the middle of a delectable flank steak, freshly ripped from a young human, my telephone rang. All my people knew I was not to be disturbed when eating new flesh, so this would be an important call. I delicately wiped the blood from my hands and mouth and answered the call. The two professional hitters had eyes on one target, but the other was out of the country. Damn it. My Italian hit team was one of the best in the business, and there was no way for them to hit the first target and get to the second target in time. A fifty percent success rate would not be advisable, because although the Sky Lords were inept, they could be malicious, and they had time on their hands. All the time in the world, apparently.

A piano could fall on my head while walking down the sidewalk fifty years from now. It would not kill me, but it would ruin my suit and cause me to be the butt of jokes for decades. I looked forward to the day that I would have full access to that time travel technology. I had heard of the dangers of not creating paradoxes, but I relished the idea of going back and killing my enemies when they were still infants. Although that supposedly would not end them in my timeline, I was planning on experimenting. And I still wanted to go back to old Rome and sit on the throne as emperor for a few weeks at a time. That seemed like a fun vacation.

But back to business. I called around while my fresh meat turned cold and slowly went into rigor mortis, and I hated tough flank steak. I would have to pull the loins off the body before it cooled much more, so I had better find another contract team quickly. A friend of a friend knew a guy... This was turning ridiculous, but there were no good teams listed for the Netherlands that could go to work on short notice.

I ended up with two low-life flunkies that did protection work for a drug dealer near Maastricht. I handed the phone to my assistant, who then filled in the details and logistics with the two contractors while I went back to my interrupted dinner. But it was now ruined. Between the cold meat and the worry that the D-team I ended up with would botch the job, my evening was unsatisfactory. I decided I should go into town and kill someone to cheer me up. My only pleasure in the entire event was using Paolo's name for the Netherlands contract. At least if they botched the hit, the local authorities could grab and beat it out of Paolo. I smiled, as I thought it might be Michael dealing with Paolo instead of the police. Then the Church could blame their own person for the hit, which I thought was quite devious. That provided another layer of insulation between myself and Michael as well. I also did not mind sacrificing Paolo, since nobody gave me lip, especially a Church flunky, when I'd just had a poor dinner.

The last insurance policy was sending one of my more useful servants to dispose of the two idiot shooters in Rotterdam. They had to go since they were amateurs and a loose end. The Italians I could trust, as we had done business before.

The news came back from the Italians first. A perfect hit, the target shot in the car while driving, and the car forced off into a ravine or gorge or something. They could not check the body but doubted there would be anyone coming back from that alive. A few hours later, the Netherlands stooges reported the target shot twice and left to die in a field. That sounded like success as well. I had my assistant send the message that both targets were down. I did hope that Michael would find Paolo and choke the life out of him. It was a good day so far. I had my assistant prepare another young human for the evening meal. I rarely ate two humans this close together, but I needed a fine meal. Also, I did not expect to be interrupted this time. My only decision was to pick the next wine for the evening. Perhaps I should begin a blog about the best wine pairings with blood and raw flesh. Surely there would be a following, especially as I was so witty and cultured.

I had a servant refresh the herbs I always kept burning in my rooms. It had been such a habit over the years, and a nice cover for the smell of blood and other things that came from my special dining room. Starting as a rough perfume to smother that hideous camp odor all those centuries ago, I had gotten used to the powerful smell. It was now somehow comforting. That reminded me, too, of that troublesome jinn. He had a smell that was reminiscent of my burning herbs. I remember that as my men put him in that boat to kill him. Not sure it meant anything, but it was odd.

Those herbs sent me back to the old Roman camp days, with memories both bad and good. I remember the night my trusted henchmen had bound and gagged a member of my cohort and dragged him to a tent outside the camp. Nobody disrespected me in my cohort and lived. We had this one in the tent and were slowly removing parts of him as he screamed into his gag. Eventually, he would be dead, and my men would chop him into enough small pieces that the hogs we always had in camp would finish disposing of the evidence.

I dreamed of the day that my family influence would rise in Rome, and my obsequiousness in the Legions would propel me to own my Legion. For it would be mine, not Rome's. I did not want it for martial glory, but to punish all those that didn't bow to my greatness. So far, I had only killed men in my cohort, but when I had my Legion, I could kill anyone I wanted. I would also milk that Legion of every penny to buy more influence in Rome. For that was my dream, to return to Rome as a senator, then destroy anyone that disrespected me. With enough time, I'd even be Emperor. Then there would be no limits to my excesses and demands. I would be the next Caligula.

Then all hell broke loose and brought change into my life. On the way back to camp, we heard an uproar. The men tossed the body parts into the woods as it sounded as if the camp was being attacked. We crept back and were astonished to see the soldiers fighting each other. Then a group came from behind and attacked us. They were literally trying to tear us apart, and they were not even using weapons. We fought them off, and other than bites and scratches, we were unharmed. We moved away from the fighting, as I had no intention of getting involved and possibly injured. An hour later, I fell violently ill, with high fever, vomiting, and diarrhea. Then I began hallucinating that I was running through the nearby town, grabbing people and trying to eat them. Soldiers were all around me doing the same. There were some soldiers killing us, and they seemed to move so fast. Even in my delirium, had the sense to crawl into a hovel to keep away from those soldiers. Besides, the child I found hidden inside there was so warm and tasty.

I woke up the next day, covered in dried blood that was not mine. A massive headache and a strange feeling in my gut were all I remembered from that day. I fell asleep again and woke some hours or days later. The town was empty and partially burned. I got up and realized two things. I was starving, and I was too fast and strong to walk properly. It took some effort, but I finally regained control of my body and walked through town. My hunger was specific, as I only wanted raw meat. I soon found an opportunity to get it, as I fed on the newly dead villagers.

After I fed, I no longer had the urge for raw meat at all and went to join the camp. I found it as deserted as the town. I gathered up food, a sword, and more clothes, then I then traveled south, as I knew eventually, I would run into more civilization in that direction. Other than a powerful urge for raw meat once a week, and my new physical enhancements, I felt normal.

And so, I began my real life. I did not get to command and own a Legion. I did not get back to Rome and become a senator, nor an emperor. But with my new powers, and occasional hunger to be sated, I used my talents to take over small settlements whenever I wanted. Then another creature similar to me found me and set me in a new direction. He told me we would live forever, and if we banded together with others like us, remained patient and hidden, then we would rule the world. World Emperor sounded so much better than Roman Emperor.

It had been rewarding, but the advancement was slow. I lived better than almost every human on the planet, but I still was not emperor of the world. I had believed my colleagues were too conservative, and I was a senior vice-president for the world's most successful corporation. But it was not enough as I needed to be the CEO and on the Board. It would be wise to keep that desire hidden, however, as one of my vampire colleagues, who lived in the future with the people called Sky Lords, was scary even to me. That only meant I had to quietly kill all my colleagues on earth first.

Aarrrgh! I sat upright with a pain in my head. That only came from one thing; one of my elder servants was dead. I tried to think who was out this evening, but there was only one away from the compound. Damn, this must be Michael's doing, as his people killed mine on sight. I only hoped the servant had done his job first. I would need to send another tomorrow to confirm the task was complete. Something always seemed to interfere with my plans. I made another note to self to turn another human to replace my loss. There were so many willing subjects these days it would not take long to find a candidate. What idiots they were, romanticizing the life of a vampire. Television did not tell them that only the master vampires, which they would never be, lived in opulence. All my servants were nothing more than abject slaves, living only until the Church or I killed them. Sucked to be them. Yes, vampire humor, obviously I was still funny.

Chapter Twenty-Six

Michael and I rapidly left the room. We looked at each other questioningly, as the situation had turned from a budding nuclear disaster to a much quieter anticlimax. We walked down the hall toward a pleasant garden at the rear of the building.

"Care for a coffee and a talk outside?"

"If you are buying, since I think I lost my wallet after getting run over by that bus. You know, the one you threw me under."

"Yes, well, it had to come out, eventually. You must admit that, however inexplicably, it ended much better than you expected. Imagine if it had surfaced during a large staff meeting at the Center."

"Yeah, I know, but you didn't have to enjoy it so much."

"I must thank you for your theoretical decision to place a tracker on the car. I assume that is how you knew where to find her."

"Yes, and I already told her. You don't get to explode that grenade in my foxhole."

He just smiled and kept walking to the stairwell. We went down to a coffee machine in a common area, grabbed two cups, and wandered outside. I never liked hospitals, so would just as well be elsewhere if possible. We walked over to a vacant bench to sit down.

"I did not bring it up earlier, but it certainly seems that master vampires could be travelers, making this entire project even more dangerous," I said. "But I also firmly believe that there are masters with good intent out there at work, and that's why the screening project has to be set up to protect them."

"You then believe that there are both good and evil masters at work in the world?" he asked. "Similar to how both good and evil shapeshifters are present in the world?"

"Yes, and that's a good analogy."

"I agree. I think we understand each other. We will make preparations to protect those that are inadvertently exposed."

We finished sipping our cappuccinos and sat quietly.

"I have some questions that are a bit off topic," I said. "Regarding shapeshifters, what information does the Church have? Is the phenomenon a supernatural issue, more of a natural occurrence like our virus, or something unknown?"

"We have studied many creatures and human hybrids, but I am afraid the information on shapeshifters is rather limited. Most of the information originated from the two hundred years of the Spanish colonization of Central America and southern North America. You probably know, or may have possibly experienced, that it was a time and place not given to study and research, but more geared toward the collection of wealth. Along with enormous appetites for rape, torture, and murder. After the priests realized shapeshifters existed, a great deal of effort was made to collect them. Once it seemed there was no profit to be gained, they were hunted, and they executed the few that were captured. Almost no data was collected that would address your questions."

"Then nothing useful is available on them. They no longer interest your group?"

"Most were thought to have been exterminated or went into hiding, so there has been little interest within my organization. There have been some recent outbreaks in northern Mexico of the bad sort of shifters associated with the drug cartels. That is the issue I mentioned to you previously, where we might need to intervene if it does not improve. I don't know enough to answer your first questions. It could be a unique type of virus and microbiome change that has somehow been infused with animal DNA, either by accident or with intent. But other than removal of those problem shifters in Mexico, the topic is not one the Church is interested in pursuing. Personally, I see the good shifters as mostly human, a benefit to their people, and therefore I include them in the flock that I protect."

"Thanks for the information."

"There is some evidence that Odin, among all the other things attributed to him, was a shapeshifter," Michael said. "Duality is a concept that originated very early among humans, so there must be a basic truth to the mythology."

"Something like how Uriel is also Prometheus."

Michael nodded. "I see someone heeded my advice about reading up on the angels. That is very astute of you. And quite a story for someday."

"Was Odin's shape a crow or a wolf?" I asked.

"Both. He was quite adept at that, plus many other things. He can be a most dangerous entity."

We continued sitting quietly on the bench. I was debating whether to go back and see Jo. But I sensed there was more to come with our conversation.

"This changes everything, you know," Michael said. He turned his head to look directly at me. "You did the right thing for Jo, and for the right reasons. But your unintended consequences are now in play. No longer can I predict likely outcomes for either of you. I don't think the next decades will be easy for her, and her despair could come at your expense. I hope you decide to stay near her for the next centuries."

I nodded agreement. "I have the same thoughts and I don't think that she will adjust easily to her family dying, as I don't think any of us do."

He nodded as well.

"Someday maybe you can tell me about yourself," I said to him.

"Probably not," Michael said. "We both still have our secrets. But I suppose we have a long time together during which I can reconsider."

We stood up from the bench.

"Meanwhile, we have a great deal of difficult and extremely dangerous work to do," Michael said.

I agreed wholeheartedly. And I would start immediately after I came up with a good Uranus joke to tell Jo. I might as well live dangerously, assuming I had the balls to tell her.

That afternoon, I drove back to Amsterdam. I thought about what I had done to Jo and if that would be chalked up on the positive or negative board. Probably both. She was still reserved around me, but perhaps that would improve with time. I got to my house, changed, and took the bike out for a long ride round Amsterdam. As I crossed a bridge over the Ijssel, I looked to the right, where a yellow maintenance boat was tied up to the bank. Three police boats were also there, and they had the bank cordoned off with police tape. Several police vehicles lined the bank.

From the location, I did not have to guess what they had found. I thought back to how many weeks the partial body had been in the water. I could not think of any evidence that would have survived long enough to implicate me in that crime. As I continued riding, I delved down deep into my inner self, searching for guilt or remorse. There was none evident. I would need to work on that, or at least stop killing, if I could. Based on what I felt was coming, I might need to hone that skill instead.

A ping from Monk showed up. I called him, as it was not an encrypted message.

"Hello. I have your coded message from Utrecht."

"What?"

"Ah, I have caught you asleep? The photos you sent me to look at. My hobby is puzzles and codes, especially in other languages. The graffiti was a simple code of Arabic letters and symbols. It reads 'Lords of the Sky return to end this earth. Prepare in haste', or something very close to that."

"OK, at the risk of sounding stupid, any idea of what that means?"

"No idea, and your risk of sounding daft is always high. It is your code, so you can interpret it however you want. Probably a rant from a disturbed person."

"Thanks for that." Another smartass computer guy. "I do have an easy request for you, maybe it will take you ten minutes. But I'll pay you for a day."

"Of course, you will. And I will be worth it. What do you have?"

I told him what I needed, and we hung up. I kept riding and thinking. The jinn was a harbinger, but I didn't know what the message meant, or if the graffiti was even relevant. But my gut feeling told me it was real, and the reason the jinn was executed. My killing days were not over. As I rode on, I thought about Jo. I didn't know what her future held, but I would try to be there for her in the new life she would find.

I was in Rotterdam three nights later. For some reason I didn't like Rotterdam. The people were nice, the new city was unique and attractive, and yet it had never grown on me. Just one of those things. Monk's information had led me to a dingy street in a ratty neighborhood on the outskirts of town. Graffiti tags were on trash containers, building, and even some vehicles that looked to no longer be in service. A place neither the tourists nor the new businesspeople in town would ever see.

The little line of two-story row houses backed up to a rail line, which helped me as I was perched up there on a concrete support overgrown with vines. I had been here nearly two hours just watching the grubby place on the end. It was annoying as a fast train went by every few minutes, with overwhelming noise since I was twenty feet from the tracks. I was getting ready to drop down and move to the back of the place to finish my operation. A completely off-the-books action nobody would ever trace to me, nor would I ever tell anyone. I had decided to commit my last murder spree of humans.

I had moved one leg to get in position to drop. I saw something move nearer to the back of the residence I was casing. It was a man, dressed in all dark grey form-fitting clothes. Somehow, he seemed to detect my movement. He was looking my direction as I froze. Then I saw him sniffing. That was odd and instantly alerted me that he might not be human. I saw his eyes, and they had a weird glow; weird because there was no light shining in them to cause a reflection. This might pose a problem, as he was either here to protect those I was about to kill, or he was here to kill them. Either way, he was not going to spoil my plans.

I waited five minutes until the next train came through, and dropped down beside the tracks, even though the passengers might have spotted me for a half-second. The man creature could not have spotted me yet as I was on the opposite side of the tracks from him. I pulled my weapons into each hand and sprinted at an insane speed across the tracks straight to where I had last seen him, jumping the fence between the tracks and the residence. He moved unnaturally fast as he saw me coming and spun to meet me. I guess he was expecting a human as he readied his body in a martial arts stance. I shot him in the chest three times with my suppressed pistol, as I never intended to fight fair with something like him. Amazingly, he shook it off as my momentum plowed me right into him. We wrestled for a few seconds as I had lost my gun when I ran into him. Not that it seemed to matter if I shot him or not.

Another few seconds and he lay still as I rolled him off me. He was fast, strong, and seemingly impervious to bullets, but the knife currently sticking into his kidney, coated with binder potion, had ended things in my favor.

I found my gun and shot him three times in the head. That did the trick, as dark black gunk drooled out the bullet holes, ears, and nose. I had gotten a good whiff of him while wrestling around, and the stink of Caius' burning herbs was on him. I suppose I had offed my first vampire, although I wouldn't be telling anyone. I took a moment to check the area, but there was no one else around. I left the body and went to the back of the house. A ten-second wrestling match and a few suppressed shots had not alerted anyone of the happenings in the backyard.

I used another knife to open the door without leaving obvious marks. I crept through the kitchen and heard voices and a television in the front. I dropped down to the floor, which was sticky and nasty, and slid forward. Two guys were watching the television. Various leftover take-away and pizza boxes littered the place, between them on the sofa, on the floor, and on the table in front of the sofa. I saw a gun on the table under one box. Very sloppy. I eased myself up and bolted into the room, landing on my knees on the sofa between them. They were quite surprised, but not for long. I stabbed one in the eye with a knife I'd brought from the kitchen as I landed and shot the other one in the throat with the gun I had swept up while gliding across the table. I waited a few seconds to ensure the throat shot was lethal, then wiped the gun and knife handle, then placed each man's hand on both the gun and knife.

My job finished, I sprinted out the back. Twenty seconds after firing the gun I was out back, dragging the vampire's body up and over the tracks. It was a nuisance I had not planned for, but I couldn't leave it at the scene. I didn't know what happened to dead vampire bodies, but they obviously didn't disappear in a puff of smoke after death. A few hundred yards down the tracks was a dairy farm, and I stashed the body under the bank of an overgrown ditch full of putrid water. I had hacked the head from the body just to be sure it stayed dead.

Another mile down the tracks, after dodging two trains, I was back at my car. Overall it had been a productive evening. The two goons that had shot Jo were dead, and as a bonus, one dead Caius-employed vampire.

Since Jo's shooting I had thoughts that both the vehicle and sloppy methods were familiar. I gave Monk some names and details, and these two had popped up. They worked in the Netherlands as goons for hire, typically for drug dealers, collecting debts and pushing around other small dealers. They had even worked as muscle for the drug dealer I had killed in Amsterdam. The idiots had left the vehicle from the tulip field parked out front of the Rotterdam house. Nothing like a Range Rover in a ratty neighborhood, with old mud on the sides, to give me a hint of who they were. Now they were gone, the police investigation should find that they had killed each other, and I just had to keep my mouth shut.

I really wanted to tell Michael, as this linked Caius and the Church. Michael had already alluded to it so I didn't know how much use my information would be. I eventually decided on a compromise. If there was any further threat to Jo or anyone else I knew about I'd tell Michael, but for the moment I'd keep quiet. Ultimately my best course of action was killing Caius and ending the threat forever.

Last night had felt a lot like the old days. But I had decided these two would be the last of my bad habit, both out of respect for Michael and to clean up my conscience, regardless of how fun it had been. It was past time to clean up my actions and hunt other things. My conscience was already bothering me, both in the act of killing two humans and keeping information from Michael.

Chapter Twenty-Seven

Jo

It seemed so surreal that I may now live twenty centuries. A few months ago, I would have believed that to be impossible for anyone. A few days ago, I believed it would be impossible for it to happen to me. I alternated between disbelief, fascination, and dread. I had nothing else to even remotely compare it to. Worse, other than Michael, I had no one to talk to about my feelings. He gently recommended I keep in contact with Senecus, as he was the one and only authority on what I was facing. But I was being stubborn in not doing so. I knew I would, but for now, I wanted time to work through it. It was all the control I had over this new condition so far.

Michael had been concerned about me having blackouts or falling into a coma while I was away, but I didn't think I would. There was not much of a scientific reason for my logic, it was my gut feeling. It made some sense that Senecus would manifest serious problems from assimilating all that alien DNA and whatever else was floating in that river. Actually, I didn't see how he didn't die. All that protein should have set up a fatal allergic reaction, or at least a serious rejection reaction. I could not explain how he survived. But since he did, all the proteins would have adapted to his human body, and would likely transfer more easily to mine. There could always be some residual allergic reactions still to come, but I felt it was unlikely.

What was happening to me was amazing, but that euphoria quickly wore off thinking of all the people I knew I would get to see die. I had been given a great gift, but at a great cost. The only positive to that was I would not have to pay that cost for a few decades, as my family died off. I had gone back to England to visit with family during my recovery. But after a few days I began thinking it was a mistake, it was too much. While I was with them, I kept imagining how they would look in fifty years, while I would look the same. I think I was already developing survivor's remorse. The best way to deal with it was to get busy.

Michael called every other day to check in. I appreciated the concern, especially as he didn't press me on anything. I understood why people thought so much of him and how he'd become a father figure for many. Of course, most of them did not know that he was also a ruthless defender of the Church and people. Because of my research topics, I had heard stories about how Michael had taken care of some supernatural problems. Until lately I had discounted those stories completely, but now realized they were probably true. Even knowing that Senecus had displayed some supernatural capabilities had not really convinced me that supernatural beings were real.

I thought about meeting Sen at the cottage, and how he and Michael had seemed such an odd pairing at first. But now I was understanding they were much more alike than different. I knew Sen was struggling to be a better person, and I was glad Michael was guiding him in that direction. If successful, Sen would be quite something, but I didn't need to go down that path yet. I really had no use for men at the moment, and thoughts of a family were not even on the distant horizon.

How did I feel about Senecus? I had not given him much credence at first, and perhaps I was a little short with him. But he grew on me. It initially surprised me he had so much background in my subject areas, but that made sense later when he told us how old he was. And how many degrees he had accumulated. Now my feelings changed depending on the day, the hour, the minute. I needed to sort it out, and I could not be around him whilst I did. Revulsion, fear, wonder, attraction, disgust, lust, and anger were all words I could use. His casual approach to killing did not sit well with me, regardless of his background and early cultural experiences. He certainly must have had plenty of time to adapt and adjust to our modern expectations, unless he was a monster incapable of change. A good-looking and interesting one, but that made him even more dangerous. I would need to keep my distance and perspective on him until I sorted it all out, and had time to watch him and what he did.

But he had been a gentleman to me, maybe too much so. He seemed interested, but was always a little aloof. I was not sure what to make of it. Traveling with him had been fun. We were comfortable together, as he had been less distant than when we were at the cottage. There were times on the trip where he had been almost too much to resist. Walking with him on the beach had been the most romantic thing I'd done in a long time, at least until the squid attack. Despite the attack, he had been oddly calm and shrugged it off as if it were nothing. I suppose seventeen centuries of life as a soldier and vigilante would do that. But it had been another attractive aspect of him, so calm under pressure, dealing with weirdness that might have paralyzed most people. I secretly had to admit the attack had been thrilling after the initial terror wore off. I nearly tore his clothes off right there on the beach.

Michael told me how he had saved me in the field, then stayed with me at the hospital. He was a walking anachronism. So violent when necessary, so kind at other times. A sharp mind, a sense of humor, good looks, and years of experience. I really needed to stop thinking that way. Yes, enough of that. I needed to stop with those thoughts and feelings.

My transition was going smoothly, I suppose, but new things kept coming up. One thing I had not expected was that I was hungry all the time. I was emptying my fridge daily, yet not gaining weight. If anything, it was redistributing into muscle without me even working out. I would shop for clothes soon, so I would put the raise from Michael to good use. I had to admit that the evolving figure in the mirror was improving by the day. Perhaps that shopping trip would include a bikini for the first time in years. I wasn't sure whether it was part of the transition or something else, but I also thought more of going swimming, especially on a warm sandy beach somewhere. I decided that was much more because of wanting a vacation in Greece.

The first days, I did not notice any massive increase in speed or strength, but I figured those physiological changes could take days or weeks to manifest. Only two days later, they began. Another visible change was that the scars from my two bullet wounds and the associated surgery were almost gone. That would be good for the bikini as well, which was also strange, as I had always been modest. Since secondary school, I normally kept as much covered as reasonable, with a one-piece, shorts, and shawl when at the water. I attributed that to my evolving positive body image. I had no more issues with my body than most women, but normally had no thoughts of parading it around. But now, maybe I could see it.

After a week, I could tell my eyesight was much better, including at night. Hearing was much improved, and I was getting fast enough while running that I only ran at night so no one would see my unnatural speed. The only worrisome part of all this was my hyperawareness. All the visual and auditory input sometimes overloaded my brain. That did not include all the incredible smells now assaulting me, both the bad and the good ones. I understood why dogs and cats took so many naps. I suppose it gave them time to process everything, plus was a way to turn things off.

Beyond that awareness, I was developing a new sense. Senecus had mentioned it, but living it was something else entirely. It felt like things were appearing in the corners of my vision, and sometimes when I closed my eyes,

I could see things highlighted in the darkness. I also sometimes felt whispers brushing my mind. Somehow, I was sensing other people, even when they were in other rooms, when I couldn't see or hear them otherwise. It alarmed me at first, but I realized how valuable it would be in my new role if I could control it.

Confidence was building overall, but especially in my physical abilities. And yes, again, in my appearance. The only thing that felt different that might be a concern was a slight uptick in aggressiveness. Nothing major, but I thought I was not as courteous whilst driving or running errands in crowded places. Might be the hyperawareness, but occasionally I still felt like thrashing someone that had crossed me by not responding to a traffic signal. I needed to keep that under control, as I could now seriously injure someone rather than giving a rude hand gesture.

I was only getting two or three hours of sleep at night, but I was fresh each day and not sleepy. I was a little worried about my dreams. One that kept recurring was both alarming, confusing, and reassuring all at the same time. I was walking alone at night and came to the edge of what seemed to be a river. I had the irresistible urge to plunge in. My clothes disappeared as I dove into the... water? But it was more viscous than regular water, more like a Dead Sea thickness. It was easy to float in it, and it had a delightful smell, sweeter than river water.

Something large in the river was moving towards me. It was the color of an ever-changing rainbow pulse, more phosphorescent light than solid. When a few feet from me, it stopped. I really could not see what it was, but it felt like a water creature of some type, but it was too blurry to get an idea of any fins or tentacles or limb, or even a head. It was neither friendly nor a threat. I knew it was studying me. The phosphorescence in the water increased as millions of tiny light spheres began coalescing around us, almost like all the stars in the universe were in the water with us. The entire river was glowing, and I felt myself glowing as well, bright silver with a hint of gold. I felt like the glow was also inside me, almost as if there were two of me. The glow in the water faded as the entity began to slowly move away. Then it quickly shot into the sky like a rainbow kaleidoscopic missile. But I was still glowing as I left the river and dressed. I always woke up at that point. Sometimes I swore I was still glowing those first few seconds when I awoke.

Each morning I spent some minutes analyzing the strange but beautiful dream. I was aware of the symbolism since I had spent my career on myths and folklore and knew how often dreams and signs played a part in those stories. Was that entity Senecus and was this dream just a way of signifying the action of him changing me? Did Senecus have this dream or similar ones? I should ask him about that. Why would a river creature shoot into the sky? But then it was a dream, so crazy things should happen. I didn't dream it every night, but it showed up several times a week. I'd probably have a chat with Michael about it. He would have a better perspective on whether it was important or only my subconscious working out my turning. Regardless of the dream or its meaning, I had to move forward to my new reality. That included leaving England and getting back to work.

Instead of worrying about my dreams or thinking of Senecus, I knew what I needed to do, and that was concentrating on what to do with all my extra time and abilities. The one thing I knew for certain, and had already told Michael, was that I wanted to change my career. I was no longer afraid of dying young or taking the risks that I knew were out there. A research librarian had been interesting, but safe. I now had this second chance, with what should be incredible physical skills coming along, and I wanted to live my life differently.

All the things I had studied for years had scared me. But now I would have the strength to confront them as they came at me, or as I hunted for them. I didn't intend to do anything stupid, but I intended to learn about weapons and skills to go after the bad guys, rather than just reading about them. I aimed to be the baddest bitch that the Church had seen, maybe a Joan of Arc on steroids, with firearms. That attitude was new to me and I wondered if the change was making me more aggressive, or confident, or perhaps both. Regardless, I'd use it to accomplish my new goals and begin a new phase of my career.

Epilogue

The ancient bearded man leaned against the ice-crusted boulder. The top of this mountain at night in the Alps was a good place to have conversations. No humans around. Not much of anything, really, other than the wind noise. Just his two companions, a massive hirsute biped, and an ephemeral shadow, seemingly made of smoke.

Not that they had to be anywhere physical to meet. But they were all impervious to cold or dark, and certain conventions, such as meeting in this place, spoke to their awareness of tradition.

"Do you think he will be ready in time?" asked the shadow.

"Unknown," answered the large one. "What do the links show?"

"Too many variations for a prediction," answered the old man. "Peculiar. Almost as if he is being shielded or hidden."

"By whom or what?" asked the shadow.

"I can't even get an eye on that either. Which is even more of a reason to think there is interference."

"Has Michael given any input?" asked the large one.

"He has been unusually circumspect regarding our subject. I believe he suspects something of importance but has chosen not to reveal it yet. Because of who he represents, that is the wise course."

"Then we must work with what we know," continued the shadow. "He may not be ready. Can we speed up any actions?"

"Yes," answered the large one. "As always, there may be consequences. But our calculations show there is no viable alternative."

"Agreed," spoke both the old man and the shadow.

"On a different matter, he has created another," the old man said. "I did not think that was possible."

"We did not think so either," said the shadow.

"Neither did we," said the large one.

"Is there an advantage to us with this development?"

There was no answer.

"We should put the matter to more thought. We must have more allies to meet our adversaries," said the old man.

"If your latest timeline is correct, we have at most a century," said the large one.

"Yes," said the old man. "This planet may be lost if we cannot find and organize more allies. The inhabitants are already likely forfeit. This new virus aspect is problematic."

"Yes;" the large one replied. "The future humans have created a most successful, insidious strategy. To stop it, we would destroy the human's virtual network, which will put them in chaos for millennia or longer. Or not destroy it and risk losing humanity anyway."

"That is why they are already likely forfeit," said the shadow. "We must have a new strategy. We can't count on turning the remnants of the Legions like we did during the previous incursion."

There was nothing left to say. The shadow melted into the wind, the old man disappeared into a door of light, and the large one was simply not there anymore.

AUTHOR'S NOTE

All the physical places described in the book are real. At least all the ones described in the current century. And most of the more ancient places exist as well and can be visited today. Certain liberties were taken with dates, however. For example, the town of Pendleton exists as described and developed as described. But the establishment of the town proper was moved approximately forty years to accommodate the story.

All characters in this book are fictitious. Any references to actual historical figures were also fictionalized to fit the story. Governor Tryon's brutal end was fictionalized, of course, but was considered appropriate as he actually did hang my great-great-great-great-great-grandfather in North Carolina in 1771 after the Regulator insurrection. Fortunately, he and his wife had already produced several children before his untimely end.

This book was originally published as *Resilient* in 2021. This new version has substantial deletions, new material, and edits compared to the old version. Although the story is similar, it simply had to be substantially improved as the old version was not good enough to tell the story.

If you like this version, please consider leaving a review or at least a rating. That information is priceless, and what led to this current rewrite. I read reviews, process the information, and use them to improve the next book, or in this case, the current book. Thank you for purchasing this book and thanks in advance for any reviews you make.

The next book in the Fisher of Time series is *Shifting Ground*. Read on for an excerpt of the book.

About the Author

Doug Smith, PhD, is a former scientist, professor, and non-fiction author. He is now recovering from those distractions and writing fantasy fiction.

Formerly a resident of The Netherlands, he is now living near Asheville, North Carolina. Visit his website at www.douglaspaulsmith.com for more information, including short stories and excerpts from the Fisher of Time series.

Shifting Ground Preview

Chapter One

Hanging from a cliff face reminded me of how much I hated heights. Really, really hated it. My quarry had led me here, showing that it was smarter than I was. I scrambled up the rock face, which was cold in the cracks and shadows, even in the late summer. If I messed up, it was two hundred feet down to the next ledge that would catch my body. Not lethal for me, but it would be painful for a day or two. Nowhere to go but up.

I finally reached the top, with one last ledge of crumbly rock to crawl over. Not a good time to hurry, so I took my time easing my body against the rock face, then over the lip. Those yoga classes really helped.

It was surprising to see a forest of massive trees before me. The vertical, barren landscape I had just climbed was now horizontal and lush. I sat down and drank some water and rested for five minutes and looked myself over, with cuts and scrapes covering my hands and lower arms, and my pants were shredded as well. The thing I was chasing owed me some new clothes. I thought about how I had gotten here.

I arrived in Anchorage four days ago. Alaska is like few other places, as you immediately notice how vast the place is. Anchorage is on flatland by the ocean and distant mountains hem everything in and fill the horizon. Despite the distance, they seem so tall because they start at sea level, where you are standing, and rise quickly to 14,000 feet. Within that bigness are few people as the population density is just over one person per square mile. Density in the Netherlands is over thirteen hundred people per square mile. So people easily go missing in Alaska, and with that vastness, abductions and murders remain hidden for years. But when too many go missing in a specific area, people notice. The corollary to that was that crimes against nature weren't noticed, much less prosecuted.

I was here because of a spate of missing humans over half a decade in a small town. And lately the sighting of an odd dog-like thing and lots of dead Dall sheep in the surrounding mountains. Another weird convergence of coincidences. The Church had documented the incidents, but several factors had prevented them from investigating until now. They did not have anyone local; the European teams had no experience in Alaska; and seven people missing plus dead sheep were not high on the priority list at the moment. But that is why they had me. Experience in Alaska, time to investigate, and I was cheaper than most alternatives. I had volunteered just to revisit Alaska. I spent the past two days in the mountains where the dead sheep were reported, waiting for something odd to show up. When it did the chase was on. A simple trip to catch a killer, yet I did not know how life altering this trip was to become.

Time to renew the chase as I followed a trail into the woods. These were genuine woods, a mature arboreal forest. Not redwood-sized, but still plenty big. I thought this elevation was too high, for both the type and size of trees growing here. Trivia dredged up from one of hundreds of college classes, in particular the one on biogeography. The greenery underneath was a cool jungle. Fern-like plants, and unfortunately some devil's club, grew waist high. The ground was covered in moss so thick it was like walking on a mattress. A mattress interspersed with deep hidden holes that were just large enough to swallow a foot and break a leg.

I stopped worrying about that when I sighted my quarry again. Hard to describe, but basically a dog person. The hind legs and bushy tail of a dog below the waist, while above it was a human torso clad in a flannel shirt, with small human-like arms and hands. The face was hairy, but I never got a close look to see whether it was more dog- or human-shaped. It was agile and fast, almost scampering up the cliff I had labored to climb. No wonder the Dall sheep were getting massacred.

Michael, my occasional employer through the Church via contract, had briefed me before coming over, with files on supernatural beings reportedly in Alaska. I assumed most were myths, but this one was likely an Adlet based on the descriptions provided. This unlikely myth was true.

I started running again, but carefully. Then I sensed something more than saw it, and came to a dead stop. A very large humanoid shape in the shadows ahead and off to the side. I stared at the place but could not quite see it. As I stood there, the shape became a tree. I took a few steps closer, then sat down, crossed my legs, and kept my hands on my knees, palms up. I closed my eyes and waited. An Adlet, woods where they should not be, and now this. So much for my simple Alaska venture. But sitting and patiently waiting seemed to be the polite thing to do while going down this rabbit hole.

"Ah, you must be a sensitive one as you have discovered me, even with my cladding. You are not the average hairless being. Well met." Those words vibrated through me as I felt them more than heard them. My skin and bones were slightly ringing with each one.

"That is amazing. I was not even aware that it was possible to shift into a tree, so I still have much to learn." I said the words aloud but wasn't sure it was necessary.

"You are correct on both counts. You have much to learn. And I hear your thoughts, but only when you wish to speak. I would not read your thoughts otherwise, unless you were a threat. Then I would determine your intent. But otherwise, no, that would just be rude. And my people are not rude."

"And who are your people?"

"Ah, that is a tricky question to answer. Regardless, I would defer an answer until I know more about you, and who your people are."

"I am not exactly sure what I am. But not exactly human, which is what I suppose you mean when you call me a hairless one. I believe I am the only one of my people."

"Hmm, now that I study you, you are silvery. Not like the typical hairless ones. Unusual."

"You can see that? Nobody ever told me that but my wife, or our kids. I don't know any other silvery people, but I could always see that my wife and children were golden."

He said nothing for a long moment. "Your wife was a shape shifter that aided the Cherokee tribe? Some time ago, in the low green mountains far to the south and east of here?"

"Yes. How could you know that?"

"I know of you, and that you are the one called the Silver Walker of the Southeastern Mountains. We thought you had gone. But welcome back, it is nice to meet you."

Now I was really confused. How could an Alaskan Bigfoot, or whatever he was, know who I was? Or my wife Hia, a shapeshifter that had died two centuries ago?

"I sense your confusion. We keep up with some of your world closely for different reasons, but usually where your people do the right thing that most helps other species. We are aware of what you and your people did in the Southeastern Mountains, saving substantial portions of it. Your efforts there also helped our kind in that area. We know of your family, especially those of my kind that still travel to that part of the country."

I was not sure what to say, so I kept it simple. "Thanks, and nice to meet you too."

"You are welcome. To thank you properly, we invite you to stay with us for a few days. We can help you with your slant since you already have a talent for it. Could come in real useful someday. I sense you are going to need it."

Once again, I had no clue to the "slant" he had just referred to. But I was continuing to play along. "The entity I was just chasing. I should take care of that while I can."

"That being is of no consequence, as she only hunts sheep. I have persuaded her to leave this area. The one you seek is another hairless one that revels in causing pain. Very ill, that one is. You will capture him after you leave here."

"OK, not sure how you know that, but it is reassuring."

"I should introduce myself. Your wife's people called us the Tsul Kalu, roughly interpreted as 'those that slant'. Many names have the different hairless tribes called us. Our real name is more of a concept than a word. It is not possible to pronounce in your language and defies translation. Our personal names are the same. But in honor of your wife, simply call me Kal."

"Thanks again, Kal. I heard stories that your people existed but was not sure if it was a myth or not. Some tales described something like giants in the forest that could control the animals, and even the trees."

"Part of it is true. As you can see, despite the translation, I am not slanted. It refers to our way of changing things by slanting them with thoughts. Slant is really a discipline or a purposeful way of thought, and how we look at the world and change it, or ourselves, on occasion. A simple trick for us is to slant light to look like something else, which affects your perception. Or persuade someone they need to change their direction if they approach too close. A more complex form of slant is where we actually bend what you call physics. One thing can become another, distinct thing, if done correctly. For us, slant is a belief, philosophy, process, and way of life that we incorporate to interact with the universe in a way that is foreign to your people."

"Then instead of seeing you, humans would normally see a tree or boulder."

"Precisely. It's a neat solution to alter the perceptions of humans, that we call hairless, and all animals at a superficial level. But I can also be an actual tree and if you approached, you would even feel a tree trunk. Slightly unique process of slant with an application of interdimensional energy. That approach delves into aspects of physics your people have yet to discover. Or you can call it magic. I sense you know something of this way of thinking. You think enough like slant to do the same, with training."

"I have never heard anyone say that I can think slant, but I do realize I think differently. And I think my world just got a lot stranger than I imagined it this morning."

"Your world has been small so far. Stay a few days and learn. It will enlarge your universe."

The prospect of learning from a nine-foot-tall, hairy forest dweller about shifting into animals or objects, using interdimensional energy, just made too much sense to turn down. So, I stayed, and my world changed, as Kal said. The next days were filled with revelations and learning that began transforming my life.

As I passed the days there with Kal, I learned more about his people. They were so much a part of the forest it was easy to overlook them. I think I saw about six different individuals. Kal said there were more around, but I could not tell. They rarely approached us, but Kal said they were listening to us through him, and sometimes he would relay a statement or a question from one of them to me.

I asked how their communication worked. He told me that telepathy connected all of them. They did not read each other's minds unless by mutual

9 781737 368045